Jade in the Snow

Louise Dawn

Jade in the Snow
Copyright © by Louise Dawn

Cover Design by Syd Gill/ Syd Gill Designs
Formatting by Polgarus Studio

ISBN-13: 978-1-7321837-7-3
Ebook ISBN-13: 978-1-7321837-6-6

To sign up for Louise Dawn's newsletter, go to:
http://www.louisedawnauthor.com

The energy of the warrior is buried in the snow.
Oh, cardinal Jadeite, dispel my fear,
and wrap me up in your sweet light.

To all the wounded souls who have fought the good fight.
And who'll always sit with their backs to the wall.
You deserve undying gratitiude and respect.
This book is dedicated to those who battle wars waged on the spirit.

Prologue

Salt Lake City, Utah.
The day they met.

Derek should've come earlier. He swore as he shifted through the mass of runners. Most operators hated crowds, and Derek Banez was no exception. The bodies crowding around registration tables made his skin itch, and he kept reaching for an imaginary holstered weapon. When he saw a flash of neon pink hair in the crowd, Derek zeroed in like a missile.

"Casey," he called.

His cousin didn't hear him. Derek yelled her name again as he dodged an elderly lady stretching in line. Casey turned and squealed. He hadn't intended on participating in the 5K race, but as he planned to stay with his cousin for a week, and since it was for a good cause—a charity called sweat4schoolsupplies—here he was. Sponsoring school backpacks for underprivileged kids in the area was a no-brainer, so he'd run his tired ass down to the local park. He'd just returned from deployment, the last one serving as a Green Beret. Now, Derek was about to join a newly formed covert Taskforce—Mobile Intelligence Team—as their Protection Specialist and Sniper on Team Two. MIT2.

Even the name sounded bad-ass, and he'd just met the first members of his team. His team leader—Erik Andersen—seemed solid, and a little anal. James Cane was the team medic, a huge beast of a man.

They were still selecting a fourth team member. At least Derek had some time off, and he supposed he'd need to up his already strenuous fitness game. A leisurely Saturday morning jog wouldn't hurt, especially at such a pretty location. Early June saw blue skies, green fields and avenues of leafed trees.

Casey jumped into his arms, and Derek staggered under her enthusiasm. As kids, they'd always been inseparable. She wasn't just his first cousin, she was one of his closest friends, and he hadn't seen her in over two years.

Derek stood back to assess his short and curvy sidekick. Her blonde hair was now cotton candy pink. A colorful tattoo wrapped over her right shoulder, and yet another piercing decorated her left ear. She grinned up at him. He forgot how darn cute she was.

"You're back from crusading through mysterious lands." Her eyes sparkled.

"Aye, Aye, milady, and I bring gifts. They're in my car."

"Two years, that had better be a big-shitting gift."

Derek laughed. "Damn, I missed your clever ass. Now where do I sign up for this gig?"

"Relax, we've got you covered. Here's your race number."

"We? Hell no, I'm donating to those kids."

"There's a separate donation table towards the back of the pavilion." Casey pointed to a teeming table. "And there's one at the finish line. And 'we' as in Kate's cute derriere and my reluctant one. Kate is my best friend in Utah, you haven't met her yet—she's walking up behind you."

Derek turned, and for the first time in his life, words eluded him. Derek wasn't a recluse. When he wasn't deployed, he dipped his toe rather generously in the dating pool. He enjoyed women and prided himself on never getting too involved. Some might call him a commitment-phobe, but Derek's first priority was his career. He was one ambitious son of a bitch. Criminal Justice classes on the side, and Counter Terrorism studies kept him busy. He didn't have time for relationships.

The goddess stretching her shoulder spoke. She had a slight Irish lilt, so subtle, it was barely noticeable.

"Case, don't try and pee. That bathroom is a disaster zone. Find a bush, it might be more sanitary. And I'm not using a porta-loo, not after the last time."

Her skin glowed, it literally glowed like an angel—a stark contrast to her blue-black hair. Derek studied her ultramarine eyes framed by dark lashes and brows. A stubborn-looking chin jutted out slightly, matching a gaze so direct that it took his breath away. His eyes ran over her hourglass shape. She looked like a 1940's pin-up girl.

Casey giggled. "That was different. It was a rock concert." She turned to Derek. "While Kate used a porta-potty at a Twin Peaks gig, a bunch of drunk dicks decided to brawl and fell into the potty, almost toppling it over."

"Thanks for the reminder." Kate shuddered. "And you're spilling my secrets to a random jogging dude? I know he's a hotty, but seriously?"

Derek felt himself blush—that was a first.

"My mute sidekick is actually my cousin—Derek." Casey nudged him. "Say something so she knows you're real. Not just a six-foot cardboard cutout for a Calvin Klein commercial. He talks, I promise."

"Six-two, and are you girls done with making me feel like a

piece of meat?" He elbowed Casey back and put some power behind the move.

"Ouch. Stop, you big lug."

Kate didn't say anything, just studied him. A couple more of Casey's friends joined the group.

"Kate, don't wait for me. I'm walking the 5K." Casey grimaced. "And I'm taking my time."

The announcer came over the system and told everyone to shuffle to the starting line. Kate turned and walked ahead. Derek's eyes drifted to her shapely ass molded by athletic leggings. She had an ephemeral quality, yet she was curved in all the right places. He lengthened his stride to catch up. A beefy-looking man pushed past her, and Derek glared his way. The eager beaver barely noticed. With long strides, Derek caught up to the raven-haired beauty and watched her six. The crowds lined up as Derek stepped up behind her. A river ran along their right side. The route would follow the water all the way into the city.

"Do you jog on a regular basis?"

She looked back and raised her brows, pausing before answering. "Often enough to complete a 5K. Try to keep up."

"Ouch. Why do you run?" Derek jogged on the spot and shook out his arms.

Kate sighed. "Because I love chocolate milkshakes and beer."

"My kind of girl."

"I doubt that. I think a Victoria Secret model is your kind of girl," she said, stretching her thigh.

"You think I'm a player." Derek grinned.

"I think you're dangerous."

"You don't like danger? I can be a meek little lamb. Or a puppy? A Golden with a waggy tail."

She tried to hide a smile. "Oh, you're something else—I'm

more of a cat person."

"Liar. I bet you love all furry beasts."

She shook her head and let her smile show. "Are you calling yourself a beast?"

"You said it, baby. I'm the beast to your beauty."

"I think it's the other way around. That girl over there—just walked into a tree while gaping at your pretty ass. No thanks, I like my men a little rougher around the edges."

Leaning down, Derek whispered in her ear. "I can be as rough as you want me to be."

He was close enough to see goosebumps break out on her arm. Her chest rose, but she kept her eyes trained ahead.

The gun went off and they shuffled forward. As Kate broke into a run, the overexcited dick-bag from earlier cut past, shoving a child aside, then ploughing past Kate. She stumbled, and Derek saw red. Surging ahead, he smoothly tripped the bastard, and the guy rolled into a ditch. "Oops," Derek muttered as he kept running.

"I saw that," Kate said from behind. "I also saw the dirtball push that kid."

"Don't know what you're talking about. Poor guy tripped over his own feet." Derek dropped back beside her. She set a comfortable pace, and they ran in silence. It felt right, a symbiosis that needed no words. He kept looking her way, her breaths came out in quick rasps, and her nostrils flared slightly with each breath. For Derek, a 5K run was the warm-up to an additional two-hour training session.

"Kat, are you okay? Do you want to slow?"

She glared at the nickname. "You're seriously trying to have a conversation while jogging, and you're not even out of breath. Are you secretly Superman?"

He grinned. "C'mon, don't let me jog alone. My poor heart won't take it."

"I need to babysit a big, brawny man's heart?"

"Maybe. It doesn't like to eat alone either. In fact, it's craving a juicy burger—with fries."

She snorted and rolled her eyes. "You've got some plums on you."

He grinned at the Irish saying but still persisted. "What do you say? After the run, we grab lunch, with a double chocolate milkshake on the side?"

"Oh, you're dangerous all right."

"Is that a yes, Kat?" Derek jogged backwards and clamped a hand on his chest. "Be still, my brawny heart. You're smiling. That's a fucking yes!" She couldn't stop a giggle, and Derek whooped, running silly circles around his gorgeous jogging partner.

◊ ◊ ◊

Three and a half years later, December.
Denver, Colorado.

Kat stood in the rain. Warm tears leaked from her eyes, as drizzle cooled her cheeks. It was dark out, too dark for the team to see her hovering on the sidewalk as they sat in the warm booth of the restaurant. Agony ripped through Kat's chest as a hard knot balled in her stomach. It was meant to be a surprise. She'd canceled the last day of her workshop seminar to be with him— Derek *Slater* Banez—on his birthday. The love of her life. The man she'd shared a bed with for the past three and a half years. The asshole who now swayed in his seat while a brunette colleague pawed at his chest. Kat recognized the woman, some work friend from Fort Bragg. Derek and Kat had run into her once at a dinner.

Another minute ticked by, and Kat couldn't tear her gaze away. The rest of the team seemed pissed, and Max and his new fiancée, Abby, stood. Abby glared at the woman as she gathered her coat. The bitch didn't seem to notice. She whispered something in Derek's ear. Clearly drunk, he leaned back and laughed, and the sound felt like knives to Kat's heart. Johnny and Donnie exchanged words, then also stood. Johnny grasped Derek's arm and Derek jerked it away.

The team took offense on Kat's behalf. She knew they felt protective towards her. They'd all been that way since the Black Friday bombing. Thanks to that tragic day, Derek's PTSD slowly expanded until it had taken over their relationship, and now it ran the show, destroying their love connection months ago. Although they still lived together, Derek avoided Kat whenever possible. When he was Stateside, he made excuses about catching up with the boys, while she sat at home. Always hoping he'd come around and let her into his damaged heart. She should've fought harder. Kat kept hoping that things would get better, that Derek just needed time to heal and he'd come around.

Except they'd drifted farther apart, and her training schedule didn't help. Kat was a corporate trainer who helped entrepreneurs grow their business. Derek's covert team had just held a training exercise in Colorado near Derek and Kat's hometown of Denver. When they'd finished up a week earlier than planned, he'd called Kat and asked her to meet up with him and the team—to celebrate his birthday. She'd felt overjoyed that Derek had reached out, but was already setting up workshop trainings in California. After months of avoidance, he'd contacted her again—earlier in the day—and told her where they'd be in case she changed her mind. Kat's workshop was too important to cancel. Still, she'd regretted her answer almost immediately after hanging up with Derek, so she'd re-scheduled her workshop and caught the first flight back home. With Derek's last deployment, and her tight schedule, the last time they'd seen each other was three months ago.

Kat looked down at her red heels. One of the birthday presents she'd bought earlier in the week for Derek. He loved her in heels—wearing nothing else. They'd always had an explosive sex life, even through the rough patches. That was their safe place, fucking each other's brains out without saying a word.

"Fuck him." Kat turned away from the skinny woman sliding closer to her soon to be ex-boyfriend. Forcing one foot in front of the other, Kat walked to her car. She didn't want his friends seeing her this way, broken and standing on the street like a pathetic stalker.

Climbing in her Mercedes took effort. Kat eyed her luggage in the back seat. That would stay. Kat swiped at her wet cheeks and headed home. No. Derek's home, not her home. Not anymore.

◊ ◊ ◊

The car sat in the shadows but offered an excellent view of the apartment steps. Picking at a scab on his finger, the man watched the drama unfold. His heart rate sped up as the woman emerged with a second load of bags, slipping on the sleet-covered steps. Her lover tried to help, and she shrugged him off. He could see the allure, a dark angel with plum red lips and flashing eyes. He hadn't meant to eavesdrop, but he'd swung past to see a friend. Now, he picked up his digital camera, and slid down his window to catch the couple's angry words only a few yards away.

"How did you even know I was there?" she said through tears.

"Donnie saw you as he walked out the restaurant. I'm so sorry. It's not what it looks like. When she tried to grope me, I—"

"Derry, how could you let it get that far?" She tossed a pillow into the front seat. White snowflakes clung to her damp hair. Zooming in, the man snapped a photo of her flushed cheek, watching how the wet flakes melted on her skin. He then zoomed in on the shape of her full breasts, peeking from her jacket. They heaved with each breath. So damn pretty.

"I arrived early and sat at the bar. It was a coincidence that she was there. We both drank too much. She invited herself to the dinner. It's not a big deal, she knows the team."

"That's our problem, you drink too much. You're angry all the time. You barely look at me anymore, and I feel like a naïve fool."

"Kat, please—"

"You need help. I'm not enough, and I never was. I want you to find peace…"

"Don't, baby. I love you. Please don't leave me—"

"Derek, you're breaking me. I cry all the time and I worry that you'll hurt yourself every time you drink too much or sink into that depression. We're both sad and I need to smile again. You need to get help—professional help. I love… love you so much." She swiped at her eyes. "I need you to be safe. Derry, promise me that you won't do anything stupid."

He pulled her into a hug, muttering unintelligible words. She drew back and placed a hand on his chest. "I have to go. Keep that brawny heart safe."

"You're my angel, please don't leave me." The tall man rubbed a hand over his eyes. "Baby, stay. I'll try harder and I'll get help."

Ignoring his pleas, the girl got in the car. With one last look she pulled away. The man swayed then collapsed on the steps, swearing then howling. Finally, he rested his head on his hands, rocking as the snow began to fall.

Heartless bitch. The scab came away and the man sucked at the welling blood. He reached over and checked the photos he'd captured. A good angle, she was a pretty one. Six girls in six months. Each kill was a cleansing. His next target was a man in Texas, the first male kill. Then, he'd write this snow-covered darling into the schedule. She needed to be taught a lesson in respect. He wasn't sure when he'd purge the black-haired beauty, but he had a feeling that the feisty girl would sanitize his soul.

Chapter One

Salt Lake City.
Twenty months later.

"I had the dream again last night."

"Walk me through it."

Slater tensed at his therapist's words. This was the second time they'd connected remotely, and he respected Seth, the man who had also once served and was now Slater's newly assigned MIT therapist. The previous head doctor was an older lady, a nice enough biddy, but Slater couldn't relate.

After Slater had been blown up by a grenade and had left his tier one team—Mobile Intelligence Team Two—he'd had a heart to heart with his MIT supervisor about his ongoing PTS issues. And a MIT registered therapist was assigned to Slater's case. MIT therapists were able to discuss sensitive and classified mission programs due to their high clearance levels, and without their guidance, Slater would not have survived the last year.

"I've laid this out before with your now retired colleague." His coffee had gone cold, and Slater grimaced as he sipped.

"You know it helps to talk about it. I can offer a different perspective," Seth pushed. "Let's run through it again."

Seth had a point—he had combat experience. Slater reached over the kitchen counter and adjusted the angle of the screen. "The night terror is a re-enactment of the Black Friday bombing that happened just over four and a half years ago. It was the second time our team had operated in the field together. We were still short of a fourth team member—Dave "Donnie" Wilson joined our MIT2 team months later. Erik "Max" Andersen is—was—the team leader. He's a force to be reckoned with—intellect and lethal energy. James *Johnny* Cane was the medic. The dude is a massive, muscled teddy bear, and a laidback bastard like me. As the Protection Specialist, it was my duty to keep my team safe—work out the layout and logistics, but we were backing another team. It wasn't our mission, and I was on overwatch that day."

"You hung back to watch your team's six?"

Slater nodded. "The op was supposed to be a quick in and out. We were to retrieve a converted asset—Sharon Nasari— from a busy mall in Manhattan. A beaten wife who was married to an extremist in a sleeper cell based in New York, and she was ready to give up the cell's secrets. My team received bad intel— from Simon *Sully* Cook."

Slater grabbed a carton of orange juice from the fridge, noting that he had Seth's full attention.

"Sully sympathized with Sharon Nasari. Due to his emotional entanglement with the asset, Sully arrived ahead of the rest of the task force and it turned into a rushed mission."

Slater paused to rub his brow. "When we arrived, we were on the incorrect level—one floor down from Sully and our target package. So, Max and the rest of the team took the escalator up to the facing food court. I intended to stand guard at the bottom of the escalator.

"You never made it that far?" Seth asked.

"No," Slater replied robotically as he poured a glass. "As I approached, I glanced up and spotted Sully and Sharon sitting on the top level. Sully suddenly lunged for Sharon Nasari's little girl and that's when the suicide vest detonated."

"Describe what you felt in the blast?"

Slater's hands began to tremble, and he sat back down to hide them from view. "The shockwave blew me off my feet, and it felt like I'd been hit in the chest by a grenade. I blacked out. When I came around, my ears rang, but I could still hear those screams. My teammates were the priority. Max—my team leader—had shrapnel embedded in his thigh, and I applied a make-shift tourniquet. A guy called Mike on the other team was in a bad way. His arm had been blown off, and he'd fallen one story down to the lower level. Aside from the knot on his head, Johnny seemed groggy but stable. One of the other operators applied pressure to Mike's arm while I saw to the kids. The food court had collapsed on the families below, crushing a children's play area."

Of the sixty-two deaths, twenty-two were tiny kids. Slater had tried so hard to save as many as he could. He paused before continuing.

"Take your time."

Grief tore at Slater's chest. Four and a half years since the bombing and he still couldn't find the words. He cleared his throat. "The first child I came across was around eight years old. He was banged up, but his vitals were good. I pulled him from the rubble and handed him to a fellow operator. I kept digging and finding kids, mothers, fathers, and infants. That's when I saw her—the little girl in the pink dress."

Slater swiped at a tear and stared at the orange pulp floating to the top of the glass. Seth didn't interrupt, and Slater appreciated his tactful reserve.

"She was so tiny, around three years old and still holding onto her deceased mother's hand. Crying for her mommy to wake up. The small tyke took her last breath as I lifted her into my arms."

That fateful moment had driven him over the edge. He'd served with the Green Berets for almost four years before joining the elite MIT2 team. Five months on the new job and he'd been PTS-fucked in a small shopping mall in Manhattan.

"Last night, that dream crossed over into my Nigerian nightmare. It melded with the grenade blast in Lagos."

Seth looked up. "The reason you left your team."

Slater nodded as he picked up his laptop and carried it to the living room. Almost a year and a half ago, a bouncing bomb in Lagos had buried Slater in a basement. The explosion shattered his left shoulder and arm. He'd been flown to the Landstuhl Regional Medical Center in Germany, and after returning to the States after a slow recovery, Slater left MIT2 to start a career with the FBI who'd offered him a lucrative and unique position. Slater would be in charge of running *The Stational Preparedness Facility* which would train agents for deployments. This project was an extension for the FBI's National Training Academy. It's focus would be on an agent's defensive tactics in war zones.

Slater had completed the basic six-month FBI training, and was immediately shoved into additional training and promoted to a SAIC, a Special Agent in Charge.

He had the exact training and know-how from his time with MIT, along with a degree in Criminology. This was a first for the bureau as they usually outsourced that kind of training to independent contractors.

Someone like Slater possessed unique capabilities in training agents for overseas assignments. FBI agents were required to work alongside Special Forces Operational Detachment Alpha (SFOD A) also known as an 'A-Team'—the primary fighting force of the Green Berets.

FBI agents were widely known as expert evidence gatherers who were also exceptionally well-trained with interview techniques. Lastly, when it came to tracking bomber syndicates, the bureau sent their best forensic experts to global hot zones.

It was Slater's responsibility to prepare agents for war zones at the new facility. The training would include mounting and dismounting operations, weapons training and handling, land navigation—escape and evasion techniques, medical and first aid training, and of course, basic P.T.

The FBI began designing and building a smaller agency version of the famous Guardian Center in Georgia, six months before Slater was placed in charge of the project. They'd first approached Slater as a consultant, before offering him the senior position and he felt privileged to be in charge of such a ground-breaking facility.

The agency had a solid reason for head hunting a super soldier like Derek *Slater* Banez. MIT operators were responsible for preparing overseas military units for combat—aside from tracking down extremists. MIT Special Forces warriors trained up indigenous black ops teams in various regions and that skill was coveted by U.S. government agencies.

Sitting on the sofa, Slater placed the laptop on the coffee table. "My relationship with my girlfriend fell apart four months before my injury. I keep seeing Kat in my dreams, just like I did in the moments after I was blown up. Thought I was going to die, then as clear as day, I saw her beside me. It was just a hallucination—Kat lying in the dirt as I waited for my team to dig me out."

The therapist leaned into the screen. "What does Kat say in the dream?"

"Don't leave me…. It's so cold… Derry, I'm scared."

"Did you ever mention this to Kat?"

"No," Slater said, trying not to sound bitter. "She'd cut off all contact with me. Wouldn't even answer my calls, even after I was injured."

"Because of your breakup? Did it end badly?"

"Yeah. I was a jerk, but I hoped Kat would put aside the pettiness once she'd heard about my injury in Nigeria."

"I'm sorry." Seth offered a sympathetic smile.

Slater shrugged. "Everything around me dies. People, relationships, my damn soul."

"That's a destructive assumption that prevents you from healing."

"Bullshit. I now drive around in an armored vehicle, thanks to some hoo-hah's email threats. Apparently, being a famous sniper paints a target on your back."

"I heard MIT provided you with the armored Raptor." Seth smiled and leaned back.

"They sure did—still protecting their former super soldier."

"You'll be fine. A trained operator like you can watch your own back."

"Perhaps I'll hold off on building a bomb shelter and prepping cave. Don't hate, meditate."

Seth laughed at Slater's joke.

Turning serious, Slater circled around to the grenade blast. "I don't understand what it means—seeing her that day in Lagos—the only explanation is that I have a TBI."

"Did you display any other symptoms of a Traumatic Brain Injury?"

Slater shook his head and leaned back into the sofa.

"How's your week shaping up after the press frenzy?"

Slater snorted at Seth's question. "Frankly speaking, they want my bones and fucking marrow. I've turned my phone off."

Someone had leaked Slater's records from his army days, and the press had got a hold of it. The military listed Slater as one of the most lethal snipers in U.S. Military history with over 150 kills. The statistics were all pre-MIT, when he'd served as a Green Beret. Undoubtedly, his file with MIT would never see the light of day and if it ever surfaced—which it wouldn't—that number would be much higher. Unfortunately, Slater now had to deal with news stations and reporters knocking at his door. He'd even had some publisher chasing him to write his biography. He'd told them all to screw off.

"I'm available anytime you need to talk," Seth offered.

Slater grinned. "Because you can't fix crazy, but you can document it."

After ending the call with Seth, Slater took a moment to calm himself down. Talking about his sorry-ass shit always got the adrenaline pumping. The old Slater would've probably used alcohol to drown out the memories. The new Slater grabbed his backpack and headed out the door to the job site for the pending facility. He had a new life that didn't include killing, explosions or angry ex-girlfriends. Now, he'd be training and saving lives, instead of exterminating them.

◊ ◊ ◊

Kat's phone lit up with an affirmation app reminder, and she used that as an excuse to check the time. Nine pm and she couldn't wait to get home to her bed. Her blind date didn't seem to notice as he spoke about his work day. From what she'd gathered, he was an installation electrician? He prattled on about a junction box. Kat smiled at the appropriate intervals, nodding as she sipped her wine.

Thirty-one.

Kat's thirty-first birthday and she spent the evening with a stranger. *Way to go, Kat.* She could have chosen any other night to start her dating adventures. Hell, she'd waited this long. Despite the slow start to the evening, Kat needed to meet new people—new men. Hoping to find a second great love? She studied her teal retro-style, swing dress and picked off a speck of fluff—nude heels complemented the look.

"Kathleen, everything okay?"

A deep voice jarred her back to the present, and her eyes darted to Rolf, the clean-shaven electrician staring across the table, hands folded in his lap.

"Please call me Kate."

That's the name most of her friends used. She preferred Kat. That's what her parents called her, and of course, it was the name Derek used when they'd dated. She always thought of herself as a "Kat." Strangers like Rolf weren't privy to that small detail.

His eyes traced her cheek before traveling down to her mouth. Kat adjusted her hair and stared down at the table. He was a large man, a quality she'd sought in the past. She'd loved that sheltering feeling of burrowing into a broad chest. Now the thought made her claustrophobic. A vision of a tall, athletic and broad-shouldered Adonis flashed. A symmetrical bone structure that could stop you in your tracks and whose hazel eyes sparkled with humor. A warm and toned body that embodied the term "shelter."

Pushing away the memories of Derek, Kat said, "Sorry, I don't know much about fuses and circuits."

"Well, if you paid attention, you might learn something."

"Wow," Kat growled the word.

"Just a joke. You seem distracted, what can I do to help?"

"I'm sorry, I didn't mean to be rude. It's been a long week." That was an understatement. Building up her clientele in a new business while preparing for a book launch took up all of her time.

Rolf smiled, his overly white teeth glinting as he pushed the platter of cornbread her way. "You barely touched your salad, have some cornbread."

A sticky, golden liquid coated the cake-like loaf, that now sat beneath Kat's nose and she shoved the plate back to the center of the table. "I can't. I'm allergic."

"To cornbread?"

"No—to the honey."

"That's ridiculous. You're allergic to honey?"

Kat nodded.

Raising brows, he asked, "Who's allergic to honey? It's natural—it comes from bees. Shit, it's in everything these days."

Kat tried to keep her snarkiness at bay. She refused to be embarrassed by her allergy; she'd lived through the "weird bubble girl" bias as a kid in school.

"Aye and I can't help my anaphylactic reaction."

"If I'd known, I wouldn't have ordered the cornbread—what a waste."

Kat traced her stainless steel medical ID bracelet with a thumb. "I have an early start in the morning, and I still have work waiting for me on my laptop. It was lovely meeting you." Tapping out a text message, Kat stood and reached for her bag.

Bodies suddenly surrounded her, and she flinched while clutching the tote to her chest. A waiter placed a giant brownie with a fizzing sparkler on the table as staff members broke out in song. Rolf fiddled with his fork.

Sinking back to her chair, Kat waited for the birthday ditty to finish. She thanked the band of singers, and as they walked off, she crossed her legs awkwardly.

Her phone dinged, and Rolf cleared his throat. "Jayden told me about your birthday."

Casey's boyfriend meant well. He'd been the one to set Kat up on the blind date. And he was also the man she'd texted earlier—now waiting out by her car and ready to follow her home.

"Thank you. That was sweet. Perhaps I'm not ready to date. I thought I was—"

"No need to explain." Rolf stood. "How about a box for that brownie?"

◊ ◊ ◊

Jayden met them at her car and Kat ignored Rolf's frown. He may think her paranoid, but she wasn't a sheep. A single woman needed to take precautions when dating strange men, and Jayden was a big-ass precaution. Over six feet of muscle. His dark skin glowed under the street light as he stepped forward to greet her date. He wore his uniform well, and Kat glanced at his police vehicle parked next to hers. The sight reassured her, and she relaxed as her tough-looking friend chatted with Rolf.

Kat hoped that Jayden and Casey stuck it out for the long haul. They were the cutest couple. Her colorful and eccentric friend deserved happiness, and Jayden's heart lay in Casey's hands.

Kat knew Jayden long before she'd set him up with Casey. They'd met many years ago at her father's pub in Colorado when they were in their early twenties. Both their fathers were Irish. Kat's Irish parents grew up in Dublin whereas Jayden's Jamaican mother met his father in Kingston before they were married. Then Jayden had joined the military and they'd barely kept in touch. The move to Utah after her breakup with Derek had placed her back in Jayden's world when she'd discovered that he lived in the city, and now worked for the Layton PD.

Rolf said his goodbyes and Kat heaved out a sigh.

Jayden watched him drive from the lot before turning to Kat. "Didn't go so well, huh?"

"It went arseways, but he seems… nice."

Jayden raised his brows. "Nice? That's the worst compliment you can bestow on a guy."

"I'm sorry. I know Rolf is a friend," Kat said as she rubbed her arms. Despite her light cardigan, the summer night was unusually chilly; a sign of the unpredictable Utahan weather.

"Relax. We're not all that close. I briefly served with Rolf's brother a couple of years ago—back in the day."

"Back in the day." Kat snorted. "You make out like you're sixty damn years old. You're a year younger than me and only left the army last year."

"Hey, grouchy pants, get your ass behind the wheel. Unlike you, I'm on the clock."

With a quick hug, Kat unlocked her Mini Cooper and climbed in.

Jayden eyed the Mini, and Kat shot him a look. "Leave my wee car alone."

"It's green—like a giant clover."

"The shade is British Racing Green, and it's savage looking. Every time you see it, you have to tease me about the color."

"It's a cliché Irish green. Only you could pull that off."

With a roll of her eyes, Kat put the car in gear.

Jayden stepped back. "Don't forget about your birthday brunch on Sunday. Will you be back in time?"

"Just a one day trip to Idaho. I'll be back by tomorrow night." Kat pulled off. Jayden followed her but turned off—lights flashing—a few blocks from her apartment. Her phone buzzed with a message from Jayden.

Domestic. Sorry. Text me when you're inside.

Kat parked in her usual spot and let out a shaky breath. Letting go of the wheel, she unclenched stiff hands. It wasn't a big deal. She only had to walk around the corner, down the path, and up the stairs to her apartment. Fifteen minutes later, Kat unlocked her car door and slammed it shut with shaking hands. She raced up the path, stumbling in her haste. Damn heels. She loved stilettos and found any excuse to wear one of the numerous pairs of heels lining her closet. So what if she had a shoe addiction… clothes addiction… make-up addiction. Looking pretty cheered her up.

Kat hurried up the stairs, shoved through her door and slammed it shut. Next came her locking up ritual. First was the Thumb Turn Only Deadbolt. Next, the silver door guard and chain and lastly, the Barrel Bolt. Once inside, Kat checked all the windows, the angle of the blinds in the two bedrooms and her office and finally tested the sliding doors in the lounge.

With a tired sigh, she kicked off her heels and wandered into her bedroom at the end of the passage. Her blue and cream haven—accented with a dash of lemon. As Kat slipped out of her dress, her phone rang with an incoming call. Kat admired the pink satin bra and matching panties she'd recently bought online. Maybe she'd buy the same set in more colors. It had a great vintage vibe. Grabbing the phone from her bag, Kat grinned at the name on the screen before answering.

"How're ya, chicken?"

Casey's snort echoed through the line. "Dying of curiosity. How did the date go?"

"Okay. I guess."

"Oh, shit. That bad? Why didn't you hang out with me instead? I have wine!"

"Because I'm trying to be brave."

"Wine makes you brave."

Kat giggled while grabbing a sweater from a drawer. The lights went out, and she froze.

"Goddammit," Casey swore. "My power just shut down."

Closing her eyes, Kat took a breath. "Mine too. It must be an area-wide outage."

"Well, that sucks. I was just about to watch *X-men*." Casey crunched down on something that Kat assumed was popcorn.

"You've watched every X-man movie like a thousand times."

"It's *X-men*—not X-man. And so what. I like Wolverine. He can stroke me with his knifey hands anytime."

"Euw. You're doing my head in." Kat felt her way to her bedside table. "Does Jayden know about your creepy Hugh Jackman obsession?"

"Hey, Hugh keeps me awake until Jayden gets off his shift. My man is more than grateful."

Bingo. Kat's hand wrapped around the flashlight. "I don't want to hear about your sex life. I'm heading to bed."

"Come over to my place. I'm like three blocks away."

Casey lived in an adjacent newly built apartment building, just across from the even newer fancy strip mall. Kat loved being this close to her best friend. If they weren't hanging out at each other's homes, they were having coffee at the waffle shop overlooking the fountains.

"Fine. Let me pull on a pair of jeans. Give me a moment. I need to—"

"I know. Do your 'leaving the house' ritual. It takes a while. I'm here, and I have coffee ice cream in the freezer. If this outage lasts a while, I'll need to eat it before it melts."

"Damn you, Casey. Why don't you just come to my place?"

"You know why. I'll see you in a bit."

Kat cursed as she threw the phone on the bed. Her friend had her best interests at heart. Kat chose an oversized sweater and sneakers—a perfect match for a full glass of wine.

◊ ◊ ◊

As soon as Casey opened the door, Kat stalked over and threw herself into the curved velvet chair. It matched Casey's seventies decor, and thanks to the poufy cushions, it was the perfect sanctuary for Kat's tired ass.

"Well, hello to you too. Don't you look like a little lady."

Kat looked down at her splayed legs. "I'm wearing jeans. And how can you even see me? It's pitch black in here."

"I have candles lit."

"One weak-ass candle," Kat said, stretching further into an inelegant pose.

"The rest of the candles are at the top of the closet." Casey started to drag a chair towards the hall closet.

"Screw that," Kat said. "It's kind of peaceful. Let's drink wine. Besides, your orange hair lights up the room."

"Hey, I like my neon orange look. I am thinking about yellow next."

"God, poor Jayden. He's dating a walking candle wick."

"I'll pour this glass over that perfectly blown-out hair..." Casey handed over a glass of wine. Flowery patterns decorating the glass matched the mish-mashed decor of the small flat.

Kat grinned. "Try it, pixie nerd."

"Bleh." Casey took a seat on the deep sofa. "God, it's quiet without all the appliances running. Creepy quiet. How was your date?"

"Probably would've been better if I wasn't my usual paranoid self. I did try, but all the fella spoke about was circuit breakers and currents." Kat took a long sip of the light wine, savoring the slightly bubbly flavor.

"Ouch. Seriously?"

"Yip, and he didn't ask about me once. Also, when I refused the cornbread drenched in honey, he huffed about ordering it."

"That's madness. In that case, I think you've had a lucky escape."

"Case, if you're going to set me up on a blind date, find someone compatible. You owe me. Jayden owes me. Historically, I was a kick-ass matchmaker when it came to the pair of you."

"Rolf is more Jayden's friend. and he's supposed to be quiet and sweet."

Kat took a long sip of the sparkling wine. "He is sweet-like. Quiet, not so much. I could've received an electrician's diploma tonight."

Casey leaned forward. "Ooh, ooh! One of my online gamers friends just broke up with his girlfriend. He seems fun."

"Hold your horses. If you haven't met him in the flesh and performed a background check—"

A knock at the front door had both women jumping.

"Are you expecting someone?" Kat rose to her feet and edged to the wall.

"Relax hun; it's probably just a neighbor looking for a flashlight or matches." Casey walked towards the door, careful not to trip.

"Case, don't answer the door."

"I have a peephole. Honey, relax." Casey pressed her face to the door, and Kat held her breath.

"Shit," Casey swore, backing away.

"Oh, God. Who is it?" Kat clutched the stem of the glass, ready to wield it as a weapon.

"Casey? Open up." A deep voice boomed from the other side of the door.

They both froze, and Casey's horrified glance turned Kat's way.

Chapter Two

The Ford F-150's headlights lit up the side of the building—the only light in the dark lot. Slater switched them off and assessed his surroundings. Casey lived in a newly built, upmarket neighborhood in Layton, and her apartment sat in a mixed-use development consisting of an upscale, open-air shopping center, offices, and residential buildings. A simulated creek flowed through the paved design, and foliage-lined walkways covered a three-block radius. In essence, the modernized area was reasonably secure. That meant a lot to Slater. His cousin could never stay in a dump, and thanks to his jaded brain, he needed her to be safe.

Although she now dated a burly police officer, Casey lived as a single woman. Her job as a computer programmer allowed her to work from home, and she earned enough to live in the luxurious development. Except now, the dark area had his nerves tingling. He'd noted the outage as he'd driven into her area. Probably a downed pole that needed fixing. A power outage wasn't a big deal, and Slater knew he should relax the hell out, but the soldier in him had him climbing out the truck.

Slater paused after locking the vehicle. He felt like an ass. He'd been in Utah for over six months and had seen Casey a total of five times. Granted, proving himself in his new career had taken up much of his time—endless days and nights of working onsite. When he wasn't overseeing the build, he was training. But shit. Growing up, Casey had been like a best friend. They'd done everything together. Casey wasn't just family; she'd been his rock when he'd had no-one. Aside from his old MIT2 team, she was the only person he trusted with his life. That wasn't entirely true. There was Kat, but he couldn't go there.

Slater bypassed the elevator and sprinted up the stairs. The only sound was the echo of his footsteps in the quiet building. Stepping out onto the third floor, he approached his cousin's door. After knocking, Slater waited. Hearing no sound, he rapped again and called out. He'd seen Casey's car parked in her covered, assigned spot. Still nothing. Maybe she was in the shower?

A scrape on the other side of the door had him straightening. "Casey, everything okay?"

The door cracked open. "Uh, hi." Casey looked pale, and tucked a trembling hand into her pocket.

Slater frowned. "Yello. What are you doing? Open up."

"Now is not a good time." Her eyes darted to the side, and the lack of eye contact raised his hackles. Since he'd moved to Utah, his cousin had been acting a little strange around him. Awkward. But the way she clutched the door, stiffly blocking his form didn't sit right.

Slater eased a hand behind his back and felt for his piece. "Are you alone, Cuz?"

"Sure." She glanced down, shifting. Her demeanor had alarm bells ringing. Power outages provided the perfect opportunity for criminals to target homes. When the lights go out, crime rates increase. Security systems fail. Sure, it had probably only been a few hours and Layton wasn't exactly crime central, but Slater wasn't taking any chances.

Lightning quick, he shoved at the door and slid past Casey. Ignoring her squeal of surprise, Slater pulled his gun and searched the dark space. A shadow near the wall moved, something glinted in the bogey's right hand.

"Drop the weapon and raise your hands."

The dark form cringed against the wall. Although Slater had only met Jayden a couple of times, he immediately knew that the shape of the suspect was too small to be her boyfriend.

"Derek, stop." Casey tried to step past, and he blocked her way.

Making out dark jeans and a hooded sweater, Slater eased closer. "FBI. I said, drop it!"

"It's Kate!" Casey shrieked at the same time as the unknown stepped closer. A flash of black hair falling forward over an oval face had him lowering his weapon. Slater staggered and swore soundly before bracing his free hand against the wall.

"Holy hell. I nearly fucking shot you."

"No, you wouldn't have fired your weapon without reason." Her husky voice adorned with that perceptible lilt, sounded pure in the quiet space.

"I'm going to be sick." Slater holstered his Glock and swiped at his now clammy brow. "I pointed my damn Glock at you. What the hell is wrong with me?"

"You were protecting your cousin."

"Why didn't you just let me in, Casey?" Slater asked, and pulled in a steadying breath.

"Umm. Because Kate is here, I knew it would be awkward… after all this time."

After all this time.

Yeah, twenty months later. He'd kept track. Slater knew he'd run into Kat at some point, maybe at the gym or a wedding or a coffee shop. Casey and Kat were best friends; how did he not figure out this scenario. Slater needed a moment. Sucking in deep breaths, he ignored the two women hovering in the periphery. Finally, he pushed off the wall while Kat still stuck to the shadows. Casey looked even paler than before.

"Awkward is an epic understatement." Slater ran hands through his hair as he walked in a circle. "I feel like I'm wearing a damn shock collar, I'm shaking like shit."

"I should go." Kat leaned down and placed her empty glass on the side table. He'd thought that was a weapon in the dark space. Slater could've shot her over a wine glass. Her hair fell back over her face, and before he could take her in, she retreated to the corner.

"I'll call you tomorrow," Casey said before opening the door.

"Wait." Slater stepped towards Kat. "We haven't seen each other in twenty months, and you're hustling out?"

She shuffled along the wall, avoiding him like he was a rabid circus monkey. Kat probably wasn't far off the mark, he felt like he'd just leapt through rings of fire while foaming at the mouth. Heart-hammering adrenaline still coursed through his veins.

"Kat, say something."

"I… I'm glad you're well. Casey told me that you're now working for the FBI. Congratulations." She reached into a back pocket; keys jangled as she ripped them free and Kat dashed for freedom like she was escaping a zombie apocalypse. Casey slammed the door shut behind her friend and turned to Slater. "Derek, I need candles. They're at the top of the cupboard. Oh, and I think there's a flashlight in one of the kitchen drawers."

Slater stared at the door.

"Derek?"

"What the hell just happened?"

"Kate has an early flight in the morning." Casey shuffled towards the kitchen.

"Bullshit. I know what happened in Denver, I acted like a dick, but the way Kat just reacted…"

"Derek—"

"Fuck it." He exited the apartment and headed for the stairs, taking them two at a time. Kat was halfway across the lot by the time he'd caught up. The lights of a green Mini Coop flashed.

"Kat!"

She froze—her back to him.

For a moment, they both stood as Slater's mind raced. He'd rehearsed his lines a thousand times—how he'd beg for her forgiveness, and ask for her friendship. God, he missed her and ached for every inch of this woman. Her body, those lips, her soft hands. That intelligent mind. Slater needed her back in his life, even as a friend. Probably a self-destructive move but he'd beg for a smile, a coffee, a sliver of her time. Of all the hurtling emotions, his mind chose the anger and frustration he'd bottled for so long.

"Why didn't you come to Germany or call—after I was injured?"

Kat didn't move.

"I didn't expect you to fly over. Just a simple phone call would've worked."

Still nothing…

"We had only been separated for just over four months." Slater swallowed past the lump. "I thought we loved each other regardless… even as just friends. Common decency—"

She still refused to face him.

31

"While I lay in Landstuhl, I messaged you. Twenty-eight texts. My teammates called, leaving numerous voice mails and messages. You knew about my shattered arm and my shoulder." Her hands clenched into fists as Slater continued with his rant. "You were never a vindictive and petty person. Did you hate me that much? That you couldn't even check—"

"Stop." Kat choked on a sob. "You're right. I'm a cold bitch—"

"I never said—"

"Derry, you deserve better. I'm not worth your time. It's best if we stay away from each other."

"If we can sit down and talk…"

"It's over Derek." Without turning, she jerked open her door and climbed in. Within seconds, Kat had pulled out of the lot.

Yeah, it was over. The Kathleen Flynn he'd known would've turned and faced him, looking him in the eye. His Kat would've contacted him after his injuries sustained in Nigeria. Hell, she would've been on the first plane to Germany. Revenge would've been the last thing on her mind. For three and a half years, they'd shared everything—hopes, dreams, breakfast, ice cream, bike rides, popcorn at the movies, their bed. Never once had he seen this side to Kat, and it hurt. It fucking ripped his heart out all over again.

◊ ◊ ◊

The next few days were busy. Slater worked his ass off at the range alongside one of the construction crews. They dug trenches and hollows for a series of ponds in the wetland area of the training facility. The hard manual labor took Slater's mind off his disastrous encounter with Kat. His injured shoulder burned but he couldn't regress. He'd come so far in the battle with PTSD. For the first time in years, he could breathe. The nightmares weren't as severe, and there had only been two flashbacks in the last three months. Maybe it was the new job and the physical exertion involved in building the training facility. It was his project—he'd adjusted the original designs for optimal success. Instead of all the killings and dissimilation he'd experienced in the military, he now raised a structure—numerous ranges and training areas. By designing a future facility and a training schedule for new agents, his life no longer included destruction.

At midnight he winded his way down the hillside from the purpose built village they'd recently erected—reflecting realistic conditions that provided a truly immersive experience. The twenty structures varied from one to three stories and included intersections, alleys, roof access and stairwells. Simunitions and munitions training had just been authorized by the county for the onsite village.

Slater pulled up at the Command Center. The rest of the team had left hours ago. His arm throbbed and Slater stretched out his shoulder. He'd take ibuprofen when he got home. Grabbing a Coke from the cooler, Slater stepped out onto the back deck of the newly built main office. So far out of Salt Lake, the stars lay clear across the sky. The distant Wasatch Mountains smudged the horizon, and Slater sat on the steps as the breeze cooled his damp shirt. The facility lay on an isolated stretch of farmland, away from the prying eyes of the media. Here, agents could train in privacy in an indigenous landscape that had striking similarities in terrain and weather conditions to places like Afghanistan. By the time they'd complete the training installations, it would feel like the agents were on foreign soil.

Giving in to temptation, Slater pulled his phone from his back pocket and dialed Casey's number.

"Hey, Cuz." Slater stretched out his legs.

"Uh, hey."

"Are you free tomorrow? I want to swing by and—"

"I have—I'm busy. I have work stuff."

"Let me guess. You're hanging with Kat?"

"Kate's away at the moment. I have projects lined up, and I'm stuck behind my desk."

"Why don't I bring lunch over tomorrow?"

"I won't be home. Can we chat another time? I'll call you."

Without waiting for him to say goodbye, Casey hung up. Slater stared at the phone. That was a first. He missed the long phone calls with his cousin when they'd talk for hours. Maybe he'd left it too long? Or perhaps she was swamped. He missed the good old days when they'd spend the summers on some lake, or winters in the Rockies. A big family vacation with his crazy sister, parents, Casey's family, and loads of other cousins.

Slater's mind drifted, and like many times before, he wandered back to memories of Kat. Their first vacation together was spent near Denver—in Summit County—and Slater rented a cluster of cabins for all their respective family members. They'd all enjoyed ice fishing, dog sledding, and skiing. Her parents were the last to depart. Finally, Slater had his girlfriend all to himself—just the two of them in a remote cabin in the snowy mountains.

He remembered walking out onto the deck, pausing and taking in Kat's quiet profile, curled in a chair. An oversized, thick, red cardigan had enveloped her delicious curves as she'd held a steaming cup of coffee in gloved hands.

"Don't you love the silence?" she'd asked, looking up at him from under a beige capped beanie.

"After both of our tribespeople have left. Hell, yeah. Now our vacation begins."

Slater had surveyed the ring of trees surrounding the cabin, weighted down with snow. Brilliant white contrasted with tree bark and the hushed woods looked like it slept under a white blanket, occasionally shuddering with falling chunks of snow.

Slater enjoyed the cooler temperatures knowing he'd soon face baking heat in East Africa. He was eager to work with his new team in the field. MIT2 had trained for months in preparation for their overseas deployment. But first, they'd support a local U.S. task force, running a joint mission in New York. Then came setting up a new base in Nairobi. Slater couldn't wait for his first MIT deployment. In the meantime, he'd relish the time spent with Kat.

She'd stood and walked down the steps, and he'd followed, pausing to pull her into his arms and give her a soul-blistering kiss. His hand had found its way under her layers, tracing warm skin. She'd grinned against his mouth at his exploration.

"We can't..."

"What? Can't make love against a tree trunk?"

"Derry."

"We'll warm up in a hot tub after. I promise."

"Someone may see us."

"No-one comes up here. We are truly alone." He pulled her between the tall trunks until he found a secluded spot.

"It's just the trees... you... me... my dick slipping into your tight—"

"Bloody hell," she'd said, pulling him around for a kiss. "And you get to keep your pants on, I'll have to take mine off, but if my naked ass gets frostbite..." She'd slipped her leggings down, balanced to remove one socked foot from her casual suede boot, and pulled it free of her pants. Slater had lifted her immediately, and Kat had wrapped her legs around his waist.

He'd unzipped his pants and placed his cock at her entrance. "Let's pretend that we're the only two people on the planet and this is our mountain." He'd slowly pushed in, watching her groan. "We're leaning against our favorite tree." Slater had then slid out. "I'm your favorite primitive boy toy."

Kat laughed as she clung to him. "And let me guess... I'm your favorite...?" He thrust up, and her head fell back. "Oh... don't stop... that feels... God, Derry!"

Slater pumped his hips and felt her tightening. "You're my favorite everything." Her fogged breath mixed with his as he groaned in pleasure. "I love you... so... damn... much."

That was the first time he'd said the words to anyone, and Kat had rewarded him by coming hard around his dick. Slater had followed and held her to him as they both spasmed out their release in that sacred space.

Later that night, when they'd taken a long bath together, he'd pulled out the Jade necklace from beneath a towel.

They'd lain in the tub, her head resting against his chest as water lapped around her shapely breasts. "What is this? It's not my birthday."

"I saw this in town, and it reminded me of you. Red Jade is the stone of strength and passion and has a life-force energy. It's not the most attractive pendant but—"

"It's perfect. I never want to take it off."

Once he'd fastened it around her neck, Kat kept to her silly promise. She'd worn the clunky bauble in the bath and to their bed, and had never taken it off in the years they'd dated.

Slater rubbed a hand over his neck and thought of all the ways he'd destroyed their love. Kat had every right to ghost him. If Slater were Kat, he'd also avoid his destructive-ass. Locking up for the night, Slater climbed in his truck and headed over to his lonely rental home. Howling at suffocative walls would be penance for his past sins.

The airline ground personnel were finally back at the boarding gate, and Kat suppressed a yawn. Her flight back to Salt Lake City had currently been delayed by three hours. She'd tried to get some work done while running between gates and had eventually given up. Kat couldn't concentrate anyway. Her mind kept wandering and settling on her run-in with a sexy ex-boyfriend. Even in the dim light, Derek was still drool-worthy. If anything, he'd seemed somehow more capable and intense. Who was she kidding? Derek had always possessed an incredible intensity. His sharp brain and quick humor backed that lean and muscled body. The man was like molten lava and she'd never been able to resist his catastrophic charm.

For this reason, Kat needed to walk—no run—in the opposite direction. How had she not planned for this scenario? Of course, she'd run into the man at some point, his cousin was her best mate.

Kat watched the other passengers begin to line-up at the gate. They were in for a long wait. She hadn't seen the new crew members arrive yet, and the gate hadn't made a boarding announcement. One of the passengers stared her way. A surly-looking man that looked to be in his mid-forties. She met his unblinking stare and refused to look away. Finally his face flushed, and he glanced down.

Arsebiscuit.

Kat wondered if Derek was seeing anyone. She tried to imagine what his girlfriend would look like. Tall, tanned and blonde? One of those Instagram stars with the perfect life?

They'd go hiking together—and probably choose a spot like the Kalalau Trail in Hawaii. They'd pose with perfect smiles, and have a wagging Labrador by their side. Their penthouse would have a crackling fireplace, matching treadmills and twin sinks. Derek had always been a basin hog. He'd want his own space.

The crew stalked past, jolting Kat out of her bitter imaginings. Her nose crinkled as she pulled out her phone. A game of Candy Crush would distract her. After all, Kat wasn't planning on seeing Derek ever again. It was better that way. She harbored a dangerous secret that could destroy his world.

◊ ◊ ◊

"I'm done with negotiating the minefield called family. I need answers." Slater glanced around the table at the other nine members. The *Veteran Assistance Program* held meetings twice a week at a local church. His therapist recommended a support group. This was Slater's fifth session, and he liked the camaraderie with fellow veterans. Like Slater, many had PTSD. They didn't always talk about traumatic issues; most of the time, they chatted about everyday challenges and how they assimilated to civilian life. Finding stable work outside the military was the biggest challenge, and many took what they could get—construction work, sales, or working in the fast food industry. A fellow veteran named Red Hill who came from Slater's original support group in Colorado, had moved up to Utah and reached out to Slater, asking him to join the Salt Lake crowd. Red was a nice enough guy, and now took his supervisory position seriously. Slater called him a "stats gagger." The guy puked up endless facts about veteran affairs. He probably spent hours online memorizing that kind of shit. Aside from Red who sat to his left, two other men at the table that garnered Slater's immediate respect were former Special Forces soldiers. Logan Jenkins and Elliot Elsworth. Both men never said much. Slater was much the same way when he'd first left the military. Now he couldn't shut up.

"Your sister?" Tiana asked. Slater smiled at the former National Guard specialist. He held nothing but respect for the 12B Combat Engineer. He'd heard she'd done her unit proud for over three years—a warrior who now watched him with genuine concern.

"I've mended my relationship with my sister. Well, kind of. She's a pain in the ass on a good day, but she resides in Santa Barbara. It's my cousin who lives here, that worries me. She's acting cagey, and her attitude is confusing. We used to be so close, and now it's like she's avoiding my sorry ass."

"When did it start?" Logan asked. "The distance thing?"

"After Germany." Slater wouldn't go into details. The veterans only knew he'd been injured, having no idea about his black ops career or who he'd worked for. Some of the vets suspected he'd gone off the grid. "Casey flew over and visited me in the hospital. Wait. Even then, she was acting weird. I thought she was just worried over my injuries. I'm not so sure now."

"You're overanalyzing this shit." The new guy piped up as he scratched his palm. "Half the time, these chicks make no sense; they don't even understand their own shit. She probably had a bad day. You know—menses crap."

Slater immediately took a dislike to the arrogant prick, trying to recall his name. Brock... Brock the bonehead.

Slater turned to Tiana. "Do you wanna kick his ass, or can I take a swing?"

Bonehead raised his hands. "I'm just saying. You're acting like a damn wimp. Civilians have no idea what we've experienced and if your cousin wants to act like a bitch—"

Slater surged to his feet. Red stepped in between, shoving Brock back. "Whoa. Dude! Are you insulting one of the deadliest snipers in history? Quit with the smack talk!"

The rest of the table stood, watching with wary eyes.

Slater vibrated with rage. "Apologize for the 'bitch' comment."

"Easy, buddy. I never called her a bitch. I said she was acting like—"

"We're not buddies. I don't know you from shit, but you're a fellow vet, so I'll give you a pass. Next time you insult my family, I'll punch that smile off your face." With a glance and nod to the others, Slater grabbed his keys and walked out. It took some minutes to calm down. Adrenaline lapped at his healing mind, tearing up old memories and Slater stopped himself from punching the dash. Hunting, pulling the trigger, death around every corner. Slater wasn't that raging soldier anymore.

Over the past year, he'd worked hard at mending his soul and adjusting his attitude. He wouldn't allow one angry prick to set him back. Picking up the phone, Slater called a person who knew his past, who'd lived through the same agonies. Max Andersen, his former team leader, picked up on the first ring. After chatting for what seemed like hours, Slater knew what he had to do

Chapter Three

The door opened before Slater had a chance to knock. Casey stepped back with wide eyes as Jayden picked up their car keys from the side table behind her.

"You look nice," Slater said, inwardly cursing his timing.

Jayden's tie matched her fitted blue cardigan which she wore with a smart black skirt. Casey swallowed and blinked.

"I hoped we could talk."

"We're on our way out." Her face colored and she glanced down at her shoes.

"Wedding?"

"No."

She hadn't yet looked him in the eye, and Slater wanted to yell out his frustration. If he knew what he'd done to hurt his cousin, then he could make amends.

"We're late. I'll call you tomorrow." She clasped her handbag strap in a tight fist.

"That's what you said when we last spoke, and the time before that."

Jayden curled a hand around his girlfriend's waist and guided her forward. "We'll catch up later, buddy."

Slater stepped out of the way, and Casey shot him a tight

smile. After closing the door, Jayden led Casey down the hall.

"Tell me what I've done wrong, Cuz. Tell me how to fix this."

"Don't be silly; there's nothing to fix." Casey waved as she stepped into the elevator. Slater still hadn't moved. Instead, he scraped a hand over his face and leaned against the wall.

"Sweetheart, I'll meet you at the truck," Jayden said to Casey as the doors slid closed, silencing her protest. He turned and walked back up the passage. Slater braced himself for an awkward conversation; he hardly knew the man.

"Listen, bud. I'm not sure what you did, but she hasn't been herself since you've moved to Utah. It's pissing me off. Casey's happiness is all I care about, and I don't know your history. I don't know you, but I swear to God if you ever hurt her—"

"I've hurt a lot of people over the past four years—tore my sister's heart out and did the same thing to Casey's friend. I've been a fucking asshole, but I'm trying to make amends. I've never hurt Casey; I swear man. I may have kept my distance while healing, and that's why it doesn't make any sense. We've barely seen each other."

"Well, she's freaking out," Jayden said with a frown.

"She hasn't said anything to you?"

"Not a word. Changes the subject every time I ask about you."

Slater swore, and his head began to pound.

"Look, we're going to a women's event—some charity breakfast. Why don't you meet us there, and pull Casey aside afterward for a coffee? It's at that fancy conference center near the mall. Kate's the guest speaker."

It took a second for Slater to respond, as blood rushed from his head. "Kat will be there?"

"Yeah, that's what I said. She's pretty nervous; it's a lead up to her book release."

"She wrote a book?"

"Look, bro, we're now fucking late. I gotta bounce. If you decide to come, I'll give you guys the space that you need." With a nod, Jayden jogged to the stairs.

Slater stared at the wall before taking a breath. He could see her one last time. Kat wouldn't even see him—Slater could stand near the back, and once she'd finished her speech, he'd slip out. No harm, no foul.

◊ ◊ ◊

Glancing around the lobby, Slater headed for the registration table. Banners advertising "The Empowerment Symposium" decorated the generous space. A polished lady stood behind the desk, packing pamphlets into a box. Smiling, she waved him through. "You've missed the breakfast, and the first fifteen minutes. You're welcome to find a seat."

Thanking her, Slater slipped through the heavy doors. The packed room—filled with mostly women—all watched a matronly-looking speaker on the stage. Slater scanned the crowd, looking for Casey and Jayden. They sat near the front, most likely at a reserved table. The speaker mentioned Kat's name and Slater zeroed in, frowning at the words.

"Some of you may know Kathleen Flynn's story. She's never spoken of her journey in public, and this will be her first time sharing. Please show her the patience and respect that her bravery deserves. At ten, we'll break out into workshop groups for the warrior brainstorm, then those joining us in the 'Standing with Strength' charity drive will meet in conference room 23."

The speaker then turned and introduced Kat to the stage. Slater knew she'd left the corporate world to start her own motivational training company. Some life coaching gig.

Curiosity piqued, Slater folded his arms and waited for her speech to commence. The moment she walked on stage, his palms grew clammy. She looked even more beautiful than he'd remembered. A fitted dress clung to her curves accenting a narrow waist and shapely hips. Her hair hung loose, pinned over on one side in an elegant sweep. Her usual cherry red lipstick matched a slim red belt cinched around her waist. Kat walked confidently to the podium in killer heels. Slater couldn't see her clearly from the back, but flat screens scattered throughout the room focused on her side profile. Her long neck exposed to the camera, a shoulder rising with one deep breath. The slight tremble to her lower lip surprised Slater. Thanks to her long career as a corporate trainer, Kat embraced the public speaking aspect. That stage was where she felt most comfortable, so why the nerves?

She took her time arranging her notes. The room collectively held its breath, and the pensive energy had Slater glancing around.

Kat began to talk. "We all plan out our lives, thinking we know what our future might hold, but the universe has different ideas. Generally speaking, many of the women in this room are starting over. You're struggling through a divorce or recovering from an illness. You're a single mum with mouths to feed. Perhaps you're changing careers and trying to be brave. Some of you might be immersed in a hopelessness, facing an upward battle against a blue funk that's pulling you back down. Sixteen months ago, my life took a different path. I'd already veered away from my ideal 'white picket fence' life. Fate took over when a traumatic incident shoved me into a tailspin."

Slater did the math in his head, working out the timeline. Was she speaking about Nigeria? About him? Muscles tensed as he studied her quiet profile, craving to know the thoughts in her head.

"Since that moment, I've been crawling on hands and knees in the dirt, figuring how to stand back up. Admittedly, it won't happen overnight, but that's okay. Starting over is a challenge many women face. You're stronger than you'll ever know, and believe it or not… you are in control. We all have different mountains to climb, and this is my story."

Kat placed her papers aside and raised her chin. "April sixteenth is a day I'll never forget. April Seventeenth and every day after that was when my struggle began."

Nostrils flaring, Slater planted his feet apart, restraining himself from rushing the stage. How dare she speak of that day— that hot Lagos day when a grenade almost ripped his arm away. Kat had no right to use his injuries or his now famous sniper career to further her own. Was she planning to talk about how his misfortune adversely affected her psyche? If Kat mentioned his MIT2 team to civilians, she'd be wading into restricted territory. Vision grayed as betrayal seared through Slater's veins.

"My best friend Casey is sitting here today." Kat pointed her out. "Casey, do I have permission to tell this story? Are you okay with this?"

Casey nodded as Slater's blood pressure soared. Was Kat asking Casey's permission to tell Slater's fucking story? The urge to run had him backing towards the door. He lived a damn nightmare in a room of enemies—loved ones who now used his infamy as a covert sniper and Green Beret superstar to further their agenda. A camera flashed and Slater spotted a couple of photographers huddled in the corner.

Kat's fingers tapped her papers as she began talking. "I took the Monday and Tuesday off of work. Casey and I decided to spend a long weekend in Park City. At that higher altitude, and thanks to the long winter, there was still snow on the ground. We rented a holiday home in town and snowshoed, hiked, laid in the jacuzzi, and drank wine. Monday night rolled around, and after wandering through town, we chose to sit at a local pub. By ten at night, we were ready to call it quits."

Wanting to see how this would circle back to him, Slater waited, ready to pounce or walk away. Kat hadn't yet spotted him, neither had Casey.

Smiling, Kat turned to her friend. "Casey had just started dating a lawyer who decided to surprise his new girlfriend by traveling up to Park City. He turned up at the bar just as we were about to leave. I decided to give them their space."

Kat's mouth turned up at the corners. "Sorry Jayden—Casey broke up with him shortly after. Honestly, that wee man has nothing on you."

"Gee thanks." Jayden rolled his eyes, shifting uncomfortably.

The room laughed. After taking a sip of water, Kat no longer smiled. Slater had never seen that strange look on her face before, and he began to suspect that this wasn't about him—this was Kat's story.

"The walk to the hotel was a short one, five minutes at the most. Casey offered to come along, but I didn't want to ruin her grand evening. Besides, the quaint ski resort is one of the safest places on the planet. I walked up Main Street on a chilly Monday night and passed one other couple. Halfway up the hill, I turned down a quieter side street and must've decided to cut through a small wooded path. I don't remember much after that. Snapshots of pain."

Slater dropped his arms at the words spilling from Kat's mouth. It made no sense. Ears roaring, he dreaded the words he thought he'd never live to hear.

"My attacker didn't try to rape me or drag me to a remote spot. The bastard was intent on murder, and a metal pipe was his weapon of choice. The first blow caught me on the shoulder, the second slammed into my thigh. Blow after blow. The pipe shattered my wrist as I tried to protect my head and face. The edge caught me on the temple, splitting my cheek. I've had two facial surgeries for that scar." Kat pulled hair back from the shadowed side of her face.

Slater's mind howled against the horrors being re-told. There had to be some mistake. Was he living in one of his fucked-up dreams?

"The surgeons did a great job. Up close, you can still see the scar. Initially, during the first six months, I looked like a monster, but that was the least of my troubles and injuries. Some of you know the story or at least parts of what went down through the media." Kat clutched at a gold chain that disappeared beneath her neckline. "My assailant would've killed me. Once I was immobile, he climbed on my chest, leaned down, and told me I'd landed on his naughty list. He then drew a knife and began to stab. I knew he'd kill me, and I was powerless to stop him. I vaguely remember staring up at the starry sky through snow-covered branches, and knowing that would be the last thing I'd see."

Kat paused to take a sip of water. The glass shook in her hands and the sound of clinking ice filled the room. Shock had Slater rooted to the spot and his temples pounded as he tried to pull in air.

"That's when Jake Calvin and his wife walked by. Jake is the hero who saved... saved my life. He dragged the evil arsehole away... and fought him off." Kat gripped the edges of the podium. "Jake almost died, saving me; he chased the bastard while bleeding out from a knife wound. By that time, I was so out of it—due to blood loss and the head injury. I only later heard about his heroics during my recovery."

Choked by rage, Slater yielded to the rising nausea. The room swung as he plowed into a waiter and stumbled for the door. Plates crashed. He glanced back at Kat, who now gaped at him as recognition dawned. Slater tried to say her name, but could only croak out his horror. Slamming through the double doors, he ran for the exit to the parking lot and headed for the nearest potted plant. After emptying the contents of his stomach, he collapsed to the curb.

Slater's brain denied her words as he rested his head in shaking hands. He'd been the one who'd been hurt—buried and bleeding—who'd lain for weeks in a hospital bed in Germany, and spent months recovering, and Kat had been safe in Utah. After his vision in Lagos, at his request, his team had reached out to Casey. His cousin had sworn that Kat was fine, except she'd lied, knowing her friend lay on death's door. Some fucker had put his hands on sweet Kat. Beaten her with a steel... God.

"Derek?"

Every muscle froze as he continued staring at the painted curb beneath him.

"I'm sorry. Let me explain."

No, he didn't want to hear pathetic excuses from his traitorous cousin. Rolling to his feet, Derek dusted off his jeans, then turned his back on Casey. Jayden stood a few feet behind her, his hands on his hips.

"Bro, did you know about Casey's lies?" Slater asked Jayden.

"This is between you and her. I'll support her, no matter what, and lower your voice."

"Don't pull that cop act on me. You went along with Casey's deceit?"

"Jayden knew about the attack on Kat. I didn't tell him any details about your relationship with her or about..." Casey stepped closer as tears ran from her now black-smudged eyes.

"About my time in Germany? So you lied to him too? Wow, you're a piece of work."

"I was trying to protect you." She touched Slater's sleeve, and he jerked away.

"Easy, bro." Jayden stepped closer. "Honey, leave him be, maybe you should wait to explain."

"There's no damn explaining her way out of this." Slater turned to Casey then shook his head and spun away. "I can't even look at you."

"Derek."

He ignored her sobbing plea. "I asked you over and over if Kat was okay. You sat beside me in Landstuhl—in Germany—held my hand, and damn-well lied to my face. For months—sixteen months, you've allowed me to despise her—to think that badly of her. Jesus! Kat would never have turned her back on me, regardless of our circumstances. How could I have bought your shitting lies?"

"I wanted to tell you for so long."

A couple of bystanders paused on their way to their car; Slater ignored their curious stares.

"But, you didn't, Casey. You destroyed the best part of me—Kathleen Flynn—you systematically disassembled everything I loved about her with your deceit. Nothing you say will ever make up for what you did."

Casey stumbled back, and Jayden grasped her shoulders. "That's enough. You don't get to talk to Casey that way. Go home and calm your ass down. We'll sit down when you're ready to talk and not yell in her face."

"I'm not sitting down with either of you." Slater's hands trembled as he placed them on his hips. He swallowed past the expanding lump in his throat and turned to his cousin. "You're dead to me. I don't want to see you ever again."

"Derek, no, please."

Ignoring Casey's outstretched hand, Slater walked towards his truck.

Jayden pulled her to his chest. "Dude."

"Don't contact me." Boiling rage ate at his control and Slater sped up, almost tripping in his haste. He wound his way through the packed rows of cars.

"Please don't drive in that state."

The voice to his right had Slater pausing, and he slowly turned to face the woman who'd just brought him to his knees.

"Are you okay?" He couldn't hide the tremble in his voice.

Kat's eyes glistened with unshed tears. "No. You?"

"Jelly bones." He raised his shaking hand. "No easy day, right?" His shattered heart would never be okay. Desolating images of a broken and bleeding Kat threatened to bring him to his knees.

"This isn't Casey's fault."

"Bullshit." Slater tried to swallow past the pain. "Aren't you supposed to be finishing up your mighty speech?"

"None of that matters." Her lips dropped off at the corners.

"Jesus, Kat. My brain is about to explode, and I'm gonna toss up my groceries—again."

"I know it's a lot to take in." Rearranging her hair over the scar on her cheek, she stared down at her feet.

"Let me get this straight, because my numb brain may have

mistaken the words you uttered in that room. Some fucker maniac ambushed, beat, and tried to murder you, on the same night that I was blown up in Lagos?"

"Aye—yes."

"Did… did they catch the son of a bitch?"

"Not yet."

"Shit, shit, shit." Slater paced in a circle. "Why didn't you say anything—after you'd recovered? And when did you learn about my injuries overseas?"

"Casey waited two months until I was well enough to handle the news. By then, you were already in rehab, back in the States. I hoped you'd never find out, but after writing my book, I knew that you might."

Feeling like he'd run a marathon, Slater tried to slow his harsh breathing. Subterfuge peppered the last sixteen months, and he couldn't discern the truth from the fabrication.

"Are you angry with me?" Kat asked.

Slater shook his head. "Jesus, never, angel—you've dealt with such brutality. I'm furious with myself and at Casey. I should've known—I think I knew—but I didn't trust my gut."

Kat looked confused. "What do you mean?"

"Hell, I'm not sure. None of this makes sense. Look, Kat, I need a minute, but I also need answers. Can we meet? Can I call you? Shit. I don't even have your number, is it still the same?"

"I swapped out numbers after… the attack." She licked her lips and swallowed.

After the attack…

He couldn't imagine what she'd lived through and he'd give her whatever she desired, including his retreat. "I need answers, honey. Once I have them, you never have to see me again."

"You're getting it all wrong."

"Then explain it to me—when you're ready."

After another moment of indecision, Kat finally nodded and gave him her number. Keeping his distance and allowing her to walk away was damn hard. Soul-shredding anger jeopardized his sanity.

Chapter Four

Groaning, Slater rolled up off the sofa. The sunlight bouncing off white walls threatened to sear his eyeballs. The pounding in his head had him glancing frantically around his unkempt living room. Had he been drinking? Slater hadn't touched alcohol for the last year. Technically, he hadn't enlisted in an AA program and never classed himself as an alcoholic, although his sister might disagree with that assessment. He did, after all, spectacularly ruin her engagement party after his breakup with Kat. Someone banged on his front door. That was what had woken him. What day was it? Saturday? No, it was a Sunday. Slater glanced at the time on his phone and winced. A Sunday afternoon. Five missed calls and a stack of text messages from his MIT2 team. Shit, he should never have called Johnny after the conference showdown.

The hammering commenced.

"Go the hell away!"

"Open up, Slater, or I'll smash the door in."

And Johnny could easily do it. Slater didn't want to see his cheerful friend. The whole team was now like the damn Brady Bunch—all happily married to good women—except for the new guy. And all the kids? It was like a damn zoo. Slater did adore the little critters, and they loved him back. Uncle Slater—the cool dude who showered them with toys and chocolate. The team now lived in Utah, and it made things a hell of a lot easier to keep in touch. Although with Slater's workload at the training facility, he rarely saw his brothers-in-arms.

"I'm fine. Screw off."

"You have ten seconds to open up—before I hulk up," Johnny yelled through the door.

"Open up, Slater."

Ah shit. Max. Slater ran a hand through his hair and stood. "Coming, sir."

He took his time, having to step over a discarded jacket, a Chinese takeaway container and a half eaten bag of tortilla chips. The second he opened the door, Johnny shouldered through.

"Well, if it isn't the Ogre Lord and his Ice Princess," Slater said, digging at Johnny's body mass, and Max's frosty-colored eyes.

"Jesus. This place stinks." Johnny paused to look around. Slater did the same. The fully furnished, one-story rental fitted his needs. The passage opened onto an open plan area, including a modern living room and kitchen. Sliding doors led out to a laid out yard with a swath of grass and a cluster of trees. Three large bedrooms and two bathrooms sat towards the back of the modern house. Johnny was right, Slater hadn't cleaned in three days and also hadn't bothered to crack open any windows while at work, or camping out on his sofa.

Charlie eased in behind and slapped Slater on the arm.

"Hey, hun."

Slater raised his brows at Donnie's wife, Charlie. "You too?"

"And me." Donnie popped his head around the door jamb holding a car seat. Slater couldn't help smiling at the squirming baby. He'd been at Willow's birth four months ago.

"Can I hold her?"

"If you change that shirt and wash your hands. What is that? Ketchup?"

Slater glanced down at the stain on his white t-shirt. "I think it's orange chicken sauce."

Walking in behind the couple, Max shut the door.

"Where's the rest of the tribe? And the other MIT2 ghost hunter?" Slater asked as he pulled off his shirt.

"Abby and Lizbug took the kids to their swimming lessons. Atlas is hiking up at Powder Mountain." Johnny wandered into the small kitchen.

Slater turned to join him, but Max grabbed his arm. "Have you been drinking?"

If any other man had asked Slater that, he probably would've decked them, but this was his old team leader. A man who Slater respected and trusted more than any other soldier. The concern he saw reflected in Max's eyes had him shaking his head.

"Tempting, but I drank a shitload of soft drinks and ate a bunch of crap. I need an antacid and a shower."

Max surveyed the messy living room, his eyes pausing on the open laptop perched on the corner of the coffee table.

"Do you have Kat's file?"

Damn, the guy was quick.

"I haven't looked at it yet. I can't get up the courage to do a simple google search on the attack. How the hell am I gonna examine the evidence?"

"How did you gain access?" Max asked.

"I have a contact in the agency—a friend of the Agent in Charge on the case."

"Slate, this could get complicated. You're not authorized to investigate."

"Solid point, but I need to know the details."

"You need to trust your agency to do their job." Max walked over to the windows.

Slater rubbed his shoulder. "They have no suspects or forensic evidence. The case is stagnant."

"Does Kat know that you'll be digging for answers?"

"It doesn't take a rocket scientist. Anyone who knows me…"

Charlie lifted her baby from the seat and settled on the clean end of the couch. Donnie walked out of the kitchen with a garbage bag and began clearing a path as Johnny watched Slater cautiously.

"Don't look at me like I'm about to morph into beast mode. There are three other barbarians in the room. What are you assholes eating on your deployments? Testosterone Teriyaki?"

Charlie giggled, and Slater shot her a wink.

"We've had a heavy training schedule." Johnny grinned.

"So have the Avengers and it looks like you could kick their asses."

"I'll kick your ass, if you don't climb in the shower," Max said, pointing at Slater's shirt clutched in his hand. "And scrape your face while you're at it, you're starting to look like a transient."

Grinding his teeth, Slater stalked to his bedroom and snagged jeans and a shirt. Climbing under the hot water felt good, but he ached to punch out at the white tiles. His old team had his back, and they were concerned about his mental welfare. Slater got that, but he no longer wallowed in a deep Black Friday hole. It had taken years to heal, even though he'd lost so much along the way—including and especially the love of his life. If the wheels hadn't come off… if he hadn't flirted with another woman… if he'd married Kathleen Flynn… would she still have been attacked? He doubted it. She would've remained in their home in Colorado. Guilt had him leaning his head against the shower wall. Even without Slater's accountability, he still had to make it right. He'd spend the rest of his days hunting the asshole-prick who'd harmed Kat, and once Slater had the bastard in his sights... A blood fog clouded his vision. *Target acquired.* Slater braced himself for the next step—opening her case file and grinding down on every last detail.

Max watched Slater emerge from his bedroom with forced bravado. He still looked as pale as all hell—despite his perpetual golden-skinned glow. The guy was pushing himself too hard. On the surface, Slater looked fine. He'd gained back most of his field muscle. Tall and broad-shouldered with that "James Dean" attitude. His arm looked great, with a seemingly good range of motion, but Max knew that meant little. Derek *Slater* Banez knew how to cover his wounds—both the internal and external ones—with charm and comedic grace. This latest development could have Slater veering into bedlam, and it might destroy his career and sanity.

Max tried to imagine himself in Slater's shoes. If some deranged nutcase ever attacked Abby while Max was on deployment? Jesus. The thought made him ill, and he clenched his teeth against the horror. Granted, Kat wasn't Slater's wife, but they'd come damn close to uttering those vows and Slater still loved her. The schmuck hadn't dated anyone since their breakup. Instead, he'd concentrated on overcoming PTSD and starting a new career.

And by crazy chance, they'd been attacked around the same time. Essentially on the same evening. That was some fucked up fatalistic shit. Max wanted to help his friend sort through the maze of emotions, but their next training exercises were rolling around. Then they'd face another possible deployment.

Slater sat next to Charlie, and she handed over her bundle of joy. Donnie stood proudly to the side, looking down at his tiny daughter, and Max couldn't help smiling. That feeling of being a new dad, hell, nothing beat it. And holding your daughter for the first time was like a punch to the balls. Visions of her growing up and eventually dating? Oh, hell no. His Lucy would be locked up in a covertly designed tower. Max's world revolved around his little Gabe and Lucy. They grew so fast.

His team had come a long way. Johnny and Donnie now both had families of their own. Atlas—the youngest member and the sniper on the MIT2 team—raced around like a wild kid. The only teammate and friend who worried Max was Slater. He'd always be a MIT2 brother, no matter where he ended up. Max had a feeling that the attack on Kat, could end up destroying his friend. Max's skin itched with dread for the broken couple.

Johnny now held the discarded bag of tortilla chips, crunching down on handfuls of chips. He eased up from his laid back position on the sofa's arm, and turned to face Slater.

"Max and I brought our vehicles."

"Uh. Good for you?" Slater said while tucking Willow's arm back into her soft, pink blanket. "Willow is so quiet—like her daddy." He rubbed a finger across the kid's cheek.

Charlie agreed. "I know, she sleeps through the night and hardly ever cries. She's such a content baby."

Johnny persevered, interrupting the cooing session. "I'll be rolling out with Charlie to pick up the rest of the gang and take them all home. You can hang with these two analytical assholes and get their input—their assistance—with Kat's case file."

Pausing, Slater looked up. "I can handle her file. Opening it will be brutal, but I'll be fine. I don't need coddling."

Max purposely kept quiet, allowing Johnny to handle Slater's defensiveness. Of course, they were worried about him, and Max didn't want his friend regressing in any way.

Slater's relationship with Kat was never toxic, but at the time, the violence he'd experienced on the job had tainted every aspect of his life and soured the love affair. Re-establishing contact with her might bring back rough memories. That, and the desire to find Kat's attacker would place Max near Slater's side. Kat might not know it, but she would always be family to MIT. News of her attack a couple of days ago had come as a big shock to all the operators who knew her. Regardless of Slater's relationship status, Max should've kept in touch with Kat. Irrespective of how busy the last couple of years had been, he'd failed her.

"Bro, you have two of the biggest covert brains in this room who are willing to help. Unclench that uptight ass and get to work." Johnny tossed the bag of chips onto the coffee table, and wiped his hands over his jeans.

Slater nodded. Max relaxed, exchanging a look with Donnie. The savage bastard who hurt the woman they all cared about, now had an even bigger target on his ass.

◊ ◊ ◊

Slater placed Willow gently back in her car seat. Johnny and Charlie said their goodbyes as they carried the baby to the truck. Shutting the door, Slater took a breath and walked over to his dormant laptop.

Taking off his jacket, Donnie then rolled up his sleeves. "I'm going to grab my tech from the trunk." He reached for Max's car keys and exited.

"You sure you want to do this?" Max asked as Slater picked up his laptop and walked over to the dining table.

"I'm meeting with Kat tomorrow afternoon. I need to know what we're dealing with and why the authorities haven't caught this bastard."

"Let's examine the intel." Max sat at the table and waited for Slater to enter his key codes and open the documents.

Donnie slipped back in and fired up his brick of a laptop on the other side of Slater. He paused and stared at the men. "It was big news that week in Utah, but none of us ever heard about her assault. How is that possible?"

"Because you were fussing over my injured ass across the globe," Slater replied.

"And Abby wasn't in Utah at the time," Max added. "She was pregnant and on forced bedrest with my family back in Colorado."

"I should've known," Slater said. "Kat would never have avoided my calls, knowing I was injured."

"But you trusted Casey." Max shot Slater a sympathetic look.

Slater couldn't reply. He swallowed the betrayal and flexed his fingers, ready to open the case file. "Time to track this piece of shit down."

The brutality of the attack floored the men at the table, and there were details that Kat hadn't mentioned in her speech. Set on the craggy Wasatch range, buildings built in the nineteenth-century mining era lined the main area of Park City. Named one of the prettiest towns in the States, it was laid out in a multi-storied and layered hillside. As stated by the investigation, she had cut through from Main Street to Swede Avenue and then headed past a parking structure towards a wooded clearing. Her intention must've been to head up the path and up the stairs to Marsac Avenue, a level up from the main area. The chalet they were staying in was then just a couple of blocks away. She never made it that far. Kat had just entered the wooded pathway when her assailant ambushed her.

According to the statements taken from both victims, and Jake Calvin's wife, the perp wore a customized wet suit described as a black latex catsuit, including a mask with eyes, nose and lip holes. The agents in charge had matched the suit to similar rubber "Gimp Bondage Costumes" found online, except, it looked like the suspect's get-up was custom made. The creepy attacker first wielded a galvanized 2.5 inch, three-foot pipe which the detectives recovered at the scene. He'd shattered Kat's wrist, broken two of her ribs, cracked her collarbone and aside from splitting open her face, had caused a hairline fracture to her cheekbone. Scrolling through the aftermath—the photos of her lying in ICU had Slater mentally weeping. She'd been unrecognizable. Her face so battered that her eyes were completely swollen shut.

Slater stood; the chair crashed to the floor as he turned away from the intolerable screen.

"Do you want to break?" Max asked as he rested his elbow on the table and cupped his tired mouth.

Shaking his head, Slater paced the room. "I want to get through this as quickly as possible, and catch this asshole."

Donnie still studied the report. "He uses multiple weapons. He tossed the pipe and swapped over to a knife."

Remembering Kat's recounting of the attack, Slater asked, "How severe were her injuries?" Needing a break from the savagery on the screen, Slater continued pacing.

Donnie didn't answer as he and Max leaned forward, focusing on the same passage.

"What is it? What do you see?" Slater ran a hand through his hair and returned to the table to lean over the screen.

"That's a fucking miracle," Donnie muttered.

"Shit, yeah," Max replied.

"What?" Slater shoved them aside, taking a moment to find his place.

The unsub tried to stab her in the chest three times. The first attempt caught her arm as she tried to block him. The second strike nicked her ribcage and the last struck the pendant on her necklace before glancing across her chest?

Scrolling down to the evidence photos, Slater sunk to his chair, staring at the image of a red Jade pendant. The techs had photographed it at various angles. First lying in the snow and then back at the evidence lab. A large gouge running down one side—indicated the path the knife had taken when striking the ornamental rock.

"Didn't you give that to her when you were dating?" Donnie asked, tilting his chair back.

Slater nodded, not taking his eyes off the screen. "On our first vacation." At the time, her attachment to the gift had touched him. A sales lady in a jewelry store had roped him into buying it. He'd wanted something red—Kat's favorite color. The pendant wasn't small, it was a heavy disc, circled in gold. He'd first chosen a pair of delicate ruby earrings, but when the sales lady told him that red Jadeite represented life force and the energy of the warrior, and also symbolized purity, Slater decided to purchase the clinker. It reminded him of Kat's strength, and he'd been so worried that she wouldn't like the gift. She'd loved it.

Four months after their breakup, Kat had still worn it. After his betrayal, any other woman in her situation would've tossed the gift over a cliff. What did that mean?

"That trinket saved her life," Donnie said as they all stared at the damaged jewel. He leaned over and kept scrolling, pausing on the next image. "What the hell is that?"

"Small pliers with a gold tinsel tied to one of the handles." Max leaned back and folded his arms.

Frowning, Slater went back to the notes. They were found beside her in the snow, suspected to be owned by the suspect.

"Any of his prints or DNA recovered?"

"Not on any of the weapons. The perp wore gloves." Slater kept reading. "The tread on his shoes matches a generic, black, steel-toed boot stocked mainly in Walmart, but that's the only lead they have—aside from his weight and height."

Max cleared his throat. "Any DNA recovered from under Kat's fingernails? It mentioned earlier that she'd clawed at his cheek."

Slater scanned through the evidence collected by the medical examiner. "They came up with nothing."

"The rubber suit probably protected his face. What method did they use for collection?" Donnie asked.

Slater should've provided protection for Kat, although how could he have foreseen such horror? Focusing on the question, Slater blocked out images of Kat lying broken in a bed, as they swabbed her for evidence. Various methods were used to collect fingernail evidence, and depending on the kit used, results would vary.

"Swabbing and scraping beneath the nail," Slater said.

"No clipping or soaking?" Donnie asked.

"No. Kat wears her nails short. Clipping may not have yielded results. They also noted that there was no visual evidence beneath the nails—blood or skin."

"I'll have to look into the results." Donnie eased back in his chair.

Max's brows drew together. "There isn't much to go on. This

bastard is one clever piece of slime, and planned the attack meticulously."

"Although he also displays disorganized tendencies." Slater wasn't a profiler, but his degree in criminology would help him track down Kat's attacker. Hell, MIT2 were masters at finding elusive extremists. "He's impatient—choosing to complete the attack in the open. And he's driven by rage."

He wasn't the only one. Slater now had a scent and a feel for his target, and was on the hunt.

Chapter Five

Kat sat on a bench near the water's edge, forcing herself to remain seated. She twisted her hands before closing her eyes for a long moment. The burbling sound of the stream calmed her nerves. Off to her left, a kid shouted. A man called out to his dog. That's why she'd chosen this spot. On a sunny day, it was well populated. The back of the bench faced a picnic table, and a wide field lay to her left while the stream sat to her right. Aside from the leafy trees and riverside scrub, she had an excellent view of the park. Her position made it hard for someone to sneak up on her.

Kat pushed the significance of the park from her mind—the place they'd first met. So she liked fresh air and found safety in the everyday normality—big freaking deal. Not bothering with much make-up, she'd slipped on jeans and grabbed the first t-shirt in her drawer. A soft gray shirt with a Mickey Mouse graphic. The time on her Apple watch showed she still had ten minutes. Kat fiddled with her medical bracelet, and looked around the busy field, scanning for his familiar gait. All she could see were families enjoying the warm day. They all seemed so normal.

Not like you, Miss Scarface.

Doubts over meeting Derek screamed for her attention, pushing aside her negative inner dialogue. Reestablishing contact wasn't healthy for either of them. She'd moved on and so had Derek. He'd view her differently. Hell, he already did. That look of horror on his face when she'd looked up from the podium and met his gaze. Kat ran her fingertips along the scar on her left cheek. Dammit, the bench faced the wrong way. Slater should sit to her right.

How could she have thought that he'd never find out? A silly supposition that they'd both merrily live their separate lives and would never cross paths. She should've told him what happened to her—chosen the right time after he'd arrived back in the States. Except she'd felt irrational shame and pride. Kat had wanted him to only remember her from before the attack. Untouched, confident and perfect. Not a damaged woman who was terrified of her own shadow. And Kat knew Derek; he'd be like a dog with a bone. She needed to reassure him that she was fine. The attack and her recovery were just hiccups on her journey towards her life goals. She was a survivor that didn't need a man to rescue her.

Maybe if Kat were honest, she could admit that the last twenty months weren't exactly "hiccups." More like a never ending shit-show. Mental exhaustion tied her down from achieving her life goals. Aside from her recovery, she'd battled to start her new business as a virtual consultant. And scrounging up the energy when her mind felt empty and numb wasn't working.

Stupidly, Kat had thought that writing a book about her traumatic experience would be a kind of catharsis. It wasn't. Even as she sat on the bench, watching the animated picnickers, Kat felt imprisoned by hopelessness. Changing her mind, Kat rose, turned... and came face to face with Derek.

His vital and capable energy always made her heart pump a little harder. God, the man was a handsome fellow and looked cool and collected in a white polo shirt with gray chino shorts. Tall and broad-shouldered with that perpetually tanned skin passed along from his Brazilian father. Dark scruff covered his strong jawline and those slashing brows she'd always loved so much now frowned down at her.

"You've changed your mind?" he asked in that deep timbre.

"Maybe."

"I won't stand in your way." Hands tucked in the pockets of his shorts, Derek stepped to the side. "We don't have to do this."

"Derek, what exactly is this? What do you want to know? Because I'm pretty sure you've dug through the case files. Is this just about my assault? You want to be friends, or do you need reassurances?"

He narrowed his eyes. "Reassurances for what?"

"To assuage your white-knight guilt. Like the rest of your soldier friends, you want to rescue a damsel in distress. Except it's too late, and besides, you were never around anyway."

Derek shook his head and smiled with those damn dimples. "Why don't you say how you really feel, as I wipe your verbal vomit from my shoes."

"Euw, Derek!"

"What? I didn't expect you to go straight for the jugular."

They stared at each other as seconds passed. A father at a nearby table packed up their cooler as the mom happily corralled the kids. Their carefree attitude grated on Kat's nerves.

Derek bit his lip before speaking. "I want many things—to understand why you both lied to me, to figure out if you're okay and I want to neutralize this rat bastard. I'm not sure about the friendship bit. Seeing you regularly while living separate lives? That's asking too much."

Kat knew what he meant. If Derek met someone else and got married, could she stand by as a friend and watch him find happiness with another woman? Heat spiked in her chest, and Kat gritted her teeth against the green-eyed anger. Putting it aside, she squeezed the bridge of her nose and nodded. "Let's talk."

Kat waited for him to sit first, before taking a seat to his left so that he faced her prettier side. She heard him pulling in a deep breath as she stared at his hands, rubbing over his thighs. Those large hands with capable fingers—Kat remembered how they felt on her skin. Long, slow strokes. The way his thumb would brush over her nipple... run between her breasts and over her stomach... Kat licked her lips as Derek clasped those same hands together between his splayed legs, leaning forward to stare at the grass edging his white-leathered sneakers.

Pulling herself away from the sensual memories, Kat focused on his perfect profile, noting the tired lines around his eyes and the way his mouth pulled tight at the corners. She doubted he'd gotten much sleep since hearing her confession. She missed his wide smile and sparkling eyes and wanted desperately to see them again. His hair was a little longer on the top since she'd last seen him with a military cut. Gloriously thick, golden brown hair that looked mussed—like he'd run his hands through it in frustration. The tousled sexiness matched his relaxed and mischievous vibe.

"So this place, huh?" He looked up at the spot on the field where they'd first met.

"I come here often." She flicked a leaf off her jeans. "I'm not your responsibility, you know?"

He turned to look at her; his gaze traced her scar and a muscle ticked in his jaw. "I swore I'd always look after you."

"That was before our breakup, and I can see to myself."

"It should never have ended that way—me acting like a dick. If I could take back that night... I lost the best thing that ever happened to me."

His honesty surprised her into silence.

"I mean it, Kat. And I'm not that angry soldier anymore. I'm getting back to who I was before the Black Friday bombing."

"I'm happy for you. You deserve peace."

Derek pressed a hand over his eyes. "I want what I don't deserve."

Kat frowned. Shite, was he referring to her? She tried to think of the right thing to say as her fingers tugged at her hair.

"Why do you do that?" Derek asked, glancing sideways.

"Do what?"

"Cover your cheek with your hair?"

"You mean 'cover the scar.' I don't like people staring."

"Kat—"

"Aye, you can't bear to look at it. I see the way your face tightens when you study the damage."

"It's barely noticeable and the reason—"

"I don't want to hear your explanation. I'm not ready to talk about my face."

"Okay. Fair enough."

"It's not the only scar from the attack. I have three others. One above my right elbow and two on my chest. They aren't as unsightly as the one on my face." Kat couldn't resist giving him the heads-up. Slater needed the facts.

"It's not unsightly and even if it were, I wouldn't care."

"Stop venerating."

"Jesus, Kat." He opened his mouth to argue, then closed it again.

Gnawing at her bottom lip, she watched a kid lurching down a hill on a new pair of rollerblades—eyes wide and knees wobbling. That's how Kat felt on the inside, never imagining she'd ever see Derek again, never mind sit so close to the handsome warrior.

He leaned back and stared at the clear sky. "Can I ask a few questions about that night?"

It took a second for Kat to figure out which night. The night of their breakup or the night of her attack?

"I'll answer whatever I can."

"How much of the actual assault do you remember?"

"Bits and pieces. I've remembered more over time."

"How about his weight, height, any discernible markings or features?"

"A little shorter than you, by about three inches. Muscular but not super fit like you."

"How do you know? The wetsuit get-up covered most of his frame, plus he'd layered clothing on top."

Kat frowned, thinking back. Her hand clenched, and she felt Derek's palm cover her fist. A jolt of awareness speared through her fizzling terror. She tried not to slip back to those moments of horror.

"At some point, I shoved at his waist. He felt softer around the middle."

"Good work, Kat. The report never mentioned that detail."

She nodded and looked down at their joined hands. Slater hadn't pulled away, and his touch felt comforting.

"Maybe I remember more than I'd first thought."

"Why don't we sit down together and run through a play by play? Take our time…"

"This is all so strange. You're sitting beside me."

Derek didn't answer. He looked down at her fist clasped in

his, probably feeling her tremble.

"Are you afraid he'll track you down?"

Kat felt her eyes widen. Derek had voiced her biggest fear and was one of the first people to frame the possibility. Everyone, including the detectives on the case and Casey, thought Kat was overly paranoid.

"Do you think he would?"

"I don't know. What did the investigators tell you?"

Kat shrugged. "The Park City detective in charge thinks that I was just in the wrong place at the wrong time, and a convenient victim. The FBI hasn't updated me on the ongoing investigation. My assailant told me I was on his 'naughty list.' That possibly means that he has a list or a plan."

Derek didn't answer, and Kat leaned forward. "I'm guessing you've memorized that file by now. Talk to me, Derry."

He looked up sharply at the sound of his nickname—the name she'd used while they were dating.

"There could be ties to a similar case in Idaho. And another in California."

"A man in a wetsuit?"

"No, there weren't any witnesses in the other case files."

Kat swallowed past her suddenly dry throat. "The victims didn't survive?"

"No." Derek squeezed her hand.

"How similar?"

"Kat…"

"Answer me. I hate living in the dark."

Nostrils flaring, he looked her in the eye. "The unsub discards his weapons at the scene. A steel pipe, an eight dollar tactical spring knife and rebar pliers."

"Pliers?"

"Yeah, the tool was also recovered beside you—buried in the snow."

"One of the detectives mentioned finding a pair of pliers at the scene. I presumed that they fell out of someone's pocket. I didn't give them much thought."

"They are significant—and we've figured out why."

Kat braced herself for the answer.

"He pulls his victims' teeth."

Despite the cool breeze tracing her brow, Kat couldn't breathe. Chest shuddering, she stared at the stream. "All... all of their teeth?"

"No, a canine and an incisor. Two teeth per victim."

"So, you think he would've done the same to me?"

"If he hadn't been interrupted."

"A serial killer who—after beating and stabbing his victims—takes their teeth?"

Derek nodded. "He executes the killing blows, except your ribcage and your pendant protected you that night."

"It felt like an angel crouched over me—sheltering me. Through the fog... I saw him striking at my chest, and I kept waiting for the death strike."

Derek stood and paced, turning to the rushing water.

Kat tried to discern fact from fantasy as she thought back to that night. "I dreamed of a spirit with wings laying over me. That and your... never mind."

"That and my what?" Turning to face her, Slater's eyes held a strange light.

"Nothing. I should go." Kat stood and stepped towards the path.

He grabbed her arm as she turned. "You were attacked at ten fifteen at night."

The intensity on Derek's face made her pause as did his next words. "I was blown up around 0500 in Lagos. Five thirteen to be exact."

"What are you saying?"

"Factoring in the time difference? Our injuries occurred at exactly the same time."

Panic had her pulling away. "I can't do this."

Too much information bombarded her from all angles. A psychotic serial killer who pulled teeth... a damaged ex-boyfriend... far-fetched hallucinations.

Derek persisted, following her up the path, his eyes wild. "Did you see me? In the moments after?"

"Derek, stop." Kat swung around. "None of this means anything. Angels and visions don't exist. Yes, I had crazy hallucinations probably due to shock and blood loss."

"I saw you..."

"Stop! Leave me the hell alone."

Raising his hands, he halted. Derek's chest heaved as his eyes glittered. Backing away, Kat turned and rushed up the path, as her head spun with unanswered questions.

◊ ◊ ◊

Slater changed into old jeans and headed back to *The Stational Preparedness Facility.* Pulling into the lot, he spotted a fellow agent and good friend sitting on the steps chatting to one of the foreman. A hawkish scowl turned Slater's way. The guy was Slater's only reliable contact in the agency who'd also been the man who'd given Slater the access codes to Kat's file.

"Fletcher, welcome to my dusty kingdom. To what do I owe this pleasure?"

Fletcher Daniels rose to his feet and waited for Slater to

approach. Wolfish eyes set within blunt planes, softened for a fraction as they shook hands.

"I was hoping for a tour of the facility. You owe me."

Slater sure did. He'd execute awkward somersaults across the lot, if Fletcher demanded it.

"Fine." Hands spread; Slater turned in a dramatic circle. "Welcome to... Jurassic Park. Shit. I mean... Stational Park." He raised his hands to the mountain. "Life... will not be contained."

Snorting with amusement, Fletcher swung his backpack over his shoulder and walked towards Slater's F150. "Get your Velociraptor-ass to the truck, I don't have all day."

"At least you didn't call me a Brachiosaurus." They climbed in and Slater handed Fletcher a hard hat.

Latching his seatbelt, Fletcher said, "I've taken over Kathleen Flynn's case."

"Say again?"

"The agent running the investigation has a huge workload—five homicide cases—and he's been neglecting the investigation. I pulled a few strings."

They sat in the running truck, as Slater stared ahead. "You'll do right by her. Promise me."

"We'll catch the bastard." Fletcher rubbed his slightly crooked nose.

Slater nodded his head, and put the vehicle into gear.

"Three years ago, you saved my life. Hell, you saved my whole unit in Somalia." Fletcher clenched the hard hat tightly in his lap.

Slater remembered that close call. Fletcher's SF unit were sent on an "Advise and Assist" mission. Thanks to MIT2 informants in the region, Slater was able to warn Fletcher's Commandos about a pending Al-Shabaab ambush. Fifty militants planned that attack. Thankfully, their plans were thwarted. A reminder that Fletcher was one of the few people in Slater's new life that knew of the existence of MIT.

"That was my last mission, before joining the FBI," Fletcher said as Slater drove along the sand road. "I wouldn't have made it home without your team's interference."

"You're being dramatic, but hey, I'm glad you're now assigned to her case."

"That doesn't give you any special privileges. If you interfere—"

"I know, I know."

"They found the remains of another potential victim."

"A third one? Deceased?" Slater clenched the wheel.

"Yeah. In Wyoming. I'm flying out tonight."

"Let me guess, three weapons at the scene. Two teeth removed."

"Looks that way. There's substantial decomposition. I'll be checking in with their local medical examiner."

Slater didn't like where this was heading. The perp was comfortable with murder and had likely been killing for a long time.

"Do we have a forensic psychologist in the mix?" Slater asked.

"Not yet. One will be assigned next week."

It took effort for Slater to drag his focus back to the task at hand, as they pulled up to the first staging area. He needed answers, any clue to the killer's identity would provide an initial scent trail. The Bundy bastard needed to make just one small mistake.

◊ ◊ ◊

Later that week, Kat burrowed into the sofa with her phone pressed to her ear, as her mom chatted about her father's antics. After all the years they'd been married, they still teased and argued with each other, and still held hands. Her introverted mother always rolled her eyes at Kat's father—calling him a social butterfly. Kat guessed that she'd inherited both traits from her humble parents. An extrovert who loved the spotlight—networking and teaching—but Kat also enjoyed hibernating in her comfortable space and definitely rocked the hermit vibe.

Reluctant to hang up, Kat extended the call as long as possible. Her parents had flown over to Utah earlier in the spring and she'd enjoyed having them by her side. Now she missed the company. She was lucky to have such wonderful parents. Kat just wished they wouldn't worry so much. So she'd broken it off with her long-term boyfriend, then been brutally attacked and now she lived as a single woman. She understood their concern. She also remembered how much they adored Derek. She'd never revealed the details of their breakup to her parents. And now elected not to tell her mum about their recent reconnection.

After her mother finally ended the call, Kat turned to her side and stared at her work notes. They demanded her attention and she resisted the urge to give the papers the middle finger. Mental exhaustion ate at her control. The weekend loomed ahead, and this was her plan? Squatting in front of her laptop?

Lately, that was always the plan. Her strict schedule demanded dedication, and as Kat lay in a prone position, she rebelled. The silence suddenly felt oppressive, highlighting her isolated and self-imposed misery. Why did she always have to be strong, and what was she trying to prove?

The honest truth was that Kat couldn't stop thinking about a certain tall and handsome warrior with an easy smile. She missed his steady hugs and wide shoulders. Those memories stalked her dreams. The way Derek smelled, and his easy laugh. How he'd unconsciously trail his fingers along her skin as she lay by his side. Mostly, she missed the way he saw the world. That natural optimism combined with his affectionate heart? Like an arrow to a girl's soul. Curling her knees to her chest, Kat mourned the loss of that relationship, cursing their circumstances.

Would seeing him again be such a bad thing? Would she beg for scraps from a man who should remain in her past? Was Kat so desperate to feel his touch? Playing with fire, Kat picked up her phone and stared at the screen. Maybe they could just be friends and besides, she needed a small break from her work drudgery.

Ignoring common sense, Kat tapped out a quick message.

Chapter Six

Pulling in beside her Cooper, Slater spotted Kat chatting to an older gentleman near the doors. Slater took in the dated building with the *Creekside Community Center* sign plastered to the side. Kat didn't mention why she wanted to meet in a quieter neighborhood. Hell, Slater was just happy to get her text after the way they'd ended their last conversation.

Slater locked his truck and walked over the warm asphalt to Kat's side. She turned and grinned, and his heart paused in his chest. He hadn't seen that smile in a long time. He basked in her upbeat energy as she turned to introduce her friend.

"Derek, this is Eugene, who helps run this facility. Give Eugene bubble gum and twine, and he'll fix anything."

Slater noted the man's veterans cap and grasped his hand in a firm shake. "Good to meet you. Thank you for your service."

The older man squinted. "You served, son?"

"Yes, sir."

"Well, then back at ya. You still in?"

"No, sir. I've been officially out for a year."

Eugene nodded, exchanging a look that only Slater would understand. Then he turned to Kat. "Have you been hiding him from us, girl?"

Flushing, Kat stuttered, "Derek's an old friend."

Eugene folded his arms. "Mmm-hmm, sure he is. Is Derek joining us tonight?"

"Joining what?" Slater asked before she could answer.

"You'll see." Kat tossed him another smile as Eugene walked through the double doors. Slater stepped in front of her. "About the other day—"

"I don't want to think about my assault today. It's time to relax. Come, I'll show you around."

Slater conceded, following her into the center. He didn't want to let it go. The more he learned about her case, the more he itched to get involved. Waving at the senior lady behind the front desk, Kat led him through some turnstiles. They passed a large swimming pool and a couple of squash courts. Slater spotted a gym overlooking the natatorium as an ancient-looking man climbed carefully onto one of the treadmills. Turning left, down a passage, they walked into an open lobby that led to a couple of rooms. Glancing at the hand-drawn banner hanging over one of the doors, Slater read the words. *The Piece Club*. Loud chatter came from behind the swinging doors.

"I think they spelled 'peace' wrong."

"Nah. It's spelled right." Kat pushed through, and Slater followed, catching a whiff of her perfume. She still wore the same soft scent, and he ached to grab the back of her t-shirt and pull her into his arms. Instead, he took in the surroundings. Eight long tables covered in jigsaw puzzles in varying states of disarray. Clusters of people—young and old—gathered around the puzzles as they chatted and swapped pieces.

Slater spotted a couple of kids, some teenagers, and a few parents. The rest of the crowd looked to be retirees. Kat grabbed his wrist, and Slater almost jolted from the contact, feeling the buzz. The second time they'd touched since reconnecting. Distracted by her delicate fingers grasped around his wrist, Slater allowed her to walk him over to one of the quieter tables. He dodged a splayed-out retriever, snoring on its side.

Kat sat and gestured to the open seat next to her. "That's Roger. He's the laziest golden I've ever known. Gladys is his mum." Kat nodded at the tall, silver-haired lady to his side, who waved a hand as she picked up a small puzzle piece. Slater noted her straight posture and sharp eyes.

"Gladys works as one of the WSI lifeguards for the center," Kat said proudly.

"I'm one of the originals. The club is my second home," Gladys added in reply.

"Originals?" Slater asked. Was he immersed in the movie *Cocoon*?

"Joined Creekside when I was a senior in high school. Now my grandkids are members of the swim team."

"Gladys has a thing for the Godfather," Kat whispered.

"I do not!"

"The movie?"

"No—for wee Alfred. He manages the community center." Kat beamed as she pointed out the compact man bustling around the refreshment table. The top of his bald head would barely reach Gladys's shoulder.

"Why do you call him the Godfather?"

Kat bit down on a smile. "Because he's all-knowing. Nothing gets by that sharp-eyed gaze."

"Enough talking and start puzzling." Gladys scowled as she shoved the puzzle box into Kat's hands. "Find all the orange pieces for the sunset."

Slater grabbed a handful and followed Kat's lead. He'd never built a puzzle before, at least not one he could remember. As far as Slater was aware, puzzles were for kids. Although the pieces he held were pretty tiny, almost spilling onto his lap.

"Don't lose any or they'll exile me from *The Piece Club*." Winking, Kat sorted out colors from her pile.

"Why did you bring me here?" Slater whispered. He wasn't complaining; instead, he enjoyed every second by Kat's side. He could stare at her for hours, and the warm atmosphere in the noisy room had a comforting edge.

"Jigsaw puzzles allow the brain to relax while keeping the hands busy. They provide a calming distraction that doesn't involve a screen. Think of building a puzzle as creative meditation."

"You think this is what I need?" he asked, hearing a defensiveness in his tone.

"No. It's what I need."

"Shit. I'm sorry, Kat. I didn't think—"

"This is my safe space. It's where I've found the most healing, around people I can trust. And I don't just build puzzles at the center; I swim, and dance on a Thursday night. It helps me to relax and I needed this tonight. I haven't visited the center in a couple of months. I've been swamped with work."

Without thinking, Slater placed a hand on her knee. Kat didn't pull away. Instead, she bumped his shoulder. "You want me to show you some puzzling moves?"

Laughing, Slater raised his brows and shoved his hand into the box. "Will it make me feel piece-full?" He emphasized the word.

Kat rolled her eyes. "Clever arse."

"Oh, wise one, help me find inner-piece." He nudged her arm.

"You'll get proper slapped if you don't stop with the jigsaw jokes."

"And all I wanted was to… fit-in."

"Bollocks, you're done." Kat tried to jab him in the side, and Slater countered the move, grinning as he gently twisted her arm behind her. Pulling her close, he felt warm breath on his skin as her hair tickled his nose. She giggled, and the vibration against his neck made him stir. Twisting away, Kat's full breast grazed his side, and he almost groaned at the contact. Slater's foot brushed against Roger who jumped up and barked as Alfred bustled over.

"Kathleen! You're dropping pieces on the floor. What in the blazes?"

"It's my fault," Slater said, releasing her arm. "I have her in pieces."

Kat squealed with laughter and Slater couldn't help chuckling at her mirth as she tried to gain control under Alfred's horrified gaze. Roger kept barking.

"Oh, Alfred, leave the young folk alone." Gladys placed a piece carefully on the table. "You might want to smile for a change."

"I smile plenty!" They both turned and yelled at the barking dog. "Shut up, Roger!"

Roger turned in a circle and wagged his tail so hard that his ass wiggled wildly from side to side. He let out a howl and everyone laughed.

Kat stood. "Apologies, Alfred. We'll behave, I promise, but first I need to fix my mascara." Kat swiped at her cheek, still grinning as she winded her way to the restroom. Her swaying ass drew Slater's attention. Even without her heels, she had a sexy hitch to her walk that reminded him of their heated past. Dancing in candlelight, running his hand over her hips and raising her skirt… those shapely legs wrapped around his waist…

sweaty sex against a wall… he could still hear those throaty moans.

Slater shifted his chair closer to the table and took a breath.

"Instead of sitting there like a lump of concrete, why don't you start with this corner?"

Gladys gestured to his right, and Slater felt his cheeks flush. Had she been watching him the whole time?

Slater picked up a puzzle piece, not quite sure what to do next. "How do I start?"

"With the edges. Look at the printed picture, build the sides, and move towards the center. I've already arranged the pieces by color."

Sure enough, little piles lay sorted in different hues. Slater got to work, concentrating as Gladys hummed to herself. Minutes passed, and he relaxed, pleased with himself when he found his first matching pair.

Gladys's voice jerked him out of his reverie. "First time I've seen that girl laugh."

It took a second for Slater to figure out what she meant. "You mean Kat?"

Gladys nodded.

"How long has she been coming here?" Slater asked.

"Since about two months after that brutal attack." Gladys picked up two pieces and stood to bend over the puzzle.

"You know about that?"

"Hard not to. Casey brought her along one Bingo evening. Dressings covered Kat's injured face."

"Wait, Casey visits the center?" Slater scanned the room for Casey's signature neon-colored hair.

"She's been coming here for years and brings us home-baked cookies every time. Casey couldn't make it tonight."

Probably because Casey knew he'd be here. Slater relaxed in his chair as Gladys continued. "Kate never uttered a word. At least for her first three visits. Just stared into space. We let her be—sat her down at one of the puzzling tables and carried on like normal. Then one day, Kate picked up a piece and began."

The revelation made Slater ill. Imagining her catatonic, shattered and sitting in the corner. He'd seen soldiers marked the same way from war. A shocked vacancy in a frozen shell of a body. How had this happened to Kat? How had he allowed it? Slater shifted on his chair.

Gladys looked up. "She's come a long way. I'm not sure of your connection, but she deserves peace. If you can't give it to her—if you hurt her—"

"I've already burnt that bridge. I'm just a friend wanting to help."

"What kind of friend?"

"One that mostly makes mistakes and inappropriate comments."

The older lady ignored his attempt at humor. Her nostrils flared as Kat walked up to the table. Slater stood to greet her.

"What did I miss?"

"Just getting to know your new friend," Gladys emphasized the word, and Slater gritted his teeth. Nothing got past the stern dame. He respected her protective tone, but his mood had darkened. Kat must've picked up on his tension, and her fingers curled around his forearm, as she encouraged him to sit back down. The rest of the evening passed quietly, and Slater relaxed. He enjoyed working by Kat's side as they filled in the puzzling gaps.

Reluctant to leave, Slater made his excuses, and Kat walked him out. He needed to be onsite early the next day. At almost nine o'clock, the setting sun lit the sky with reds and oranges as they strolled to his truck.

Kat stared at the horizon and rubbed her arms. "I should also leave; it's getting late."

Slater studied her expression. "You don't like the dark."

His guess had Kat jerking her head around. "I... I don't like being out at night. Is it that obvious?"

"No, but it's a normal reaction. Pretty normal after what you've been through." He stepped closer and looked her in the eye. Slater was a tall man, and denim-colored eyes glanced up to meet his. He'd always loved her long lashes, the way they almost quivered as her gaze flitted over his face.

"Do you want me to wait? I can follow you home."

"No. I need to overcome my fear. If I keep relying on others... Jayden followed me home the other night, but that's just because I went on a blind date and—"

"You went on a date?" Slater shoved his hands in his pockets and stepped back. What did he think, that she wouldn't see other men after their breakup? His gut cramped, and he turned to his truck.

"Aye, I did."

Slater closed his eyes as she spoke, picking up her Irish lilt. He loved that melodic and husky voice. His heart broke again for the thousandth time like it always did when he thought of losing Kat. Now, she dated other men, made room in her life for a love that didn't include him.

"But the bloke was straight up boring and a bit of an arse."

Slater couldn't help grinning and turned to face her. "He was? What did he do that got you all riled up?"

"Grumbled about my food allergy."

"Bastard," Slater whispered as he reached down to tuck her

hair behind her ear. She smelled of sunlight and airy florals. He couldn't understand why a small percentage of idiots in the general population regarded food allergies as nonsense. Anaphylaxis could easily result in death. Slater had seen it first hand as a kid when his school friend's mother had died at a festival after eating a biscuit containing nuts. Hospital admissions for anaphylaxis in the United States were on the rise, and so were related deaths. As far as Slater was concerned, every kid and their family in the United States should have access to free or affordable epinephrine. The soaring prices and shortages of autoinjectors were unacceptable.

Slater paused to trace Kat's temple with his thumb, and she jerked away and held her fingers up to her scar.

"I'm sorry, Kat, I…" He hadn't meant to freak her out by touching the old injury, and she was self-conscious. She always tried to hide her damaged cheek with her hair, and the protective gesture pissed him off. Kat should never feel any shame. If anything, it was a mark of a brave survivor. Did she think he'd find it distasteful? If so, then she didn't know Slater at all. Hell, scars marked Slater's chest and back, all souvenirs of a dangerous career. Had dick-bag people judged her in the past? Did they stare at her face like she was a freak? Rage rose to the surface.

"It's fine… thanks for coming." Kat stared at her feet, looking so vulnerable and awkward in the moment.

Slater wanted to sweep her up; instead, he cleared his throat and nodded. "I had fun. Thanks for inviting me." He opened his car door and gazed at his seat before speaking his mind. "You don't need to cover up your beautiful face when I'm with you, and Kat, it is so damn beautiful. You're gorgeous, both inside and out, and I'll have words with anyone that thinks otherwise."

"Derry—"

"No, fuck them, Kat. If anyone ever makes you feel uncomfortable in any way, call me, and I'll deal with the bastards."

"You don't have to do that."

"I'd do anything for you." Slater didn't wait for her response, he climbed behind the wheel and forced himself to pull away.

Chapter Seven

Kat leaned closer to her reflection in the mirror and studied her scar. The plastic surgeon had done an excellent job. She'd always have a scar, but it was a remarkable improvement from the jagged gash she'd first received. Now, it ran from her temple, beneath her cheekbone in a long thin line, stopping halfway to the corner of her lip. Kat religiously applied a silicone gel to the site each day, with the hope that it might fade.

You don't need to cover up your beautiful face when I'm with you, and Kat, it is so damn beautiful.

Derek's words from two days ago had her leaning back and standing taller. He was right. She couldn't control people's adverse reactions, but she could control her response to the stares. She'd allowed the opinions of others to affect her self-esteem. Bollocks to the lot of them. She was alive and had a second chance at life. Ignoring the scar, Kat assessed her unmarked features. Average-sized lips with a slightly larger and pouty lower lip, set above a strong, determined chin. She had no issues with her straight nose. Her deep blue eyes were definitely her best feature. Framed by thick lashes and dark brows. Her hair took some work. In it's natural state, it had a slight frizz that annoyed the hell out of Kat. The wispy flyaways took patience and loads of hair product.

Tucking her hair behind her ear, Kat marched into her walk-in closet and selected a kick-ass outfit for the meeting with her publisher the next day.

After a quick shower, she glanced at the time—almost midnight. Kat slipped on her nightie and climbed beneath the covers. For the first time in months—even years—she felt hopeful for her future. She told herself that it had nothing to do with Derek walking back into her life, and she ignored the fluttering in her stomach whenever he was near. They'd always had chemistry, but it wasn't like they'd run into each other often. He'd probably call whenever he had an update on her case. Maybe she could invite him over for her famous Irish stew… Kat immediately nixed the idea. The man was trouble, and she'd learned that first hand. His betrayal had almost destroyed her; Kat couldn't live through that heartbreak again, and she shouldn't have invited him to *The Piece Club*.

Turning over, she closed her eyes. A loud bang echoed through her apartment. Kat shot up and out of bed. Terror had her freezing in her tracks as she listened for the source of the sound. A second bang, louder than the first had Kat jumping and racing for her gun in the drawer beside the bed. Gripping the weapon with a shaking hand, she grabbed her phone, dialed 911 and edged down the passage towards the living area. At the third pounding blow, Kat crouched against the wall. She'd seen her front door shudder that time. Someone was trying to smash down her door.

Kat pulled in a courageous breath and yelled at the top of her lungs. "I have a gun, and I'm not afraid to use it!"

Her hand shook so hard that she doubted she could hit a twenty-foot tank rolling up her passage, but she'd point and shoot if need be. Visions of a shiny, latex-clad monster holding a pipe had Kat whimpering and sliding to the floor. The eerie scratching at the door grew in intensity. A tinny voice echoing in the dark space drew her attention, and Kat looked down at her lit screen.

"911, what is your emergency? Hello? What is your emergency?"

"Someone... someone is trying to break into my apartment." Kat gave her address, and hung up, not waiting on the line but instead calling the next best person.

Casey.

Her friend picked up on the fifth ring. "This had better be good; I'm snuggling with—"

"Help... get Jayden. I need his help."

"Kate? What's going on?"

More scratching. Kat heard her neighbor from above as they walked across the floor. Their door opened. "Who's there? We've called the police."

The scraping noise paused before speeding up and memories of her attack flickered through her mind... Pain exploding in her ribs, her shoulder, her cheek. Her attacker's crotch crushed against her stomach as he raised the knife. Slashing pain, then nothing. Turning in the snow and seeing Derek lying beside her as the metallic smell of blood lay thick in the air. Having no defense against the frigid ice, as a dark crimson liquid spread in pulsing waves.

Casey's voice yelling through her phone drew Kat from her trance. The scratching noise stopped. With a shaking thumb, Kat pressed the end button and scrolled through her recent contacts. The third call was picked up immediately. "Kat?"

"Derry," she said in a daze. "I need you."

Slater broke every traffic rule to get to Kat. He lived twenty minutes away and it was too damn far. Kat remained on the phone for the first five minutes, not saying much, just that someone had tried to break in. She'd assured him that she'd called the police and Jayden. When Jayden had arrived at her door, she'd hung up. Slater saw the flashing lights from the road, turned in, and spotted Kat's small car in the lot. He slammed on the brakes beside it.

She's fine. She wasn't hurt. Jayden got there in time.

Slater repeated the mantra, as he raced past residents and neighbors milling around the central stretch of grass, and small fountains encircled by rows of central-facing, three-story apartments. Exterior stairwells led into the building, and when he spotted the uniforms, Slater ran over to the nearest block. He'd never been to Kat's home, but the gathering crowd certainly led the way. Jayden stood to the side of an open door on the second floor, barefoot, but wearing jeans and a t-shirt. He spoke with one of the uniformed officers. It took a second for Slater to take in the damage, noting the three boot-sized holes in the center of the door and scrawly lettering etched into the wooden surface. *NAUGHTY OR NICE?*

"Where is she?"

"On the sofa. Easy buddy, watch where you're stepping. The perp left her a gift." Jayden nodded to the far side of the door. A tiny, velvet draw-bag lay beside the door frame. "We haven't touched or opened the bag; we're waiting on a tech."

Slater stepped past, and a second officer blocked his way. Slater pulled his badge. Technically he wasn't a field agent, and he wouldn't usually pull his credentials, but this was Kat.

"The FBI? For an attempted break-in?"

"He's with me," Jayden commanded. The man stepped aside, and

Slater eased past, careful not to touch the evidence. From the inside, her door looked like Fort Knox with numerous locks and bolts. Thankfully, the reinforced barrier had held up against the assault.

Kat sat huddled on her sofa, wrapped in a soft blanket. Her wild eyes met his—distress palpable as he rushed to her side.

"She's not making any sense." A familiar voice called out from the open plan kitchen to his left. Slater glanced over at Casey.

"I'm pouring her a soft drink—for the sugar."

Slater nodded and returned his attention to Kat. He gently grasped her shoulders as he knelt before her. "You're safe now—"

"It's him."

"We don't know that, not yet—"

"I know... I know it. My fault. The stupid book." Her teeth started chattering.

"What book?"

"My book—I shouldn't have written it—and you're in the snow. We're both bleeding out—red sticky blood. I can't... the blood. It's all over me."

Slater frowned, scanning her for injuries. The door wasn't breached—did the scumbag access a window?

"I'm so cold... cold. The snow hurts, and I can't move. Derry, my arm is numb... it won't move."

Slater rubbed a hand over his mouth and sat beside Kat, pulling her stiff body to his chest.

"Do we need an ambulance?" Casey asked. "Is she having a giant panic attack?" She stood uncertainly next to the sofa, dressed in flannel comic strip pajamas. Her orange hair was all mussed on the one side.

"No, it's a flashback to her assault in Park City. Kat needs a sedative."

"I can check her bedside drawer. She has a prescription for her attacks." Casey ran down the passage, causing an officer to glance up.

"Don't leave me, Derry, I'm so cold."

Kat's words broke his heart; past violence trapping her in a vortex. Slater rocked her as he muttered soothing words. She smelled of fresh soap and shampoo. He pressed a kiss to her head as his cousin returned with two bottles of pills—shaking them. "All I could find were these. Prescription strength Ibuprofen that's expired, and I'm not sure what the other one is."

"What's it called?"

"Hydroox... Hydroxyzine. Wait, it says it's for anxiety."

"It is," Slater confirmed. "My head doctor tried to prescribe them for me in the past."

Shaking Kat gently, Slater asked, "Will these help you to relax, angel? Or should I take you to the ER? Is this what you use for anxiety?"

Kat stared at the container, then nodded, the glazed look never leaving her eyes. "Aye. Need them. I don't... take one... that often."

Casey handed Slater a Mountain Dew, and he encouraged Kat to swallow a pill. Then, he eased back and tucked her closer, preparing for the entourage of law enforcement while shooting off a text to Fletcher, before sending another to Max. Officially, Slater wasn't running the investigation, and the bureau would reprimand him if he interfered, but he'd be delving into the case on his own time, and fuck anyone who got in the way. Kat's trembling began to slow and she relaxed into his side. When her grip relinquished its hold on her blanket, Slater rearranged the covering, enveloping her completely. She only wore a thin camisole.

"Can you grab something for Kat to wear from her bedroom?"

Nodding, Casey disappeared down the hall.

"Thank you," Kat whispered, sounding more herself.

"You never have to thank me. Just relax; I'm not going anywhere."

Slater heard boots parading up the stairs, only to pause on the entryway. A couple of uniforms milled about. He glanced around the living room, noting the small "Saturday night special" pistol sitting on the tv unit.

"What the hell, is that your gun?" he asked Kat.

"Aye. When Jayden arrived, I handed it over, and he took out all the bullets. I hadn't fired it or anything."

Rubbing the back of his neck, Slater shook his head. "Did you plan to blow the dick's ass back to 1970?"

"Excuse me?"

"What were you aiming to do with that rusty-ass revolver? Do you even know how to shoot that thing?"

"Derry!"

"You're gonna get lead poisoning, just holding that MOFO."

"You're mean." She tried to pull away, but he held fast.

"I'm honest. Hell, Kat. The first thing we're doing is buying you a decent weapon, and I'm teaching you how to shoot. Why I never took you to the range when we were dating is beyond me."

"Because I never liked guns, remember?" She tugged at her medical bracelet with a finger.

"And you like them now?"

"No...but..."

"I get it. You're afraid, and so you bought some arthritic, piece of shit weapon."

"My father gave it to me. He used to keep it under the till at the bar."

"Well, that explains it. You dad still thinks he's Kojak."

Kat giggled, and Slater grinned.

"Daddy does kind of look like Kojak," she said with a snigger.

"Hey, you said it, not me."

Her parents ran an Irish pub in Denver. They'd opened the restaurant over thirty years ago. Slater used to love hanging with Kat's family. They'd serve traditional Irish cuisine… stews, tayto crisps, Ardglass potting herring and wheaten bread to name just a few. He missed the place. He missed Kat, and her current state worried him. It was clear that she hadn't yet worked through the trauma of her attack. Not only did Kat have acute PTSD, but she also lived in a state of constant terror. Her fear of the dark, the numerous locks on her front door, the pistol, the long wooden rod placed in the frame of the sliding door—which he'd just noted.

Casey returned with black leggings and a sweater. Kat sat up and pulled the sweater over her camisole, before sliding on the leggings. Slater shielded her from the officers with the blanket, and forced himself to look away. He wouldn't gawk at those shapely legs while she still shook from terror.

"You're not staying here tonight… or any other night until we've identified the asshole who destroyed your door."

Sleepy eyes flashed with sudden fire. "I won't let this lunatic run me off. That shite bastard will never call the shots."

"Don't be stubborn when it comes to your safety. Even if it's some teenage punk that turned up at your door, whoever terrorized you, now knows that you're a woman living on your own."

"Teenage punks leave bagged gifts for their victims? C'mon

Derry, I can handle the truth. A psycho fan has decided to visit his only surviving victim."

Slater swore. "Either way, if you refuse to leave, then I'm staying."

"No. I—"

"Agent Banez... a word?"

Fletcher Daniels stood in the entryway, and after squeezing Kat's arm, Slater walked over to his former SF brother-in-arms.

"How is Miss Flynn holding up?"

"Not great. Kat took anxiety meds." Slater turned to watch the tech open the velvet baggy with gloved hands.

"I'll need to question her." Fletcher glanced at an incoming text on his phone. His focus returned to Slater. "You need to stay the hell out of this."

"It's the scuba bastard, isn't it?"

They both paused to watch a jumble of teeth slide out of the bag onto a sterile sheet.

"There's your answer." Fletcher slid his phone into a pocket on his FBI issued jacket. "This is now my crime scene. You're here only for emotional support, you hear me?" Not waiting for Slater's answer, Fletcher walked over to Kat who stared ahead at her blank flat screen tv. Shaking herself from her daze, she smiled politely as Fletcher sat beside her. Slater noted her slow movements accompanied by resigned shock. In an unconscious gesture, she covered her scarred cheek with her hand as she answered the first of Fletcher's questions. Turning away, Slater watched the techs bag the evidence. Putting aside his rage, he considered the words carved into the door. *NAUGHTY OR NICE?*

Kat's attacker used the phrase,"Naughty List" in Park City. Casey slid up beside him, and Slater swore inwardly. He wasn't ready for a familial heart-to-heart. Her actions still pissed him off, and it was clear from Casey's body language that she wanted to hash things out.

"Not now, Casey. Kat is my only concern."

She stepped closer—stubborn wench. "I only have this to say. You might hate me, but you were badly injured. When I arrived at Landstuhl, the German doctors told me that you might not ever be able to use your arm again. Do you remember how drugged up you were—situated halfway across the globe from Utah? I'd just left Kate lying in the intensive care unit, and climbed on a plane to be with you. Her parents sat by her side, but it shattered my heart to leave her broken body because I felt responsible."

Pulling Casey down the passage, Slater rounded on her. "None of that was your fault, and I get that you were protecting Kat—by not telling me."

"No—I was protecting you. And her attack was my fault," Casey whispered. "I invited her to Park City. That little getaway was my idea. And then I squatted at the bar with some damn boy while she was getting the crap beat out of her. I should've left with her. We came together, we—"

"You've been blaming yourself for what happened to Kat?" Slater knew how it felt to live with survivor's guilt. For years he'd over-analyzed his actions in the Black Friday bombing. That helpless regret could destroy a person.

"Because the only person responsible is that evil son of a bitch. If you'd walked back to your chalet with her that night, he could've killed you." The thought made Slater ill.

Casey shook her head, dismissing his words. "I planned to tell you in Germany, but I knew what you would do. No matter how sedated or injured you were, you would've climbed out of that bed and discharged your sorry ass, raced to Kate's side and damaged your arm. I know you better than anyone else, and I couldn't allow you to go to her. You would've destroyed all the work the surgeons had done on your shoulder and arm."

"That wasn't your decision."

Casey grabbed Slater's sleeve, preventing him from turning away. "Your arm was my only concern. Do you remember when we were kids. We'd hang out every weekend. You were my protector when the neighborhood bullies rolled around. Remember our blood pact? We found that blade cutter in my dad's toolbox, and slashed up our fingers and mashed them together, swearing 'blood, bone, and loyalty.' I swore to protect you, and I've held up my end. Maybe I made the wrong call, and I definitely should've told you about her attack at some point afterward, but I'll never regret saving your shattered arm—I saved it from you. Screw being cousins, we're closer than that. You're my brother in every sense, and I'd do it all again. I need you to be whole and safe."

"What stopped you from confessing once I'd healed?"

"Kate. She didn't want you to see her face, or to pity her. She made me promise not to say anything."

"Are you for real?"

"Derek, that asshole destroyed her—and even now—she pretends she's okay, but it's all a lie. That scar runs her life and affects how she feels on the inside. She lives in constant fear."

Looking around her apartment, Slater saw those terror troves of protection. Kat had tried to build a fortress in a rental residence. Her valiant efforts highlighted how vulnerable she'd felt, and Slater hadn't been around to offer her real protection. Kat lived her nightmare in solitude. That would end in a flash. Even just as a friend, he'd never allow her to survive in a bubble of fear. Putting aside his concerns, Slater pulled Casey into his arms. She stiffened at first in surprise, before hugging him back fiercely. Her head barely reached the center of his chest.

"Blood, bone, and loyalty. But if you ever pull that shit again—"

"I won't. I swear, and I'm sorry. I'd do anything to make it up to you."

"Stop blaming yourself for Kat's attack. That's all I need from you. And are you done acting like a weirdo around me?"

Casey chuckled. "As long as the next time you swing by, you let me beat you at Mortal Kombat."

"Never. I own that game."

He walked them back to the kitchen, then headed over to Fletcher who now rested a hand on Kat's arm. The former Green Beret sat too close. Slater supposed women would find Fletcher attractive. He exuded that rough and rugged vibe with his slightly mussed, short blond hair and contrasting stern attitude. A perfect curve to his bottom lip amplified the agent's sulky countenance. Fletcher's mouth turned up as his thumb stroked her forearm. Jealousy spiked. Kat returned the smile before turning Slater's way.

"She'll stay at my place tonight," Slater stated.

Kat's stubborn chin jutted forward. "The hell I will, besides its nearly morning. I'll be fine."

Slater sucked in a breath, striving for calm. "You need a new and uncompromised door. A crazy bastard has marked you, and this apartment is no longer secure."

"I can stay at Casey's place."

"And when Jayden is on shift? Do you think your assailant is scared of your tiny friend? You're placing her in danger."

"Shite, you think he knows about Casey?"

"Probably," Fletcher intervened. He must've spotted Slater's laser-like glare and removed his hand from Kat's arm. "Derek has a point. I'll be checking in with our profiler in the morning, but it doesn't take a genius to figure out that he's been planning this for a long time. I'm guessing that he's been watching you for a while now."

"Fan-bloody-tastic. Well, I refuse to let this whack job run me off. He's constrained my life for so long."

Slater understood her struggle; this space was the only sliver of control she had left. He touched her elbow. "I can sleep on that couch, and you can get some rest. Tomorrow, we'll decide what the next step should be."

Kat rubbed her palms over her eyes and nodded. "Thanks, everyone. I'm going to bed." She gave Casey and Jayden a hug, before stumbling down the passage. Thirty minutes later, after everyone had finally left, Slater maneuvered the battered door back in place and settled on the sofa. Feeling too wired to rest, he flicked through television channels. All he focused on were those teeth slipping out of that bag—the serial killer's deceased victims. Most likely, beaten with a rod, stabbed with a cheap knife and defiled with a pair of pliers.

Chapter Eight

Kat woke to the smell of coffee, toast, and something delicious cooking in the kitchen. She donned her robe and wandered down the passage. Derek dumped two pieces of toast on a plate and turned to grin at her. "It's about time. I was about to wake your exhausted ass."

"What bloody time is it?"

"Almost lunchtime. Don't know about you, but I craved a good breakfast. Your fridge is well stocked."

Kat squinted through bleary eyes. That's why she rarely took anxiety meds; they made her way too sleepy. Derek wore jeans and a military green t-shirt that said *KEEP GOING* on it. The sleeves molded his defined biceps, and Kat had to drag her gaze away. "Wait, since when do you cook?"

"Abby's been teaching me." Derek placed a cup of steaming goodness under her nose.

"Thanks." Coffee was exactly what she needed. Kat settled in her chair. "Abby—as in Max's wife?"

"Yeah. We all went on vacation together earlier in the year—a four-day gig to Oregon. I was in charge of breakfast and Abby gave me a few tips. Lizzy taught me how to make a Malva Pudding. Holy moly, that's some addictive shit."

"The team's wives have been domesticating your laid back arse. What wouldn't I have given to be a fly on the wall?"

"Hey! If you're mean, you don't get my famous scrambled eggs." Derek shot her a heart-stopping smile—the unshaven morning stubble framing a sexy mouth. She imagined those bristled cheeks scraping along her inner thigh as his firm lips worked their way up to her...

Kat shifted and crossed her legs. "This I have to try."

Derek flashed those dimples. "Don't go all 'Gordon Ramsey' on me. I'm still learning."

Kat smiled, remembering their joint love of the show *Kitchen Nightmares*. They'd watch it together religiously when he was in-country and always tossed around "Ramsey" quotes.

"Chicklets—shitlets. So...I can't say it's like eating dried cat food?"

He grinned and adopted Ramsey's accent. "Nope. Nor can you say it's like eating a patch of soaking wet grass after a cow shat over it."

Kat giggled as Derek deposited an overly full plate in front of her.

"Derry, there's no way that I can eat three pieces of toast. Do I look like Arnold Schwarzenegger?"

Ignoring her, Derek took a seat and laid into his equally loaded plate. She only realized how hungry she was as warm food slid down her throat. The eggs were particularly good, and she polished them off immediately. They ate in a comfortable silence until she started on the grilled potato and bacon concoction.

"Blimey, this is delicious."

"I know."

Ignoring his smug expression, Kat asked, "Did you get much sleep on the sofa?"

"Aside from my usual habit of staring at the ceiling and questioning my life choices?"

"You do that too?" Kat returned his grin.

"Sleep is for the weak and the sane."

Kat smiled as her eyes wandered around her living area. The damaged door drew her attention. "What did they find in the velvet bag?"

Derek put down his fork. "Kat."

"No-one told me—you were all whispering at the door like spooks. Thanks to my meds, I was also pretty out of it."

"Let's enjoy a good meal. We can chat about it later."

Taking a sip of coffee, she asked, "That bad, huh?"

Derek shoved his chair back and stood.

"No, Derry, finish your food. I'm sorry."

"It's fine, I'm done." He carried his plate over to the sink.

Kat stood and skirted the table. "Don't be withholding information when it comes to my life and—"

"They found teeth."

"Teeth, like before?" Kat gripped the back of a chair.

"Like human teeth, yeah."

"Canines and Incisors? "She didn't wait for confirmation. "I'm the one that got away, and he's finally coming for me."

"He won't touch you." Derek opened the dishwasher and began unloading the sink.

"There's no guarantee—he's a determined killer with rage issues."

"Well, that makes two of us."

"Don't ever compare yourself!"

"I'm not saying it's a bad thing. My military training has prepared me well."

"You're not getting hurt or killing anyone for me."

"You're the only one that I'd—"

"Don't say it." She stepped closer. "Things are long over between us. You need to find an unscarred, pretty girl and—"

"Goddammit!" Derek spun and pulled her into his arms. Kat tried to look up, but he held her head firmly to his broad chest. "Don't ever compare yourself to other women and come up short. I won't tolerate it."

"Derry," she said in a muffled voice.

"I lost the perfect woman—look at you—you're the full package. Brainy, beautiful, humble and so damn sweet. If anything, you're even more beautiful than I remembered."

His grip loosened, and as soon as her eyes met his, Derek pressed his lips to hers. The taste of coffee had her melting into the kiss. Slater's thumbs traced the sides of her mouth as he cradled her head in large hands. He stroked her scar—again—and Kat suppressed the urge to pull away. Exploring old territory with increasing urgency, Kat stood on her toes, trying to absorb every delicious sensation as he backed her against the counter. Her hands ran over his familiar shoulders, and cupped the back of his neck. When she felt his hard length pressing against her pelvis, she almost purred. A hand nudged her robe open, and Derek cupped her breast through her silk camisole. The kiss obliterated every thought as it turned demanding, and his thumb brushed her nipple. Kat pressed into his heat. Derek growled his frustration when the doorbell rang, and Kat shoved him away, stepping aside. His flashing eyes echoed her own hunger. With a hammering heart, Kat shook her head at their impulsiveness, backing up against the sink.

"Baby—"

"See who it is—I can't operate that broken sucker. Besides, I need a shower." Kat tried to control her trembling limbs, her mouth still tingling.

Glancing away from the questions in his eyes, Kat waited for Derek to yield and answer the door. Once he'd physically lifted and opened the barrier, Fletcher Daniels stepped inside. Retreating to her bedroom, Kat studied her walk-in closet, looking for something to wear. Kissing Derek brought up so many memories, and she tried not to think about that sexual magnetism. Every time his gaze met hers, Kat's heart flipped in response. The overwhelming need to touch him ate at her control.

Could she survive another relationship with Derek Banez? Doubtful, and she wasn't in a mentally strong place. And did she have any love left to give? It felt like her heart lay shattered on the frigid ground, where the killer left her to die. Loneliness wasn't an excuse to hook-up with her ex-boyfriend. If anything, they should both slow the hell down. What was so wrong with just being friends? Kat battled between desire and common sense. The desire to play overpowered her urge to run, inviting an old and powerful love back into her life.

Putting aside her predicament, she chose the brightest clothes in her closet—light blue capris and a chartreuse green blouse. A bright red lipstick would finish the look. Kat may not feel cheerful, but she could look sunny.

Twenty minutes later, she returned and found the men studying the damaged door. Slater flashed a warm look of appreciation as she walked down the passage.

"Miss Flynn, we need to talk." Fletcher's formal use of her name as he pivoted had Kat tensing.

"In case you're wondering, I know who visited me last night. Why is it taking so long to identify and catch this arsehole? It's been over a year since he tried to kill me."

"I get that, ma'am, and we're trying. We've only recently

linked the perp to murders in four other states."

"How many other victims are there?" Kat asked, hoping for honesty.

"Possibly six unsolved cases. We've just identified a male victim down south in Saint George."

"He doesn't just attack women?"

"No. It's an unexpected twist."

Kat folded her arms. "And none of the victims have anything in common?"

"The only common denominator is his use of weapons. The steel piping, knife, and pliers are all discarded at every scene. Because they're every day, garden-variety brands, it's hard to pin down a suspect. Plus we think he's concealed his purchasing trail by buying them off of the dark web."

Derek mirrored her stance, before leaning against the wall. "The body count is escalating. Three profilers are now assigned to the case. So far, we have very little to go on."

Kat studied his pensive expression before addressing Fletcher. "So why are you here? To question me again? Over the past months, I've given the FBI and local law enforcement numerous and comprehensive interviews."

"We're recommending a safe house."

She was so tired of feeling powerless. The nameless entity that damaged her body and soul all those months ago, still controlled her world. He dictated her path in life, and that made her want to scream. Kat stepped away from the entryway. "You want me to move out and up-end my life and my schedule."

"If you want to live."

Considering his warning, Kat asked, "Derry, what do you think?"

"I think you should take his advice." He watched her

carefully, like she was a spooked deer who'd race past the damaged door to freedom.

"I'd be depending on strangers."

Nodding tightly, Slater agreed.

"And you trust these men?"

Derek's shoulders visibly stiffened as muscles flexed along his folded arms. "Angel, I don't trust anyone with your life. None of this sits well, and if I wasn't working towards an impossible deadline at the training center, I'd never leave your side. I'm considering a leave of absence to sort out this mess."

She wouldn't be responsible for screwing up Derek's career. The man was still proving himself to the agency and probably hadn't even accrued paid time off. Not that she'd ever allow him to use those days on her sorry arse.

"Shite." Kat paced the small room, coming to a decision. It was time for her to take charge of the chaos. Pivoting, she faced the men. They weren't going to like what she had to say, but this was her life. Derek must've sensed trouble, because he dropped his arms. His expression held a note of wariness.

"After my attack, I wondered if there were other victims. My fears have now been confirmed. For the past week, that's kept me awake at night—obsessing over the ones who didn't survive. What were their last thoughts? Were they dazed and confused like I was? Angry at the universe? Did they know their fate, or hoped that they might survive? As he landed those blows, I prayed that I would. Now I wonder if his other victims were conscious when he pulled their teeth? Did they try to fight back? What would I have done if he'd used those pliers on me?"

Derek pressed a clenched fist to his lips. Kat saw him visibly swallow and she did the same. Fear parched her throat, but she continued.

"And what about the victims' families and their suffering? I think about why I lived, and why others didn't. I guess it's what's called survivor's guilt. He's an evil maniac who extinguishes lives for his satisfaction, but I survived for a good reason. I'm meant to stop him, and I'm doing it for his future victims."

◊ ◊ ◊

Slater knew where she was heading with her heartfelt speech, and he moved towards her in an instinctive gesture. "Don't be crazy. Your only objective is to stay safe. You're untrained and if you mention using yourself for bait—"

"Use me for bait. Go ahead."

"The hell we will." His fists bunched at his sides as he thought of all the ways her silly scheme could go wrong.

Thankfully, Fletcher backed Derek's words. "Ma'am, that's not how the FBI runs our operations. We don't dangle innocent victims in the path of a human T-Rex."

Kat lifted her chin and plunged on. "Well, I'm refusing the safe house option. If you remove me from the equation, what will be his next likely move? I'm sure he'll find a fresh victim—an unknown individual. And that kill will be on me."

"Bullshit." Slater's jaw tightened at her determined defiance, and he wanted to shake sense into her.

Kat trounced over to the sofa and rearranged the pillows he'd slept on the night before. "With me, you have the advantage. Just wait for this bastard to strike."

"It's not that simple." Fletcher eased closer. "I can't assign a task-force until I have more evidence. We need physical evidence tying the victims to this serial killer."

"It is that simple and we all know it's the same brute committing these crimes." Her voice rose with frustration as she picked up a tv remote and placed it on the coffee table.

"The FBI requires a DNA match on the teeth and a revised report from our profiler. That's just to start. The previous Agent in Charge of the investigation neglected the basics," Fletcher stated.

Her nostrils flared. "I'm not allowing this butcher to win. I've been living in the shadows since the attack, waiting for his return. I knew he would, because he's always been calling the shots. Now it's my turn, and I'm not waiting for the FBI to get their shit together. Catch up or bugger off."

"Jesus, Kat!" Slater erupted. He'd reached the end of his patience. "Stop being so bullheaded."

"I'm not spending years hiding from a demon dick-bag. If you want to help, then find a solution. I have virtual meetings to organize this afternoon. I'll work from home in the meantime—that's the best I can offer under the circumstances." She picked her laptop bag up from beside the sofa and stormed up the passage to her office.

Fletcher swiveled to face Slater. "That's one stubborn gal. We can't force her into protective custody."

Slater wanted to break furniture. Instead, he pictured slaying the violent monster who'd marked their lives.

Finally, he spoke. "I need to make some calls. I have a couple of former SF boys who could help."

◊ ◊ ◊

The glass wall provided a lovely view of the library grounds, and he chose his regular spot nearest the cafeteria. The large state library was where he found his victims. Not physically, but online while he sat at terminal #26. Even that was a longwinded process. He'd first need to establish a physical connection with his chosen asset, then slowly uncover his hidden targets. Revealed like pearls in a clamped oyster. He was the one doing all the prying, but it was worth the effort.

The killer thought back to the previous night. The teeth were a nice touch, although giving up part of his collection had been a sacrifice. He'd loved the terror in Kathleen's voice. *I have a gun, and I'm not afraid to use it.*

He also had a gun, although guns weren't his favorite weapon. They were way too impersonal. Getting close to his victims, and hearing the bones crunching under his blows or feeling the knife breaking the skin and plunging through flesh and muscle, that was his nirvana. Finally, he'd use just the right amount of pressure, and a twist of his wrist to extract the teeth. By then, most of his victims were dead. However, the ones that were still alive got to experience his final mishandling of their deceitful bodies. That was where his power lay, seeing the light fading in their terror-filled eyes as he pulled back their heads and pried open their mouths.

Perhaps he could still use a gun to attain his current objective, and terrorize Kathleen in the process. Drawing out the hunt was a new concept. He usually hit his target swiftly, with force, channeling his rage into their annihilation. Kathleen was different because she'd survived his wrath. That didn't upset him necessarily; what did piss him off was her stupid boyfriend. Derek Banez should know better. She'd left Derek in his time of need, yet he raced to her side like a kicked puppy. Oh, he'd teach them both a lesson.

The man methodically shut down the browser windows, covering his trail as he went along. When the blue home screen replaced his search, he pushed his chair back and rose. A librarian bustled past with a wheeled cart, and the killer smiled. The pretty lady blushed, her fair skin reminding him of Kathleen. Thanks to him, Kathleen Flynn wasn't as beautiful as she once was. Now she carried his mark. Two large books fell from the overloaded cart, and he bent down to help the quiet librarian who now smiled at him shyly. Why couldn't all women be this meek?

"Thank you, sir. That's very kind."

He handed over the heavy encyclopedias, their fingers touched, and her eyes jerked up to meet his. Trying to infuse warmth into his expression, the killer considered asking her out on a date. Dismissing the idea, he instead rose, and nodded politely. People were all the same—humans weren't meant for monogamy or to procreate. Betrayal waited in the wings and he was above all the deceit, inevitable cheating, or a woman who thought she could defy him.

Humming his favorite tune, *Teeth in the Grass* by *Iron & Wine*, the killer left the quiet space, pushed open the glass doors and walked into the sunlight.

Chapter Nine

"Thanks for keeping an eye on her." Slater shook Elliot's hand.

"No problem, bro. I'm between jobs anyway, and available for the rest of the month." Elliot headed out of the sports bar. Slater liked the quiet operator from the support group. He had the energy of a laid back poet rather than a former SF warrior. If Elliot had a spirit animal, it would be a chocolate lab. He'd met his wife, had two children and served his country well. It seemed so simple from the outside. Slater should be in the same position. He should've handled his shit, married Kat, and started a family. Thinking of what could've been—of her as his wife and the mother of their child made his heart ache. Slater glanced around the darkened interior, and his gaze landed on Kat, who stood in a corner. The older couple standing with Kat had to be the publisher and her husband.

Slater accepted his surge of possessiveness as he watched Kat laugh and wave a hand in the air. He'd never been a hired gun, but he would shield the hell out of Kathleen Flynn, and the latest developments in her case had him wanting to throw her over his shoulder and stash her in a safe house. Scanning the sports bar for threats, and seeing nothing, Slater made his way over, noting her vintage, navy, pin-up skirt with a white, polka dot bodice, that accented her perfect curves. God, she was like sex on a carnal stick. In an age where everyone flashed their skin, Kat dressed in a feminine and put-together way that held intriguing mystery.

Slater barely took note of the introductions, wanting to pull Kat aside and update her on the case. He nodded at the appropriate times as her publisher chatted about a promotional launch, book sales and something called KDP. A rowdy group of men in the corner drew his attention. One of the men turned and stared openly at Slater and nudged his drunk friend. *Bonehead Brock.*

Slater cursed his luck; it was time to go. "Are you ready to leave?"

Kat shot him a strange look but nodded, picking up on his sudden tension. After saying her goodbyes, they exited the sports bar and made their way over to his Ford Raptor. As it was a busy Friday night, he'd parked farther down the street.

"Derek Banez!"

Kat paused at the man yelling behind them, and Slater gripped her arm, pulling her to his side. "Keep walking."

"Friends of yours?"Kat asked as she hurried along.

"I know one of the drunk twats—and he's not a friend."

"Banez, you're going to snub a fellow brother-in-arms?" Brock called.

Derek kept walking, focusing on his truck sitting under the streetlight ahead. "Have a good one, Brock."

Kat shot Slater a worried glance.

"A world-renowned sniper who thinks he's too good for us?" The voice sounded closer. Bonehead and his two buddies were closing in quickly, and Slater turned to face them, shielding Kat from the impending confrontation.

"I'm having a pleasant evening with my girl. No offense. I'll see you in the next group session."

"Fuck that! You're a slick Hollywood wannabe with a pretty piece of ass." Brock zeroed in on Kat. "Is his dick as pretty as his face?"

Slater's pulse picked up as he stepped forward. "Watch your mouth in front of the lady."

"I heard you joined some covert, black ops team after being a snake eater. That you did some 'Tier One' shit as a fancy-ass hatchet 'G' man."

Slater adjusted his stance. "You seem to know an awful lot about me."

"You're a celebrity, brother. The latest glitterati killing machine." One of Brock's douche bag friends sniggered, and the men tightened their circle.

Raising his brows at the meat heads, Slater asked, "Is this some kind of team building exercise? I think it's past your bedtime."

Brock grunted and shook out his hands.

"Sober up, buddy, it's over. Go home." Slater grasped Kat's hand. Before he could step away, Brock leaned closer. "What? Can't you share Miss Polka Dot Polly with your friends? Look at that sweet mouth."

Going still, Slater repositioned himself to protect his outside line—a technique where he could fight and never turn his back on one of the attackers. "One more word—"

Kat leaned around him. "Yo, mate. Touch me, and I'll shove my foot so far up your steaming arse, that you'll have bandy-legs for days."

One of the beefy sidekicks took a small step back. Trying not to smile, Slater almost missed Brock's swing.

Kat shouldn't have opened her mouth. She watched the rage flare in motor mouth's eyes as he struck out at Derek. He was well-trained, but Derek was faster and far more lethal. In a sidestep, Derek ducked and with an upper thrust, punched Brock in his ribs, and elbowed him in the face. In a blur of movement, Derek kicked at one of the second charging thugs. The man fell, clutching at his knee. The third man backed up with his hands slightly raised. If he'd climbed into the melee, Kat would've tried to stop him. Not that she had any idea what to do, but she'd grabbed her mace from her purse and stood ready. A small crowd had begun to form, but no-one seemed interested in helping in any way.

Not that Derry needed their assistance. Kat had never seen him in action before. While they were dating, he'd never had cause to get physical with anyone. The man was so easy-going that she'd forgotten what he had done for a living—a honed and highly classified weapon trained by the U.S. government.

It was over before it had begun. Blocking a punch, Derek grabbed Brock's wrist, twisting his arm back at an unnatural angle and bringing him to the ground. Brock groaned and tried to scramble away, but Derek held fast.

"The only reason why you're not bleeding out in the dirt is because you're a fellow veteran. Next time I won't give you that benefit. If you say anything derogatory towards this lady, I'll crush your damn skull. Do we understand each other?" Derek applied more pressure.

"Yes… shit… yes. God, let go!"

"Yes, who?" Derek eyed the other injured colleague climbing gingerly to his feet while holding Brock to the pavement, obviously watching for a possible second attack.

"Yes… yes, sir."

Releasing his hold, Derek backed up and allowed the younger soldier to roll to his feet.

Brock swiped a hand over his sweaty, grit-covered mouth. "Sorry, man. I'm drunk, and a fucking screw-up. Not everyone can be as perfect as you."

"You have no idea what I've experienced. You know better. By drinking and acting like a spiritually constipated dick, you're only hurting yourself. Get your head out of your damn ass, and I'll see you in our next group session."

Derek watched the three men retreat before turning to Kat. "Are you okay?"

"I wasn't the one fighting off multiple assailants. You're quick. They didn't lay a hand on you!"

Derek shrugged. "I've been training heavily—getting back to my fighting weight. I did however tweak my bad arm." He rolled his shoulder as he guided Kat to his truck. The warmth from his hand resting on her lower back calmed her frayed nerves.

"Let's move," he whispered in her ear. "I don't want to stick around in case someone called the police. An agent brawling in the street won't go down well with the FBI."

"You know, you could've arrested him for assaulting an agent," Kat said as he opened the passenger door and helped her inside.

Once he'd gone around and climbed in, Derek turned the ignition and pulled away. "I was Brock once. Maybe not as ill-mannered, but I recognize that glazed look in his eyes. He's hurting. Brock mentioned that he lost a couple of his teammates in Afghanistan before he left a few years ago. I'm guessing he's blaming himself."

"Is that what you did?" Kat asked as they pulled up to a light. "Blamed yourself?"

"We all do. Overanalyze what we could've done differently. The truth is—never mind."

"No, tell me." Kat placed a hand on his thigh as Derek stared ahead.

"I've untangled much of my PTSD. I still have the nightmares and the Black Friday bombing will always be a part of me. But now… all my regrets are tied up with you."

"Derry—" she said as he pulled off.

"I blame myself for all of it—for losing you. I could've done things a whole lot different. I should've been a better man."

"Derek, what you did to me—to us. I loved you with my entire being."

Taking a right down a quiet side road, Derek pulled to the side and turned to face her. "I know. I live with that mistake every day. I could make excuses that I was drunk and let my guard down. Or that I was upset because I wanted to spend my birthday with you. That I was in a bad place with a fucked up brain, but, the truth was, that I could've tried harder. I should've flown out to your seminar gig on my birthday, and surprised you. I ignored you—us—for weeks and wallowed in self-pity. I wanted to self-destruct—I can't explain that numb feeling. When you stop caring about everything that matters."

Kat considered his words as she stared out the window at the empty sidewalk. She'd done a lot of thinking over the last almost two years since their breakup, and spoke into the strained silence. "It wasn't all your fault. I didn't know how to deal with your PTSD. Whenever I tried to help, you'd push me away. Yes, you locked me out of your life, but I didn't fight hard enough to stay in it."

"Bullshit. You were an incredible girlfriend."

"No. I was an absent one. I threw myself into my work and

chose to travel out of state. I chose not to be by your side for your birthday celebrations."

"You were trying to build your career, and had to deal with an immature and selfish man."

Kat turned and grabbed his shirt, pulling him towards her. Tears pricked behind her eyes. "Look at me. Don't you ever say that. I dealt with a torn up man who was my best friend, my rock and my heart. All I wanted to do was to love you, and hold you, and take away your pain. But I failed. Derry, I left and failed you." A tear ran down her cheek, and he gripped her shoulders.

"You did exactly the right thing by leaving my sorry ass. That was the biggest wake-up call of my life. That's when I sought out treatment and when I saw my first therapist. You saved my life, angel."

He pulled her to his chest as she cried out all the old pain. His capable fingers combed through her hair, and Kat breathed in his familiar scent. He still wore Yves Saint Laurent La Nuit De L'Homme. The comforting smell of cardamom and cedar brought back old memories. Movie nights, snowy vacations in the Rocky Mountains, slow dancing in the backyard in the summer... Then she remembered the lonely nights and how shattered she'd been after their breakup.

Kat pulled away and wiped her eyes. "Look at us, two sad little tits, sitting in a truck."

Derek laughed and tucked her hair behind her ear. "We need a Disney day."

Kat huffed out a laugh. "What is a Disney day?"

"Well..." Derek dragged a damp strand of hair off her cheek. "It starts with chocolate milkshakes—loaded with whipped cream." He shot her a devastating grin.

"Keep going," Kat chuckled.

His fingers brushed her neck. "Then you get to choose a Disney movie from my extensive DVD collection. I'm partial to the Lion King, but I won't stand in your way. As long as it's not that frozen chick."

Biting her lip to prevent a giggle from escaping she asked, "You have the *Frozen* DVD?"

"The boys love it—Max and Johnny's kids." Slater grimaced. "We sing it together… often."

She couldn't control a burst of laughter, while filing away that snippet of information. Max and Johnny had children? "Anything else I need to know about a Disney day?"

"There may be some sparkly pink wigs and singing thrown into the mix—really bad karaoke type singing."

"You'd sing *Hakuna Matata* for me?"

"That I can do." He grew serious and his gaze traveled to her lips. "So where do we go from here?"

"Hell if I know." Kat fiddled with her hands.

"Let's not go to your place tonight. Stay with me."

"Derry, that's not a good idea."

"I have a spare room and a huge flat screen tv. We can binge watch a Netflix series and order in."

"I need my toiletries—"

"I have a spare, new toothbrush. You can use my soap and shampoo."

"And your face cream and body lotion," Kat teased. He was such a metrosexual. Derek's drawers were filled with so much product, that they could make a cosmopolitan editor jealous. "Maybe I can forget about a crazed serial killer for one night?"

"Well, sure. I guess that rules out watching Dexter later. Gosh darnit."

Kat smiled at his joke and the flash of those deep dimples.

The man could've easily been a male supermodel. Brock had been correct, Derek had an awfully pretty face, and an even prettier—her face flamed thinking about his perfect cock, and she pulled on the seatbelt, straightening in her chair. "The *Lion King* it is…"

Stepping into his territory was a bad idea, yet Kat didn't protest as he swiped the indicator and turned towards the freeway.

◊ ◊ ◊

This was a bad idea, Slater thought as he scooted back on the carpet, and leaned back against the couch. Kat sat on the cushion above him and attacked his shoulder, expertly kneading while watching some hospital show that she'd selected after they'd watched the Lion King. Slater barely took note of the drama unfolding onscreen. Her hands felt like heaven. He hadn't been touched this intimately in a very long time. In fact, the last person to have touched him this way was Kat. Whenever he'd return from deployment or heavy training exercises, she'd sit naked on his back and work over all his sore muscles. This was different. They were both fully clothed, and she'd offered to rub his shoulder when he'd gotten up to take a pain pill. Now he was surrounded by her perfume, and ink-black hair that fell forward and grazed his neck, and God, had her breast just brushed against his ear as she leaned into her kneading hands. His dick stood at full attention and Slater raised a knee to hide his obvious woody.

"That nurse is obsessed with him," Kat said as her palm twisted into his muscle. Slater groaned in response, not caring who had the hots for who, on the television farce.

"Too hard?" Kat asked.

It took a second for him to figure out what she meant, and

he pulled up his other knee. "No. Umm… just perfect."

"Your shoulder is one giant knot. You've been overworking it."

"It's healed. It's fine."

"It's filled with pins and a plate and you should take it easy."

"Casey told you the details of my bionic arm?"

"A little bit of hardware doesn't make it bionic." Kat's husky laugh made him smile.

"It really does. I'm effectively Robocop." Derek spoke in a robotic voice. "My friends call me Slater. You call me… Robocop."

She laughed in answer, and dug her knuckles into his shoulder blade. "I haven't seen the movie. It was way before my time—and yours."

Slater groaned as she hit a tender spot. "That's a damn crime. That's what we should've watched tonight."

"What? You don't like *Chicago Med*?"

"Nope." Slater reached back and tugged at her hair.

"Hey!" Kat slammed a pillow into the side of his head. He snagged her wrist and pulled her forward, reaching back to tickle her ribcage. Giggling, Kat grabbed a fistful of his hair with her other hand.

"Let go!" Slater warned. He'd always loved how she fought dirty. In one smooth motion, he pulled her wrist as he rose, and swung her over his shoulder. Kat yelped, and he slapped her on her cute ass.

"Stop! Derry! You're going to hurt your shoulder even more!"

Slater lowered her to the wide leather sofa and dropped her onto her back. Instead of letting go, she grabbed his shirt, and he toppled on top of Kat, almost head butting her. All he registered were her soft curves. The familiar fit had him thrusting his hips forward and pinning her delicious body to the cushions.

Kat groaned.

"Shit, did I hurt you?" He should roll off and gain control.

"No. Don't move."

"Kat?" He raised himself on his elbows and looked into her deep blue eyes, seeing a hunger that reflected his own as she settled into the cushions.

Kat licked her top lip. "I missed this—miss touching you. Feeling you up against me."

"Angel—"

She thrust her hips up to meet his, as his cock strained through his pants, pushing against her thigh.

"Don't," he said in warning, but instead of listening, she grasped the back of his neck and studied his face.

"I love that one freckle that sits just below your eye." Kat reached and traced her other thumb over his cheekbone. He pursed his lips, and she smiled. "And God, those wee dimples." Her thumb moved lower, pressing into one of the slight indentations before touching his lower lip. Slater pulled her hand away and almost growled.

"You're playing with fire," he said instead.

"Just a quick taste." The reply had barely left her lips before he crushed them beneath his. Her chest heaved, intensifying his assault. Coaxing her lips open, he reveled in the velvet warmth, and took his time to explore her familiar taste. When her fingers dug into his neck, and she moaned softly, his exploration shifted in intensity. Shoving up her skirt, Slater slid a hand up her silken thigh and traced a thumb over damp panties. Kat bucked in response. Slater didn't let up. Planting kisses along her jaw and down her neck, he bit and sucked as his thumb stroked then pressed firmly against her clothed slit. Her thighs tensed beneath him, as he increased the friction while reveling in her strangled moans. Her now damp panties had him growing impossibly hard. He wanted to push aside the flimsy barrier and thrust into her wet heat. Instead, he circled his thumb against her clit. Feeling her build so quickly had him sucking her earlobe hard before biting down.

"Oh, God, don't stop... missed this. Oh, my..."

"Come for me," Slater whispered in her ear in a thick voice as he pressed harder against her clit. Hips bucking, the climax ripped through her, and he pressed his palm to her warmth, waiting for her to drift back down. He knew that body, remembering all of her hot zones. He had driven her to the edge with just his hand. He liked that his touch turned her on.

A long ago memory surfaced of Slater tying her wrists to their bed in Colorado and playing a game. He promised to bring her to orgasm multiple times if she threw out the rules. Kat demanded that on the first round, he was allowed to use one finger. That had been a fun challenge. Next he could only use his mouth—no hands. When he'd reduced her to a quivering mess, he'd eased inside and pulled out a third and fourth orgasm before screaming her name. He'd untied her, and then it was his turn to be restrained. That had evened the playing field, because whenever Kat had touched him, Slater had turned to molten lava.

Shaking himself from their delicious past, Slater transferred his weight to his good arm, straightened her skirt and ran his fingers across her chest and along her collarbone. "I love the way you dress. Like an old-fashioned siren. All feminine and sexy."

"I've changed over the past couple of years. I might still dress the same, but I don't feel that sexy anymore."

Slater tensed at her words. Because of her scar. Kat had no idea of her vibrant beauty. She literally glowed, and her light drew people to her side. No amount of scars could ever take away her essence. Feeling a necklace around her neck, Slater drew out the chain and stared down at the Jade pendant. He stilled, before fisting the Jade stone in his hand.

"You still wear this?"

"It saved my life. I asked the detective to return it, once they'd finished with it at the lab."

"It's chipped—all smashed up on one side."

"Aye, just like me."

Dark pain pierced his heart, as Slater glanced up to study her face. "Don't say that."

"It's the truth and not a bad thing. I like that it's not perfect. This stone survived the assault and protected me, just like you said it would."

Slater jerked away and sat up. "Is that what you think? That it was some screwed up piece of fate and that silly stone was meant to save your life?"

Kat shrugged as she swung her feet to the floor, and tucked the pendant between her breasts. "The wee bugger did its job. Why are you so upset?"

Standing, Slater ran a hand through his hair. "Yeah, it did its job. That inanimate object was the only thing to do it's damn job, because I sure as hell didn't. I did fuck all."

"You were deployed and working in Africa," Kat said with evident confusion.

"You should never have been in Park City in the first place. You were supposed be in Denver, living in our home. I did this. I pushed you away, broke your heart, and left you to deal with the fallout. I fucked up and I'm not good for you. Ever since you hooked up with me, your life has been one long shit-show. If we had never met—"

"Wind yer neck in! You don't get to blame yourself for my attack. You know what, shit happens. A bus could've hit me when I crossed the street in Denver, or I could've tripped down a flight of stairs. You can't control outside circumstances. And our relationship wasn't all bad. For a long time, it was amazing. You were my everything."

Her words hurt. Familiar words that he'd whispered in her ear, against a tree trunk all those years ago. She'd always been his everything, and he'd treated her like shit. Ignoring her for weeks while he licked his mental wounds. He moved away before he did something stupid like fall to his knees and beg for her forgiveness or for her touch.

Kat stood and walked over to the passage. "I'm not playing your blame game. I am, however, going to use your guest shower. I'm tired, and it's been a long day."

"What do you want from me?" Slater asked as she turned her back.

"I want you to be happy. That's all I've ever wanted."

Sinking to the sofa, Slater switched off the television and rested his head against the back of the couch. Kat was right, it had been a long day, and they'd just waded into complicated territory. He cursed under his breath. She deserved more than a soldier with a blood-stained soul—an asshole who'd sliced up her heart in a drunken haze.

His phone buzzed in his pocket, and Slater pulled it out to stare tiredly at the screen.

Sorry about earlier. Didn't mean to scare your girl.

Slater forgot that the veteran's group had access to a cell number directory as a support lifeline for fellow vets. Ignoring Brock's text, Slater lay back and rested his eyes, hearing the shower turn on. The phone buzzed again in his hand.

For the love of Christ.

Slater opened his eyes and glanced at the device.

So how does a simple soldier land a college educated, fancy-ass corporate queen like Kathleen Flynn?

What in the living hell? Slater sat forward and stared at the screen, then tapped out a text.

What did you just say?

Slater waited for a reply, his full attention now on the phone.

She's a little above your pay-grade. Heard she had a nasty run-in with a bad-ass in Park City. Girls these days have to be careful. Wolves lurk in the shadows.

Jolting to his feet, Slater swore and paced the room. Fury dissolved into shock as he retrieved his laptop and began digging into Brock's online presence. When he found the bastard on an old LinkedIn profile, Slater pulled up Donnie's number. MIT was still in-country, and Slater now had his first big break in the case. Donnie answered, and Slater tempered his words, wanting to spit nails. "We have a suspect. I need you to run a check on a Brock Samuel Newman. Originally from Little Falls, Idaho. I'll text you the address. His parents still live in Idaho."

"Whoa. Slow down, bro. How is he a suspect?"

"This is about me. I think Brock is obsessed, and Kat fell into his crosshairs."

Donnie tapped away. "Dude, the guy is a veteran. Spc. Brock Newman, from Idaho, served as a UH-60 Blackhawk Helicopter repairer, assigned to 1st Battalion. He also worked on HH-60M Hospital Helicopters assisting combat medical specialists in transporting patients to safety."

"I know. Brock has been out for a few years. As far as I can tell, he's now a drifter. He mentioned once staying with friends on his travels."

"That doesn't explain his other victims—which by the way, have zero ties to you."

"Check him out. I have a weird feeling about this guy. I thought at first that he was working through PTS issues, but now I'm not so sure. He seems a little... off."

"Who seems a little off?" Kat walked into the room, wrapped in his thick robe. Slater stared with longing, remembering how she used to love wearing his robe in the winters before bed. Her eyes dropped under his raking gaze, and Slater zoned back in on the conversation with Donnie.

"Let me know what you find." Slater hung up and turned to Kat, bracing himself to tell her that this may all be about him. Slater wasn't good for her, and as soon as they caught the serial killing bastard, he'd exfil out of Kat's life.

Chapter Ten

There was no listed address in Utah for a Brock Newman, and after contacting Fletcher and handing over the intel, both the agency and Donnie drew the same conclusions. Brock technically may have physically been in the same states as all of the victims around the time of the attacks, but without additional information to go on, they didn't have enough cause to arrest him. Fletcher planned to bring Brock in for questioning but decided initially to conduct surveillance. They knew Brock would be at the next Veteran Assistance meeting, and Fletcher agreed to accompany Slater to the meeting, under the guise of a possible new member. The rest of Fletcher's team sat in a van behind the adjacent church, and once Fletcher was wired up, they pulled into the lot in Slater's truck.

Red met them at the door; Slater introduced Fletcher, and Red immediately got his balls in a twist. "You can't just invite random strangers. There are procedures in place for a reason. You should've emailed me ahead of time."

"Relax Red; he's just getting a feel for the place."

"Where were you stationed?" Red asked Fletcher.

"Marine RECON." Fletcher flashed a wide grin. "3rd Reconnaissance Battalion—Based out of Japan."

Red looked skeptical. "You saw action in Japan?"

"No, we were based out of Japan. My mobile unit saw action in hotspots across Asia and the Middle East."

Narrowing his eyes before yielding, Red said, "Fine, but if you decide to sign up, I need you to fill out the required paperwork by month end and I'll place you in the system."

Once they'd made it past the gatekeeper—both men entered and casually walked up to the refreshment table. Brock hadn't yet arrived, and Slater hoped he'd turn up.

"You squat in this depressing room every week?" Fletcher asked as he took a sip of lemonade.

Slater glanced around. It did seem pretty dingy and had a 1970's classroom vibe. The church rented out the old facility on its grounds to anyone who'd pay. Slater guessed that the leasing fee was a pretty minimal one.

"It works."

"I also attend an occasional meeting, but my support group is alot more laid back. We even have a billiard table and occasionally hold a poker night. You should come along."

Slater might take Fletcher up on his offer. Everyone shuffled to the circle of chairs, and once they'd settled, Red launched into his introductory speech. Every week it was the same. Welcoming new members, then Red would drone on about current veteran policies for ten minutes, and finally, he'd cover the conductory rules for the meeting.

"This is a real blast," Fletcher muttered as Slater covered a yawn.

"It's a decent group."

"If we were all 'Walking Dead' zombies."

Red shot them a glare. "You two, stop whispering."

The doors creaked open, and Brock sauntered in wearing a

cocky grin and a shiner—courtesy of Slater.

Game-on.

Slater assessed Brock's weight and build. He fitted Kat's description. A couple of inches shorter than Slater, and broader around the middle. But then again, a few of the men around the table could fit that physical profile. A fairly common body type. The bonehead immediately zeroed in on Slater, staring him down while taking the opposite seat. Brock sat gingerly— probably due to his tender ribs. Slater suppressed a knowing smile.

A couple of the veterans spoke about their current challenges, assimilating into civilian life. Red mentioned his brother, who was still deployed in Afghanistan. The whole time, Brock barely blinked, never glancing away from Slater. The guy had major issues.

"You have a fan," Fletcher whispered into his hand.

When the group took a ten-minute break, Slater and Fletcher headed over to the snack corner.

Brock sauntered over to the two men. "You brought a friend? Is he an alpha ninja like you?"

"Hello, Brock, I see you're still in asshole mode." Slater poured a glass of lemonade.

"Where's your little sex kitten? I thought Kathleen would be here holding your hand?"

Scalding fury shoved aside any rationality and lemonade spilled as Slater placed the pitcher down a little too firmly. "What did I say last night, when I brought you to the pavement?"

"Easy," Fletcher muttered.

"Relax." Brock chose a chocolate chip cookie. "It's a compliment."

"So have you been in Utah long?" Fletcher asked.

Eying the agent, Brock shrugged. "Long enough to get fucking bored. This place is damn slow. I might head out to LA."

"You've got some work out there?" Fletcher asked.

"What's it to you?"

"Just asking—I may do a bit of traveling."

"You?" Brock snorted. "Looks like you have your dick stuck firmly up your ass. Let me guess—private security?"

"I do work in security. Good guess."

"Damn hippies." Brock stuffed another cookie in his already full mouth.

"Derek tells me that they assigned you to the 1st battalion. You're an Idaho boy?"

Brock turned his beady eyes on Slater. "Did he now? I didn't take 'Mr. Tall & Deadly' for a motor mouth."

Slater shrugged a shoulder. "I told him about your dick moves last night."

"Give me a moment alone with your girl, and I'll show her 'dick' moves." Brock thrust his hips. Rage detonated and Slater didn't pause to think.

Ignoring the crashing refreshment table, he drove Brock up against the nearest wall and pinned him with a forearm. The asshat's face turned scarlet, and Slater increased the pressure against his windpipe, craving annihilation. "I will end you. Right now! You understand me?"

Brock's eyes bulged as Fletcher and the other men tried to drag Slater away. He wasn't letting go until he'd driven his message home. "Touch her and I'll obliterate you!"

Letting go suddenly had Brock dropping to his knees. Brock coughed as his chest heaved. Slater allowed Fletcher to drag him away, and once he'd gained distance, Slater shrugged the fellow agent off and headed to the door.

Red beat him to the exit. "That was unacceptable. You know the rules!"

"Get out of my way."

"No physical altercations allowed in these group sessions. You'll be written up and expelled! You can't just—"

"Back the hell up."

Slater pushed past into the night and cursed soundly at his lack of control. He'd just assaulted a suspect in an active investigation. Slater had allowed emotion to run the show. Dammit, he thought he'd worked through his rage issues, but when it came to Kat... Imagining Brock cornering or harming her had set Slater off, and now he'd face disciplinary action. He climbed in his truck and waited for Fletcher to join him. It didn't take long.

"What the hell was that!" Fletcher wrenched open the passenger door and slammed it shut behind him.

"You're right; I can't be involved in any way. I just fucked things up." Slater rubbed a hand over his face. He couldn't think past his own harsh breathing and stared at the dash as his heart slipped back to a normal rhythm.

"Look, maybe we can salvage this. Brock Newman is now pissed, and that's a good thing. He's been trying to push your buttons, he succeeded, but your level of rage threw him out of whack."

"That makes two of us."

"We'll keep him under surveillance. He might go on the hunt."

Slater stiffened. Kat was safe, Elliot was with her at Slater's place. Earlier that day, they'd packed a couple of her suitcases, and Kat had temporarily moved into Slater's guest bedroom while they sorted through this mess. Still, he needed to get back to her. Kat was all he thought about, and if anything happened to her, no amount of therapy would fix that shit.

Chapter Eleven

The 24/7 bodyguard thing was getting to Kat. Burly men now shadowed her every move. Many women wouldn't complain, but she needed to escape her walled prison. Hiding out at Slater's place was getting old. She'd caught up on all her emails, meetings, and blog posts, and canceled a speaking gig, plus two scheduled in-person meetings. The past week, Slater had been working all day onsite, he'd return exhausted and would immediately jump online with his former teammates as they worked over her case. Kat tried to stay out of his way. It was for the best. Fooling around on his couch that one time was a mistake. But, shite, the man was built like a God.

Twice she'd run into him in the living area while he wore just a towel—his naturally tanned skin still damp from a shower. The way his wet brown hair curled into the nape of his neck… water droplets dripping down his back… and a defined stomach with that rippling six pack. She'd also spotted his scars. Not just from his shoulder surgery, but a few other older ones decorating his chest and back that she hadn't seen before. She was secretly glad he'd left the military and chosen a safer profession.

Kat ate her granola at the breakfast counter, glancing up when Slater walked into the kitchen. He wore old jeans and work boots which meant he'd be back at the FBI facility for the day.

"You look nice," he said as he opened the fridge.

Kat wore a mustard yellow, button-up blouse, blue jeans, and red flats. "Thanks. I want to run a few errands."

"As long as Elliot tags along." Slater stared into the fridge, deciding what to eat.

Kat sighed, then agreed. "My front door has been replaced. I could return to my place."

"Not until we've made an arrest."

"That could take months."

Slamming the fridge door, he placed the milk on the counter and walked over to the pantry to retrieve a box of cornflakes. Choppy movements hinted at an irritation. "I know this is awkward for you, but I'm barely here. When I am in residence, I'm trying to work on your—"

"Stop. It's not that, I need some time to myself. Being constantly shadowed…"

"Look, let's talk about it when I get back later. In the meantime, do what Elliot says and keep aware of your surroundings."

"Sure." Kat played with her spoon, surprised when he suddenly grasped her shoulders from behind. "I'm sorry, angel. All I want is for you to be safe. Putting up with my grouchy ass is a sacrifice you'll have to make. How about I bring you back some cheesecake—from that awesome bakery down south?"

"You wee bastard, it sucks that you know all my weaknesses."

"Nothing wee about me, baby." Slater bent down and kissed her neck.

The doorbell rang. Elliot. Slater grabbed his pack and headed for the door.

"What about yer cornflakes?" she called.

"I'll grab something on the way. I'm out of time."

Shoving aside the rest of her breakfast, Kat rushed to her room, brushed her teeth, and applied the rest of her make-up. Elliot had barely sat down at the kitchen counter when she dragged him towards the door.

It was the perfect late summer's day. The cloudless sky and bright sunlight had Kat pausing to take a deep breath of fresh air before climbing in Elliot's Subaru. She directed the self-contained man to a large, newly built outside mall. Nestled amongst boutiques, it had an organic grocery and a lovely artisan cheese shop.

First, Kat wanted to stop by her treasured coffee spot. They wandered along the cobbled streets, and avoiding her favorite shoe store, Kat headed past the sectioned off playground situated in the courtyard and wound her way into the coffee shop. She waited for Elliot to order, and after selecting a chocolate eclair and cappuccino for herself, Kat paid for their order.

"Kat!"

She turned at the sound of her name and froze. Eyes widening, Kat recognized the elegant woman who stood a few feet away with a wad of napkins in her hand. Max's fiancée— probably now wife—walked over and immediately embraced Kat in a firm hug. How had Kat not asked Derek about his old team? All she'd spoken about was her situation. Feeling the guilt, Kat offered a tentative smile.

"You look amazing," Abby said, squeezing Kat hard.

Shoving down her awkwardness, Kat returned the hug. After pulling away, she almost gave in to the urge to cover her cheek with her hair. Stopping herself, Kat straightened her shoulders and reached over to squeeze Abby's hand. Even though they'd barely had time to get to know each other before Slater and Kat's breakup, she'd always loved hanging out with Abby.

When Kat had broken it off with Slater, she'd purposely distanced herself from his team. It wasn't right, but it had hurt too much to see them. Abby—dressed down in sneakers, leggings and a vest top—now looked so relaxed and content. When she'd first arrived in the States almost two years ago, she'd looked worn down and pale.

Kat immediately addressed the potential elephant in the room. "I'm sorry I didn't stay in touch or answer any of your texts."

"You were hurting, and I wanted to let you know that I'd always be there if you needed me."

"I knew."

"How are you, hun? Max told me…" Abby's gaze flickered to Kat's scar.

"Shite happens, right?"

Abby laughed. "Ain't that the truth. Is that your boyfriend?" She nodded towards Elliot, stirring his coffee at the counter. His bushy brows shaded pensive eyes that now glanced her way.

"Oh, hell no. That's Elliot; he's married with kids. He's my… it's complicated."

"We've got time to catch up. Come sit at my table."

"That would be great. Wait a second."

Kat got Elliot's attention. "This is an old friend of mine, can we join them at their table?"

"You go ahead. I just got a text from my wife. She's at the dentist, and USPS just delivered a large package to our door. Do you mind if I run home to retrieve it? I'll be gone for thirty at the most."

Kat smiled at Elliot. "Aye, you go ahead."

"Don't go anywhere." He shot her a warning glance.

"Like I can—I arrived in your car."

Grabbing Kat's hand, Abby led her to a table on the outside patio next to the playground. "Come, let me introduce you to the rest of the girls."

"The rest of the who?" Kat said as she slipped her sunglasses back on.

"The other wives."

Kat screeched to a stop. "Shut yer bake, the rest of the team are all married?"

"Pretty much."

"Even Donnie? After what happened with his wife?"

"Yip. He married Charlie, and she's like a ray of crazy sunshine."

"No way! Charlotte Quinn from Wyoming?" Kat had met her a couple of times when they'd traveled up to stay over at Johnny's farm.

"The very same."

Kat looked over at the table just as Charlie looked up and waved. How had she not spotted Charlie in the corner? Her flaming hair stood out like a beacon as she leaned over a pram. A petite blonde wearing a "30 Seconds to Mars" t-shirt sat beside her, eating what looked to be a giant sundae piled with bananas and ice cream. Kat immediately smiled at the early morning breakfast choice—a fellow ice cream lover.

"Gabe! Wait your turn. Don't push in front of other kids!" Abby's shout had Kat following the brunette's gaze.

She barely recognized Abby's little boy standing at the top of a blue slide on the playground. He'd grown so much since she'd seen him last—now an energetic little boy versus a quiet toddler. He was still recognizable amongst the crowd of kids swarming the jungle gym, with his wavy dark hair and thickly lashed eyes. Gabe backed up as a tiny girl pushed in front of him and slid down the slide.

"How old is he?"

"Almost four. School starts back up on Monday. Thank God. It's been a long summer." Abby smiled and rolled her eyes.

The two women arrived at the table, and Charlie ran around to hug Kat. The tiny blonde looked up, and Abby introduced her as Johnny's wife, Lizzy.

"Oh, my God. You're the 'Kathleen Flynn!'—the love of Slater's life."

"Lizzy!" Abby admonished, but Lizzy squealed in excitement.

"Holy cannoli. I heard you were gorgeous, but hell, girl. No wonder Slater never recovered."

"He didn't?" Kat frowned.

"Ignore Lizzy; she has no filter. Kind of like me." Charlie grinned and pulled out a chair. "Sit, honey. What have you been up to?"

Kat settled and spotted a baby in the pram, and the toddler in the stroller eating strawberries from a container. "Okay, whose adorable kids am I looking at?"

"This is Lucy. She's my angel," Abby said, using a wet wipe to wipe off strawberry mush from the toddler's cheek.

"Oh, my gosh! She has Max's pale eyes."

"I know. Spooky, right? And that's Willow, Donnie and Charlie's little girl."

Kat leaned over to admire the squirming babe, noting the red tint to her blonde hair. "I think she's going to have your same hair color."

"I think so. Donnie is stoked. That's all he talks about."

Something wet touched Kat's leg, and she jumped.

"Sorry!" Lizzy leaned down. "That's Ray—my service dog— she's just saying hello."

The sweetest face looked up, and Kat couldn't resist stroking the spaniel's soft ears. After a long scratch, Kat relaxed back in her chair in the cool shade, and chatted easily with the other women, picking up right where they'd left off. They spoke about how they all landed up living in Utah and how it made it easier when the men were on deployment. Kat tensed when Charlie mentioned Kat's attack.

"The team are trying to help Slater. They told us about what happened. I'm so sorry."

Kat shrugged. "It's common knowledge."

Abby leaned back in her chair. "At the time—if I'd known, I could've come over and helped."

"It's all good. We were all living such separate lives—my fault. I shouldn't have cut you out of my life. It was just such a painful breakup."

Abby squeezed her hand just as Gabe raced to Abby's side. Another little boy ran up to Lizzy, who handed him a glass of juice. Beautiful amber eyes contrasted with the boy's dark brown skin.

"That little girl pushed Gabe and he fell on his butt!" The kid pointed at the same little girl from earlier.

Lizzy rolled her eyes and introduced him to Kat. "Valentino, say hello to Miss Kat first. Show your manners."

Valentino looked sideways at Kat and shot her a shy smile before surprising her with a quick hug. Tiny hands brushed against her waist, and Kat squeezed his shoulders in return.

"Nice to meet you, Miss Kitty."

All the women laughed before both little boys raced back to the swings.

"Valentino is awfully protective of Gabe—being a year older and all."

"He's a wee darling. He has a trace of an accent?" Kat said to Lizzy.

"John and I adopted him from a children's home in Kenya. He's a character."

"That's grand. I'd love to adopt someday."

"There are so many children in need of a loving home." Lizzy smiled fondly at Valentino as he climbed onto a swing. "We've applied to adopt another little girl from the same orphanage."

"Lizzy works over there for at least three months out of the year," Abby said proudly. "And she's a singer. Her debut album is being released in October."

"Congratulations." Kat would love to hear Lizzy sing. "Do you play live?"

"At a few spots in town. It's just a hobby."

"John takes it very seriously." Abby grinned. "He shadows Lizzy like a bodyguard at her gigs. The friendly giant stands proudly in the corner."

"When he's not on deployment…" Lizzy smiled before her glance flicked over Kat's cheek. Kat pulled at her hair.

"Don't," Lizzy said. "That scar makes you a kick-ass warrior."

Lizzy's direct address took Kat by surprise. She opened her mouth to say something when Lizzy held up her hand. It took Kat a second to spot the damaged index finger—amputated at the middle joint.

"I also have the mark of the warrior. Embrace it. It took forever for John to convince me, that I've survived crazier shit than most people have dreamt about, and screw them all if they ever judge us for being survivors."

Kat gaped. She closed her mouth before nodding. Tears pricked as she leaned over and grasped Lizzy's injured hand. Knowing she'd found a friend for life, Kat never flinched as Lizzy reached over to trace the scar running down her cheek. She didn't know what had happened to the wee woman, but she guessed it was some pretty lousy shite.

"Kick-ass warriors," Lizzy whispered, her eyes glistening.

"Uh… sorry to interrupt girl time, but is that a friend of yours?" Charlie asked Kat while burping Willow on her shoulder.

Kat looked in the same direction as Charlie and froze.

Brock stood leaning against the coffee shop's brick wall, drinking from a cup and staring her way with an unblinking gaze.

"He's been staring at you for the last five minutes," Charlie added. "Sorry, I'm more observant than I used to be."

"Bloody hell," Kat whispered, squeezing Lizzy's hand in fear. She now knew he was a suspect, and panic tore at her fragile control. His creepy scrutiny felt like a hand closing against her throat, and she barely heard the other women's concerned questions. Taking a shaky breath, she focused on Abby's tense expression as Abby leaned forward and asked, "Honey, who is he?"

"He attacked Derek the other day. He's a suspect… in my case. Where is Elliot? Shouldn't he be back by now?"

"Wait." Abby gripped Kat's arm. "Has he been brought in for questioning or arrested? Why is he wandering around in broad daylight?"

Kat replied softly. "They have no proof. Not yet. He's supposed to be under surveillance."

"Well, that sure as hell isn't the case," Charlie said as she pushed the two tykes into the corner and blocked them with her chair. "Should we call the police? Our hubbies are all the way out in Idaho on a training exercise."

"And say what?" Kat gripped the edge of her seat. "He hasn't committed any crime. He's in a public space."

Brock pushed off the wall and headed in their direction. Abby visually checked on the two little boys who played a safe distance away from impending confrontation.

"You want me to call Slater?" Lizzy asked. Kat nodded, hating that he'd have to leave the work site. "You guys need to leave. If he's the killer, then he's dangerous."

"Bull. It's broad daylight, and shoppers and families surround us. We're not leaving you." Charlie folded her arms, almost eager for first contact. Lizzy placed her phone to her ear and walked away, as Abby straightened in her chair.

"This is foolish," Kat muttered as Brock paused directly in front of her. As Kat rose from her seat, Abby stood and moved closer, the quiet support giving Kat courage.

"Miss Polka, fancy meeting you here. Are you enjoying your morning?"

"I was."

"Ooh, sassy." Brock ignored her deadpan expression and glanced around the table. "Pretty girl has pretty friends."

"One more step towards Kat and this friend will punch you in the balls."

Brock raised his brows at Charlie's threat then smiled. "I'm just here to apologize to my Irish beauty."

"I'm not your Irish anything, you arrogant prat, and if I spot you lurking near me again, I'll file a restraining order and have you arrested."

"Easy. You're just as feisty as your asshole boyfriend." Brock leaned close. "Are you this brave when lying alone in bed at night? Are there monsters in your closet? I know all about the boogeyman."

Kat felt the blood drain from her face as caliginous silence descended. No-one twitched as Brock's gaze lingered on her scar.

"Hey, girls! I found a friend!" Lizzy bounded up with a security guard in tow. "Told him that this weird dude was bothering us. Hey, ass-hat." She grinned at Brock. "Take a walk."

Raising his hands in surrender, Brock turned to the guard. "Just saying hello to an old friend."

"Let's go, buddy." The guard stepped in between.

With a velvet tone, Brock said to Kat, "I'll see you soon." Walking backwards, he shot her a wink before turning to leave.

"What a horrible worm." Lizzy glared at his back before turning Kat's way. "You okay?"

Kat sank back down. "Bollocks. I'm shaking like a leaf."

"Slater is on his way, and I've never heard him that stressed before. The guy sounds like he's pooping cinder blocks."

Lizzy was hilarious, and Kat couldn't help but smile. Abby shook her head and shoved a glass under Kat's nose. "Here, drink. It's a sweet lemonade."

Kat did as she was told, sitting stiffly while running over Brock's words.

I know all about the boogeyman… Just saying hello to an old friend… I'll see you soon.

Chapter Twelve

Elliot knocked. Slater opened the door, and grabbed his shirt, dragging Elliot into the passage. Slater bulldozed the startled man, causing him to stumble.

"I'm sorry, bro. I tried to explain things on the phone. It all went to shit—"

"It all went to shit? Yeah, asshole, it went to shit when a suspected serial killer approached Kat in broad fucking daylight! But you had to babysit a delivery package and leave her exposed." Slater shoved Elliot again, and this time he careened into the living room.

"When I arrived home, my wife called to say that our kid was sick at school. I thought I could fetch him and take him home quickly. I apologize, man. I thought Kat was safe—I know that's no excuse." Elliot looked gut-shot.

"Derry, it's okay." Kat stood in the bedroom passage; her arms wrapped around her waist. She'd changed into sweatpants and a t-shirt, and her long sable hair hung loosely over her shoulders. "Elliot's family comes first."

He pressed his lips together in anger. "Tell that to Max and the boys who are just as furious. Their families were involved."

"We were sitting in a public mall."

"That's not the point, our friends could become the focus of a serial killer. If he can't get to you…"

"Then he'll hurt the ones I love." Kat took a step back. "My God, I've placed the women and children in danger."

Slater advanced, stopping in front of her. "Don't do that 'blaming yourself' thing. Focus on the next steps—I've called Fletcher, and we're taking out a restraining order."

"Is that going to stop his fixation?"

"No, but if he tries to approach you again, we'll have an excuse to arrest him, and also obtain a warrant to search his property, backpack or motel room."

"You know where he's staying?"

"The Red Texan Inn off of I-90. We had a team trailing him, but they were called back to HQ for a briefing on another investigation."

"Can they not take him in for questioning?" Kat asked, obviously frustrated at the snail's pace of the investigation. She'd faced this for months when her case had pretty much turned into a cold case—at least in her eyes. Now that they had a suspect, a hope must've stirred. She probably prayed they could get him off the streets before he killed more victims. Slater wanted the same outcome.

"Not until they have enough evidence. The agency doesn't want to spook Brock. We need a warrant to search his Chevy truck as well as the motel room."

Brock drove a blue 1989 Chevy Silverado with a silver stripe on the side. The rusted-up truck had seen better days, and Slater was sure it held most of Brock's belongings. Slater had trailed Brock's truck a couple of times, unable to stay away from suspected target. He wanted in—almost tempted to sneak over and search the vehicle which could compromise the investigation. Standing back and letting others run the show wasn't in Slater's DNA. His corrosive need to go rogue had everything to do with Kat's involvement.

"So we just sit around and wait?" Her frustration reflected his own.

"Get dressed. Let's head to the station to file that restraining order."

"I'm so sorry, man." Elliot stood slumped in the corner. "I'll get out of your way."

"Where's your kid now, is he okay?" Slater asked.

"My wife is home with him." Elliot ran a hand over his clipped brown hair. "It looks like a stomach flu."

"Go home and take care of your kid. I'll call you when I need you."

"You still want me on the job?"

Ignoring the strained note in Elliot's voice, Slater asked, "Are you going to fuck off and leave her alone again?"

"No, sir."

"If anything happens to her on your watch…"

"It won't." Elliot offered a hand, and Slater shook it.

A silent promise.

◊ ◊ ◊

"I like your yard," Kat said as she sat on the deck stairs leading down to the lawn.

Slater handed her a lemonade. The rest of Thursday had been busy. They'd spent hours at the police station, and Slater had decided to take the following day off. The center was back on schedule, and he'd worked solidly throughout the week. The foreman would contact him if anything came up.

"It's pretty basic. I haven't exactly made this place home. I spend most of my time at the training facility."

"You have good shade."

"Thanks. This place is a rental. I'm looking to buy a property, but I haven't decided on which valley."

"I'd say, choose a home nearest to your work."

"Except the facility is in the middle of bum-ass nowhere."

"I'd love to see it sometime."

Slater wasn't sure if that was a wise idea. Inviting her into every aspect of his life would get them both hurt. Maintaining at least some measure of distance would be the best decision, yet he couldn't stay away from his Irish angel.

Slater leaned on the railing. "How about we get out for a bit. What do you feel like doing? Burgers and shakes? We could go for a drive up one of the passes?"

Kat considered his words. "What about a swim? I need to exercise—we can run down to the community center."

"Uh. Sure." Slater couldn't remember owning a pair of swimming trunks. He'd visited a few beaches back in his time in Africa with MIT, but he'd worn some old pair of shorts or a wetsuit. "We'll need to stop by the mall to pick up some swimming gear."

They did just that, and by the time Slater walked into the center, he was having second thoughts. They were the youngest guests in the workout facility. Alfred walked through the men's locker room as Slater was changing, and the older man studied Slater's naked ass with his hands on his hips. "You're a tall boy, aren't ya?"

"Uh. Yes, sir."

"A thick head of hair."

Alfred obviously referred to Slater's hair on his head, maybe in comparison to his own balding head? Slater wasn't sure, but he pulled on his swim shorts in rapid time.

"You still have the tag attached."

"What?"

"On your trunks… at the back."

Slater cursed and ripped off the tag.

Inclining his head, Alfred said, "I googled you. You're a famous sniper. Tallying just short of the most confirmed kills in U.S. History."

Technically, Slater set the record of the most kills—including his MIT records—which would never see the light of day. Not something he was proud of. All his eliminated targets were viable threats and part of extremist networks, but death was no longer Slater's constant sidekick.

"Since you're new here, I'll go over a few basics." The tiny man launched into the locker room and pool rules. No, Slater wouldn't be eating, smoking, drinking out of glassware or pooping in the pool. He had no communicable diseases or leaking lesions. Trying not to smile at the long rattling list, Slater picked up his towel. The godfather trailed behind him like a small shadow, only dropping away when he saw Gladys perched on the lifeguard's chair.

Slater waved at the fierce-looking retiree, wondering how capable she'd be at dragging anyone from the gigantic pool. In her seventies, she still looked to be in pretty good shape and Slater admired her efficient spirit. The back of his neck prickled. Large glass windows looked out onto the parking lot, and Slater instinctively scanned the area. All quiet outside. As far as the direct surroundings went, a couple of old folk milled in the shallow end. They were doing some kind of water aerobics. One other swimmer swam lengths. All clear.

The door to the women's locker room swung open, and Kat

walked out. Slater sucked in a breath. She wore a full red bathing suit, looking like a slightly curvier version of a "Baywatch" babe. Kat's braided hair swung as she strolled over and paused to place her towel down on a bench. Her mouth kicked up in an uncertain smile. Slater could still pick up her flowery scent that permeated the chlorinated air as she turned her back to him. He'd missed that hitched smile that Kat got, every time her nerves kicked in.

"Help me with my wee swimming cap."

And he loved how her Irish accent played up when she felt frustrated or excited. With her direction, Slater twisted her braid into a donut and held it in place as she pulled the lycra cap over her hair. He couldn't resist rubbing a thumb over the soft nape of her neck. Kat paused with her head lowered as Slater then ran his palm over her shoulder and down to her waist. He stood close enough to see goosebumps break out on her alabaster skin. Slater studied the contrast of her pale limbs next to his golden-toned body. He wanted to lean down and scrape his teeth over the back of her neck, before nipping her shoulder.

Kat moved away, and Slater clenched a fist. Since the small bathing suit wouldn't hide a giant hard-on, he needed to stop thinking about those luscious limbs wrapped around his waist. She now sat at the edge of the pool and Slater lowered himself beside her. "I don't remember you as a swimmer—back when we were dating."

"Abby asked me to swim with her a couple of times when you were deployed. I got hooked. It's pretty relaxing once you find your rhythm. Plus, I'm sure it will help your shoulder." Kat placed her sleek goggles on her face and slipped into the water. Slater did the same, surprised how warm it was—probably catering for all the sweet old folk. He was used to executing training exercises in cold oceans, not that MIT had run those all that often. His team had been landlocked in Kenya. They still were when they weren't hunkered down on a mission. Thanks to his military training, Slater knew how to swim laps, and he joined Kat as she pushed off the side.

After lap ten, he'd loosened up nicely. His stiff shoulder burned as it pulled and stretched. Slater ignored the discomfort and pushed on. His mind ran over the investigation, and he worried he'd missed something. *Naughty or nice...* He'd guess that the killer had issues with women, but there had also been a male victim. Chances were that bastard felt the same way about his other victims as he did about Kat—he'd judged them to be 'naughty,' so perhaps they'd disappointed him in some warped way? Yet, there were no common denominators. All the victims came from different backgrounds, and had dissimilar physical traits. How had the serial killer run into Kat? Possibly on one of her business trips? Hell, these days it could even be someone delivering a mail package. Was the killer Brock Newman? How long had the killer been obsessed with her before he'd made his first move?

The laps flew by, and Slater paused for a rest. He spotted Kat hovering in the deep end, near the diving boards. Swimming over, Slater noted she'd raised her goggles. Droplets clung to her dark lashes, and his heart stuttered as her indigo eyes met his.

"Are you okay?"

"Yip. Just treading water," she said breathlessly.

"A skill you may need... when?"

Kat flicked water at his face. "It's a great way to firm my arse and stomach."

"I like your 'arse' just the way it is... all ripe and round."

"Well, it's not up to you, mister. It's my buttocks, and I'll exercise them if I want to."

Kat grinned, and Slater laughed. "So feisty."

"I've always been feisty."

"I remember."

Heat flared in her pretty eyes, and Slater swam toward her. Kat backed up against the wall.

Slater paddled closer. "The old folk have probably all headed to their respective locker room saunas."

Gladys had leaned around in her chair to talk to Alfred at the far end of the pool, and Slater drew up against Kat and slipped a thigh between her legs—caging her against the side.

"What are you doing? You're going to get us kicked out."

With a gentle tug, he peeled off her cap and placed it on the edge of the pool. "You feel so good—all slippery and smooth."

"Slater," she said in warning.

"I can be covert," he whispered in her ear, feeling her shiver. Pulling the elastic from her hair, Slater loosened her braid as he blocked her from sight. "Better…" He ran a hand over her hip and traced the back of his fingers between her thighs.

"Stop." Kat giggled. Slater slipped his thumb under her suit, and she shrieked in his ear, trying to pull his strong wrist away. "Derry, I mean it."

His smile deepened into laughter as they both wrestled for control. Conceding, Derek withdrew his hand and caged her against the side of the pool.

"I'm guessing you don't want my hand between your thighs, Miss Flynn?" he whispered hotly in her ear.

"Ask me again later."

Not expecting such a direct answer to his teasing question, Slater almost pulled away to gauge her sincerity, but her arms slipped around his waist, and Kat leaned her chin on his shoulder. The toying moment turned quiet. Water lapped as he kicked his legs, keeping them afloat. He could stay there forever, feeling Kat's warm body suspended against his, her hands curled against his back. Slater closed his eyes. Her wet hair brushed against his cheek, and he turned his head towards her neck. He needed this woman like he needed his next breath.

"Why did we see each other? When we were both badly injured?"

Slater didn't expect the question and couldn't give her a rational answer.

Kat persisted. "Was it just a grand coincidence, or was it something else—something bigger than the both of us?"

"I don't know, angel. It doesn't make any logical sense."

"When he knelt over me with that knife, the cruelty in those eyes was like nothing I've ever seen, and I had to turn away."

Slater squeezed in closer. "My sweet angel."

"That's when I saw you lying beside me... and I knew I'd be okay. I felt warmed by the ghost of you. But then pain chased you away, and frigid ice permeated my very being."

Slater curled a leg around hers. "For me, it was the heat. I couldn't breathe. Sweat and filth coated my skin. You looked so pure—lying in a single ray of light. Like an angel—my angel."

Water lapped as another swimmer dropped into the deep end.

"Derry, we're both going to get hurt."

"Probably. Except this time I won't let go."

"Aye, you will. You'll drift away again, and I won't stay afloat."

Hearing the tears in her voice, Slater pulled back to stare into her eyes. "Is that what you're afraid of?"

"History has a way of repeating itself, and that scares me."

"I'd never…" Slater couldn't find the right words. How could he convince her that he'd rather cut off an arm than break her heart again? But, she could easily break his. One look into those brimming, red-rimmed eyes, and he knew he was screwed. The old Slater had provided Kat with the tools to build defensive walls that were almost impossible to break down.

"Maybe we can do the casual thing?" Kat asked. "And get each other out of our systems."

He couldn't believe she'd said that. Slater didn't want casual—never with her. So what did he want? Reluctantly letting go of soft skin, he stroked backward. "I need to check-in with my crew. Let's get changed."

Kat nodded bravely and swam for the stairs.

Derek waited for her in the foyer. After emerging from the locker room, Kat paused to chat with the lady behind the desk, asking about her upcoming hip surgery and offering to cook and bring over some meals.

Slater loved how she cared for those around her. He remembered how she'd always throw out compliments to strangers or friends. Whether it was a waiter, teller, or colleague, Kat saw everybody. A rare trait in a busy world. Slater pinpointed that elusive quality—Kat was gracious. There was nothing fake about how she cared. She sought the human connection in a world where technology replaced empathy. That's why she'd loved her job as a corporate trainer. Helping others gave her satisfaction.

With a sinking heart, Slater realized that the worst damage he could've done to their relationship was to distance himself from this warm and caring human. His remote attitude and his breakdown in communication had smothered their love. Now, thanks to her traumatic attack, Kat isolated herself. She had

Casey and the recreation center, but she still hid from the world.

Was Kat forever changed?

◊ ◊ ◊

After handing in their locker keys, Slater followed her out of the double doors. Kat walked ahead, confusion over his pool embrace muddying her brain. Why couldn't they be together? She knew why; a long time ago, he'd broken their trust. Before that, their relationship had gone from sublime to miserable, and she was just as much to blame. What if that happened again? Were they bad for each other? Was she the Neutron to his Uranium—a nuclear bomb waiting to detonate?

Students' cars from a neighboring high school filled the packed lot, and they walked between rows of vehicles towards his Ford truck in the third row. Kat paused beside an FJ Cruiser, and Derek almost plowed into her. A school bell rang in the distance.

"What I said earlier—I don't know what I'm thinking half the time. I need to sort out what this all means. You're back in my life, even if it's just temporary and—"

"Kat, let's talk about this later, I—"

Derek didn't finish his sentence. Glass shattered behind her, as a loud crack sliced the air. Kat barely had time to feel the burning pain on the back of her neck before Derek shoved her to the tarmac. She landed awkwardly, twisting a wrist. Covering her with his large frame, Derek dragged Kat around to the front of the cruiser. Groaning, she heard him swearing as something ripped through the air and buried itself in the hood with a loud thunk. Derek removed a gun from a concealed holster beneath his shirt, leaned around, aimed and fired.

Chapter Thirteen

"Move now!" Derek hauled her up and hustled her around the back. "We need to get to my truck. It's bulletproof."

A vehicle revved and she heard it accelerating down one of the rows.

"Down, Kat!" Derek jammed her against a tire, sheltering her with his hard body as bullets punched through the metal above their heads. Kat screamed, terrified that Derek could be hurt. She flattened herself to the warm asphalt as best she could. Blood trickled down her neck, and Derek's body felt like an unrelenting weight that made it hard to breathe.

Please don't die, please don't die.

If Derry got shot protecting her... suddenly, his weight lifted, and he half carried her across to the next row. Derek's familiar truck screamed safety as he unlocked the doors and raced her to the passenger side. He threw her up and into the seat, just as a blue truck, two rows down, reversed back into their line of sight. Derek slammed her door—locking her in—and raised his weapon. Kat yelled—he had no protection against the madman's bullets. Teenaged kids who'd begun to spill from the school grounds either stood frozen, ran or crouched behind a low wall. Instead of opening fire for the third time, their assailant took off.

Derek lowered his weapon. Kat knew it was because of the kids. Such a highly trained marksman could've easily hit his target, but Derek would never risk hurting a bystander.

"Call 911!" Derek yelled at the nearest huddle of teenagers as he rounded the hood, opened his door, and climbed into his truck. He looked whole and unhurt, and Kat breathed a sigh of relief.

"Are you okay?" he asked, reholstering his gun.

Kat nodded in shock.

"Jesus! Shit, shit, shit!" Derek slammed a fist against the wheel. "I want to chase the fucker, but I'll be endangering civilians during lunchtime traffic." He turned fully in his seat, and froze the second he saw her hand clamped to her neck. Fingers wrapped around her wrist and Derek pulled her hand away. Blood coated her fingers, and he turned pale.

"You were hit." Derek dragged her damp hair off her neck, searching for injury.

"Hit by... by the exploding glass. I think."

"Dammit. It sliced the back of your neck!"

"I'll also need an ice pack for my wrist. I may have sprained it."

Derek's ragged breathing filled the cab as he dragged her to his chest, clamping a hand to her neck. She let adrenaline run the show and shook apart in his arms. "I was so... so scared for you. You kept exposing yourself... to protect me."

Distant sirens rent the air, and something sharp tapped the window. Kat looked up into the barrel of a gun.

◊ ◊ ◊

Slater met the school resource officer's terrified gaze, and slowly raised his hands.

"Don't move, don't fucking move!" The Glock 21 shook in the man's poorly positioned hold. The officer wasn't comfortable with his weapon, and that made for a dangerous confrontation.

"Easy, buddy. I'm a federal agent." Slater had to shout through the thick glass.

"You could be lying. Witnesses saw you holding a gun and there were reports of gunshots."

"My badge is in my pocket. I can get out of the truck and show it to you." Although they sat behind bulletproof glass, Slater didn't want the situation escalating into a SWAT stand-off. He'd leave Kat in the protected cab as he de-escalated the situation. She needed medical attention with a possibly broken wrist, and she looked way too pale. Slater reined in his rage and took a calming breath.

"Where's the gun!"

Slater raised his hands higher. "In my holster. You're welcome to remove it, once I'm out of the truck."

The man pointed at the door handle. "Get out. One wrong move and I'll blow your damn head off."

Slater guessed the twitchy cop would probably shoot wildly in their general direction, and he couldn't let that happen.

Slater announced every move he made. "I'm reaching down to the door handle with my left hand. I'm slowly pulling the handle. The door is opening…"

The officer wrenched back the door, and Slater raised his hands again. Perspiration gathered on his already damp brow. Kat sat exposed.

The man's wobbly aim pointed her way, finger on the trigger. "Is she your hostage?"

"Jesus! Don't point that gun at her. The shooter you're after injured Miss Flynn, and she needs medical attention. I told you,

I'm an FBI agent. Buddy… I'd rather you point that damn Glock my way."

Two patrol vehicles pulled up, and three officers surrounded the truck. Now there were four barrels on them, and Slater inwardly cursed. He spoke to the most experienced-looking officer on the scene—an older man who held his weapon confidently, demonstrating solid training.

"My name is Derek Banez, and I'm a federal agent with the Salt Lake Office. You're welcome to call them. I have the number memorized, pull out your phone. You're looking for a shooter driving a blue Chevy Silverado with a silver stripe on the side. The plate number is A34 8BA. It's owned by a Brock Newman who's being investigated by the bureau. The suspect targeted Miss Kathleen Flynn who's sitting beside me, and needs an ambulance."

"Some kids saw this man brandishing a weapon." The RSO's gun still shook in his inept hands.

"I discharged my service weapon once while protecting Miss Flynn. It's in my back holster."

The older officer narrowed his eyes. "Aren't you that famous Green Beret sniper?—I saw you on the news."

Well, at least his infamy was good for something, and Slater thanked the heavens.

"Yes, sir, and I'm now a senior Agent in Charge with the agency."

The officer relaxed slightly and directed Slater to get out the vehicle and place his hands on the roof of the truck. He followed orders. After they'd retrieved his weapon and checked out his credentials, Slater breathed a sigh of relief. Through all his missions and years of combat training, he'd never felt this level of fear. Kat could've been killed, not once, but twice. Feeling weak in the knees, Slater sat on the curb as ordered, and stretched out his legs. He wanted to hold Kat in his arms, but didn't dare make any sudden movements until he was totally out of the woods. Slater heard them calling in his description of Brock's truck and spotted Kat making her way over to him. She sunk to the ground and he pulled her into his side, careful not to jostle her wrist.

"Your neck—"

"Stopped bleeding."

Her slurred words had him calling an officer over for a blanket. Slater rubbed his hands over her chilled arms. Her dried blood coating his hands had him pausing. This time there was no excuse. He'd been by her side, and she'd still been injured. Was Slater destined to be a constant disappointment when it came to Kat?

He held her until the ambulance arrived and Kat protested about going to the hospital. Her wrist looked swollen. Rage pumped through Slater's veins as he waited for the paramedics to check her over. He'd made a few calls while waiting. Fletcher's number now lit up the screen, and Slater answered.

"I'm ten minutes out. How is Kat?"

"Being stubborn as usual, she needs to get checked out."

Glaring, Kat stuck out her tongue. Slater walked a little ways away. "This ends now. I want him apprehended. I'm tracking the son of a bitch down myself."

"Relax, the FBI SWAT team is already en route. A shooting on school grounds has escalated this shit-hole's status. A fuckload of HQ boys are flying into Utah as we speak, and I have the whole field office on standby. But get this, Brock Newman's truck is parked back in front of his motel. Four of my agents just arrived on the scene."

"I'm heading that way." Slater hung up as a text from Max lit up his screen. Walking over to the taped-off perimeter, Slater flashed his badge, letting Max and Johnny into the secured area.

"Thanks for getting here so quickly."

Pale eyes assessed their surroundings before Max turned back to Slater. "How's Kat?"

"Sore—she may have broken a wrist."

"How are you, buddy? Did you nearly crap your pants? Do you need baby wipes?" Johnny asked, clapping Slater on the back.

"When I thought Kat had been shot, yeah. I'm pissed. We're taking him down today. You guys don't mind helping with Kat?"

"Jesus! You even have to ask?" Max shot Slater a side-eyed glance.

"I trust you guys to keep her safe. There's no-one I trust more."

"You're family, so is Kat. Nothing has changed." Max squeezed his shoulder as they walked up to the ambulance.

"Thanks, you Viking bastard."

Kat's eyes widened when she spotted the two operators.

"Hey, honey." Johnny smiled. "How are you doing?"

"The paramedic says it's just a sprain." Kat pursed her lips and tried to stand. Slater placed a hand on her knee and stopped her. "Max and Johnny are running you up to the ER for an X-ray. Even if it's a sprain, it needs to be strapped up."

Johnny squeezed in beside him and gently cradled her wrist. Kat winced as the large medic felt around the joint. "It doesn't look broken, but we'll still get it checked out. How did you injure it exactly?"

"It bent the wrong way when Slater pushed me to the ground. He saved my life."

Johnny grinned. "Then he did his job as your meat shield."

Unable to resist joining in, Slater added, "A big meat shield is a good meat shield."

Kat glowered. "You think this is funny?"

"I'm just happy we're both not resembling swiss cheese and… that you're heading to the ER."

Max looked at Slater. "You're going after him, aren't you?"

"You know I am."

"Please be careful." Kat reached out. "He almost shot you today."

"He was aiming for you." Slater stepped in and pulled her head to his chest. "Do whatever Max and Johnny tell you to do. They'll protect you with their lives. If Brock has given the FBI the slip, I'll need to know that you'll be safe. I won't stop until he's arrested or taken out." With a kiss to the top of her head and one last squeeze, Slater left and walked to his truck. He unzipped his FBI-issued bag and pulled out his tactical vest and jacket. Once he'd checked his backup weapon, Slater drove his vehicle out of the lot, negotiating through the layers of law enforcement. As soon as he was on the open road, Slater gunned the engine, heading for the Red Texan Inn.

◊ ◊ ◊

Slater's career started with a bang. After the FBI training academy, he'd spent a couple of months working as a field agent, and then he'd been promoted to Special Agent in Charge, a title required to design and run the training facility. That didn't sit well with individuals in the organization who'd worked for years to gain promotion. Slater was an outsider, who'd exited the military and been placed in a position of power almost immediately. It was virtually unheard of within the agency. All because of his MIT career.

Slater and the MIT2 team had trained numerous special forces teams—indigenous to various regions—for high-level and specialized combat. No-one was better qualified to prep FBI agents for overseas hot zones than an MIT operator. That's why the agency headhunted him—his skills were hard to come by.

Slater hadn't had time to build relationships within the agency before his promotion, and that was a significant disadvantage—especially for a man with a Green Beret background. Slater's new colleagues would eventually become family. He was all about building networks. He may be a SAIC, but he had zero ties to any of his colleagues—except for the re-established contact with Fletcher, which had everything to do with the former soldier's involvement in Kat's case. Thanks to his supernova rise through the ranks, Slater now found himself standing on the periphery, in the large warehouse two blocks from Brock's motel, while agency men huddled in large groups.

Slater was just an un-involved bystander in the investigation. A couple of agents approached him, thanking him for his service. His reputation as a sniper preceded him, serving both as a curse and a blessing.

Like any close-knit organization, the FBI was a jabbering grapevine. Everybody knew of Derek Banez, and that wasn't necessarily a good thing, judging by some of the sour looks in the room.

Slater imagined the conversation surrounding the new golden boy, and gritted his teeth. It would take time to earn their respect, Slater accepted that, and many of the boys in the FBI had no clue what lay ahead. Technically accountants and desk jockeys made up much of the bureau. The men weren't prepared for scenarios that included hidden explosive devices, being kidnapped, injured in the battlefield, or driving through IED littered landscapes. Slater's role was to prepare them for war zones, and prepare them he would. By the time Slater was done, they'd be crying for their mommies.

Slater watched the FBI SWAT team preparing for Brock Newman's take-down. Now, that was a well-trained tactical team that reminded him of his MIT2 unit. Just like the FBI's Hostage Rescue Team, the FBI's Special Weapons and Tactics Team could strike with deadly force. Like Slater, many of the SWAT men were former Operators. All he cared about was that they'd take Brock down or take him out of commission. Fletcher walked up beside Slater, prepped, and ready to go.

"I want in on this." Slater crossed his arms.

"Like that's going to happen. Maybe I can sneak you inside after the take-down. Right now, you might as well have a giant neon sign painted on your head. Every agent here knows that you were the target today, and they know who you are."

Slater shrugged. "Them and the rest of America. I've said it before, thanks to my new infamy, I'm currently a liability to the FBI."

Fletcher disagreed. "It'll eventually blow over, and you'll be just fine. The bureau doesn't mind so much. Having a famous sniper now working for them is giving the agency good publicity, and we sure as hell need it. As long as you don't act like an ass— this needs to be 'by the book.' Stick to the perimeter, and be a good little observer."

Fletcher walked back over to his team and SWAT. Ten minutes later, they got the green light. There'd been no sign of movement in Brock's room; his now-famous truck still sat parked haphazardly out front.

Slater followed Fletcher's team from a respectful distance. He watched the SWAT team expertly breach the door, and listened for shots, sound of a struggle or gunfire that never came. Something felt off. Fletcher's team slipped inside. Slater remained in the lot with the backup team.

Two minutes later, SWAT emerged and exited down the stairs. Fletcher remained inside with his team. Still no signs of a cuffed Brock. Pacing impatiently, Slater never took his eyes off the door. Finally, he stalked over to one of the nearest agents unstrapping his tactical vest.

"What's going on? SITREP?"

The man didn't answer as he pulled off his helmet.

"Is Newman in there?"

The man nodded. "But he ain't going anywhere. The guy blew his damn brains out. Not much left of him."

Slater's gaze shot back to the motel, just as Fletcher walked out onto the landing and called over an EMT—most likely to call time of death. The paramedic ran up the stairs and exited a minute later. Fletcher slipped out the door and waved Slater over. Pulling thick latex gloves and shoe covers from his pocket, Slater hurried up the stairs. Barrier protection was an essential defense against biohazardous substances such as blood, and also prevented the contamination of a crime scene. Slater carefully entered the room. Fletcher's team had already donned protection, and two members filed out as Slater walked in.

Two double beds faced a cheap wooden unit containing a fridge and battered-looking microwave. Wine-red carpeting covered the soiled space.

Brock's body lay on the far bed, slumped on its side. His blood and brain matter decorated the drab, pale green curtains and seventies-style velvet chair, and a wooden table situated in front of the far window. An empty holster lay on the side table. The bed, nearest to Slater and the door, looked untouched.

Watching his steps, Slater edged along the perimeter and studied the body and the blood-soaked bed.

His time in the military prepared him for violence and gore. Death, rotting corpses, or fresh kills were part of his MIT existence…and now apparently a part of his FBI world.

Brock's right hand partially gripped a Taurus PT-145 Millennium Pro Pistol. Slater leaned closer to double-check the make and model. Then he inspected the injury—one shot to the side of the head—a star-like mark surrounding the wound.

"Any suicide note?" Slater asked as Fletcher stepped back into the living area from the bathroom.

"Not that we can see."

"Other weapons? Any other handguns lying about?"

Fletcher frowned at the question. "We haven't had a chance to check, but nothing in plain view. We still need to search his truck." Indicating the bathroom, Fletcher said, "I didn't bring you upstairs for a forensics examination, there's something I need you to see."

Slater straightened and followed Fletcher into the compact bathroom.

Ignoring the dull white fittings and the gray linoleum floor, Slater stared at the large mirror. His angry gaze took in the collection of photographs plastered across the reflective surface, and Slater had to restrain himself from shattering the mirror. Pictures of Kat… Slater and Kat together… Old images of Slater, just after the breakup with Kat and two articles on Slater's military infamy. There were also photographs of other victims, some Slater recognized from the autopsy reports and case files.

The cabinet door beneath the sink sat slightly open, and Slater nudged it the rest of the way with a gloved finger, as Fletcher leaned in to see what he'd found. A box of tools sat open in the dirty space. At a glance, Slater noted the stack of generic pliers and knives, still with the price tags attached. They'd found the weaponry stockpile for his future kills—all that was missing was the steel piping.

Slater looked up at Fletcher. "We need to search that Silverado."

"Already on it."

Leaving Fletcher in the bathroom, Slater walked back into the front room, squeezing his aching shoulder. Pausing to assess his surroundings, Slater spotted what he was looking for.

He used to be the Protection Specialist for MIT2. Donnie was the Intelligence Specialist, who'd gather evidence at a scene and prep an RFI package for the Intelligence Collection Director at MIT headquarters. Slater had seen Donnie in action many times and knew the ins and outs of evidence gathering.

Approaching Brock's backpack tucked against the wall and partly concealed by the second bed, Slater crouched and unzipped the pack. A passport, a wad of cash, dog tags, a spare t-shirt and a roll of duct tape sat in the main compartment. When Slater flipped through the passport, a small folded up greeting card fell out, along with three well-worn photographs. Opening up the greeting card, he read the scrawly writing.

Happee bird day daddy. Luv you lots and lots and lots.

The three photographs then drew his attention. A picture of a little girl sitting in a pink bumper car and waving at the camera—she looked to be around six or seven. Slater examined another photo of a woman holding the little girl. They stood in a garden, wearing bright dresses and smiling into the camera. The final image was of Brock holding the tiny girl in his lap on a towel on a beach. Slater flipped the pictures over, looking for a timestamp or identifying mark, and found nothing.

Pulling out his phone, Slater snapped photos of the images, before placing them back in the bag. He'd need Donnie's input on what he'd found.

Just as he stood, Fletcher walked up behind him. "Your time is up; the Evidence Response Team has just arrived along with some of our big brass. What did you find in the bag?"

"Just some photographs of what I think is his family."

Fletcher clamped a hand on Slater's shoulder. "It's over, man. Go home and get some rest. I'll call you tomorrow."

With so many unanswered questions, he had to force his retreat. "Treat the scene right," Slater said carefully.

Ignoring Fletcher's narrowing eyes, a worn-down Slater stepped out of the run-down motel room, still smelling the distinctive odor of death.

Chapter Fourteen

"Your decor is amazing." Kat sat curled on the sofa. Lizzy and Abby kept her company in the cheerful living room. Their two little boys were bunking together in Valentino's room, and the house sat quiet.

"Thanks, it reminds Valentino and me of our homes in South Africa and Kenya," Lizzy said, glancing around.

"That's a grand painting." Kat pointed at the abstract work of warriors with shields.

"Those are of the Maasai warriors. The Maasai people live in Southern Kenya. A fearsome semi-nomadic tribe. Valentino loves to read fables with me about their history."

Kat glanced around at the rest of the decor, noting the colorful woven baskets, the wooden rhino sitting on the coffee table, and the array of travel magazines. The ochre accent wall matched a blue and white color scheme. Johnny and Lizzy were such an exciting couple, and Kat loved their dedication to the orphanage in Kenya and the wanderlust vibe that permeated their home.

"I'm making you a cup of tea." Abby rose, and Kat smiled her thanks. She'd just arrived from the hospital with her two fearsome bodyguards, who now sat in Johnny's man cave down the hall. Kat pulled an eclectic pillow to her chest with her uninjured arm. It was just a mild sprain, but it still throbbed. And thanks to the injection they'd given her for pain, Kat's eyes kept drifting shut.

She should be icing it, but it had been a trying day, and the long wait in the ER didn't make it any easier. Kat yawned, and Lizzy placed a hand on her leg. "Why don't you take a warm shower, or I can run a bubble bath for ya?"

That sounded tempting, and Kat nodded. Lizzy bounced up, and rushed down the passage. Rubbing her eyes, Kat worried over Derek's safety for the hundredth time. He could take care of himself. Shutting down her concern, Kat unfurled herself from the couch just as Abby walked in and handed her a mug.

"That's called rooibos tea. It's a South African thing. They call it redbush tea in the States. You're either going to love or hate it."

Kat looked at the clear tea and gave a cautious sniff. "Is there honey in this?"

"Oh, shoot, I forgot you were allergic!" Abby grabbed the cup from Kat's hands and raced back to the kitchen. "Oh, my God, I almost killed you!"

"It's been a while since we've hung out." Kat laughed, following Abby to the kitchen, and watching as she placed the mug in the sink and poured a new cup. This time, Abby added a teaspoon of sugar. She handed it back to Kat, who took a cautious sip, savoring the smooth and nutty taste. It lacked the bitterness of a black tea, and the mild taste felt comforting.

Thirty minutes later, and Kat felt like a new person. She'd soaked in a strawberry-smelling bubble bath, and washed the chlorine and blood from her hair. Max greeted Derek at the front door just as she walked back into the living room.

Derek looked as exhausted as she felt. Kat paused as their gazes collided. They both moved at the same time. She rushed into his strong embrace, and he buried his face in her neck.

"You smell like berries. God. I shouldn't be holding you. I need a fucking shower. I'm contaminated."

Kat didn't know what that meant. Derek didn't feel contaminated; he felt solid, warm, and familiar. She never wanted to step out of his protective hold. Finally, he released her. Kat took a moment to rest her head on his broad chest.

"How's your wrist feeling?"

"Okay. It's not broken."

"But I'm betting it's damn sore. Did the doc give you something for pain?"

Kat nodded. Derek cupped her jaw and raised her chin. Sharp eyes ran over her face. "You look pretty drugged up. Let's get you home."

Home. He meant his home, which was beginning to feel more like hers.

"Aye. Did you catch Brock?"

Derek's fingers tightened on her chin, before he let go and stepped back. "Brock Newman is dead."

"He put... put up a fight?"

"No, angel." Derek's jaw visibly tightened, and his worried eyes glanced at the other men before darting back to hers. "It looks like a suicide."

Brock had killed himself? She tried to sort through the mix of horror and relief, feeling immediately guilty over her reaction. All she'd cared about was Derek's well-being. Now he stood before her uninjured and safe. Was it over? She couldn't decipher the look on his face that set unnamed alarm bells ringing.

Abby grasped Kat's arm. "Do you need a moment, hun?"

"No, but thank you for looking after me. Derek's right, we both need to rest." Kat said her goodbyes to the two solid men and their sweet wives, allowing Derek to lead her out by her hand. He released her and guided her to the passenger seat. After climbing in and starting the car, Derek took back her hand and placed it on his thigh, covering it with his. Kat didn't protest as they drove out of the neighborhood. She also needed that skin to skin contact, a reassurance that the man by her side was still warm and alive.

◊ ◊ ◊

Slater jerked up in bed. What had woken him? Was it a scream? *Kat.*

He grabbed his Glock from the bedside table and ran for her room. Cracking open the door, Slater noted crumpled covers in an empty bed. Early light lit the room in a dusky haze. Unreasonable panic took hold as he checked his office before moving through his living area and kitchen. Had she been taken? He'd let his guard down and slept too deeply. His muggy brain still felt half asleep, and Slater paused to regroup, relaxing when he heard water pipes humming. He walked back to the only room he'd bypassed in his clearing frenzy and paused at the closed door, hearing the shower running.

"Kat. Angel? Are you okay?"

No answer. A loud thud and a curse.

"Kat, answer me."

Slater nudged the door; steam poured out. He spotted a blurred silhouette behind frosted glass. White bandage wrappings lay on the cabinet counter.

"Honey, are you all good?"

"Derry? Shite, I woke you. I needed another shower. I had a

nightmare and felt all sweaty."

Sweaty… steamy… damp skin. Slater swallowed, clamping down on his lust. He wanted to step into that shower so damn badly. Rub his cock against her wet ass, reach around and stroke that sweet nub. Fuck.

"Do you?" Slater cleared his throat. "Do you need help… with your wrist and all?"

He waited, watching her pause behind the glass.

"I'm coping just fine."

Letting out a shaky breath, he backed up into the passage. Yeah, he wasn't going back to sleep any time soon. He now also needed a shower—a cold one. But he'd washed himself clean only a few hours ago—scrubbed away at almost raw skin as he wiped away the stench of death.

Slater turned to the kitchen and pulled out a cutting board. Loading up the blender with a shitload of fruit, he made himself a large smoothie. Kat padded up to the counter on bare feet. His eyes ran over her damp hair, down over her thick bathrobe to her bare calves and red-painted toenails. One tug on that looped tie and he'd have access to those naked curves. Slater imagined gripping her waist and pulling her to him. Her full breasts pressed against his chest.

Kat eyed his stomach, and Slater realized that he stood in a pair of boxers. He hadn't bothered getting changed.

"Do you want a smoothie? I didn't know how long you'd be?"

"Do you have chocolate ice cream?"

Now his fantasies veered down a naughtier path.

"Um. I think so."

"Do you mind making me a chocolate milkshake? I'd make it myself but…" She waved her swollen wrist in the air.

"You need to ice and strap that."

"I can't do it on my own. I need help. Milkshake first."

"It's five in the morning, and you want a milkshake?" Slater said as he opened the freezer section of his fridge.

"It's never too early for a chocolate shake, and you know they're my weakness."

Smiling, Slater remembered her obsession with shakes. Mostly chocolate, sometimes the Oreo kind. Occasionally a strawberry shake, but never vanilla.

He blended the ice cream with milk, topped it off with whipped cream and shoved in a wide straw and a spoon. Placing it in front of her, conjured up old memories. Their first date, eating burgers and drinking double malt shakes, or how he'd make her a shake when she'd had a bad day, or when they'd swing by the Farr's ice cream shop for date night.

Kat swiped up a generous helping, humming as the spoon hit her mouth. Slater shifted against the counter before gulping down his fruity concoction. Attacking it with one-handed vigor, she took another mouthful, then licked her spoon. Her darting tongue shattered his control, and Slater eased around the counter and grabbed the utensil, before placing it on the counter.

"What the bollocks—"

His hand came back up, and Slater stroked the side of her mouth with his thumb. Kat froze, watching him as he lowered his head.

"Derry—"

"Tell me to stop and I will, but I really, really want a taste."

Kat licked her top lip a moment before Slater captured her mouth with his. Her lips felt cold from the shake. Slater gripped her head as she rose to meet him, twisting for a better angle. Desperate hunger rose as she gripped his waist before sliding a hand beneath his waistband.

"Fuck," Slater muttered between kisses and gripped her ass, lifting her onto the counter. Ignoring her growing passion, Slater undid the robe's ties with trembling fingers, revealing smooth skin. Like a starved wolf, Slater flipped the material aside and pushed her back onto the granite surface. Kat complied, laying herself bare to his hungry gaze. He stepped between her splayed legs.

Bare breasts arched towards the ceiling. Slater ran a palm over the two small scars. He couldn't think about the bastard stabbing a knife into her chest—she'd been so lucky. Instead, Slater concentrated on her pale pink buds, squeezing one between his thumb and finger. Kat moaned, and he stilled her.

"Don't move. I've missed this body and want to explore every inch."

Taking the spoon, Slater dripped ice cream onto that same delicate pink nipple. Kat sucked in a breath, and he watched in fascination, as the bud tightened. That invited a long lick and a generous suck.

His hand ran between her cleavage, down to her stomach. Slater nudged her legs further apart with his hips and bent, tracing his tongue around her belly button, then nipping a path to that sensitive area, just above her groin. Kat bucked, and he smiled, remembering all her erogenous zones. Taking his time, Slater nuzzled before tracing her inner thigh, coaxing strangled cries. After parting her folds, he tasted her with one long lick before shedding his boxers.

"Condom," Kat rasped.

"Within reach." Slater opened a small drawer to his left and grabbed a strip before tearing at a packet with his teeth.

"Are kitchen antics part of your regular seduction plan?" she asked, smiling as he paused.

"Bought a pack and never used them. Just threw them in this drawer."

Noting her frown, Slater was tempted to confess. He hadn't been with anyone since her. He'd tried to move on, but she was the first woman he'd brought to this Utahan home. A couple of polite and dismal blind dates didn't count. All Slater wanted was to feel this woman around him again—nirvana to his soul. She still lay back, watching him with sleepy eyes.

"Kat?"

She widened her legs, and that was all the invitation he needed. Clasping her good arm, Slater pulled her to a sitting position. He grasped her ass, careful not to jolt her injury, and carried her to his bedroom. Laying her on the mattress, Slater pulled her to the edge of the bed. He paused to take in the sight of Kat naked and lying on his sheets.

"Rest your wrist and let me do all the work."

The head of his cock entered her wet heat, and they both groaned. Slater pulled out and drove in deeper.

"God, I need this. How does that feel, angel?"

"Don't stop. I want all of you."

"You'll fucking have me." Slater slammed home, fully seating himself. His desire overrode everything else, as she arched to meet him. Positioning a thumb over her clit, Slater paused to allow her to acclimate. His cock throbbed and he rolled his hips.

"Just like that." Her pelvis rose, grinding against him.

Slater began to thrust. Kat cried out in delight and raised her knees. Slater pounded into her wet heat, watching her eyes squeeze shut with desire. He settled over her, caging her beneath him and drew in and out with long strokes. She spasmed, clenching around his dick as she came, screaming his name.

Slater scooted her back in the center of the bed. Kat clung to his back with her uninjured hand as he paused with his lips on her temple. He still smelled a trace of strawberries, mixed with her elusive flowery scent. Emotion swelled as he slowly pulled out and back in, this time slowing his thrusts. It would be over too soon—him buried in her sweet body, her soft breath against his neck. The silence of the dawn surrounded them, and Slater absorbed every detail. The way her nipples brushed against his chest, the tickle of her eyelashes on his cheek, her short nails scraping along his back.

"You're so damn gorgeous," he muttered, reaching between them to cradle her wrist. "I'm sorry you got hurt on my watch. It tears me up."

"You saved my life and… oh…."

Slater eased out and back in. "I could do this for hours; it's a perfect fit…" He ground his hips, watching desire flair in her eyes. "Like two puzzle pieces, slotting together."

Kat smiled breathlessly.

"You like my dirty puzzle talk, baby?"

"Stop." A giggle escaped, followed by a moan. "Do that again." Slater did as she asked, shoving in deeeper. Kat pulled his mouth to hers, devouring his control. Slater pumped with long strokes, and she came for a second time. His climax erupted, and Slater roared out his release.

◊ ◊ ◊

Was it just sex? It didn't feel that way. Derek's palm trailed along her arm as she lay on his chest. Kat suppressed a shiver. He wasn't saying anything, just stared at the ceiling.

Even if it were just sex, it had been the best sex of her life, and that was saying something as they'd always had great chemistry back in the day. Now they were a little older, and a lot more mature. And God—the man remembered how to turn her on. Where to touch… squeeze… lick.

This morning had held an intimacy with Derek that Kat hadn't felt since they'd first started dating all those years ago. Before the Black Friday bombing, and the PTSD and the deployments. Before her ambitious dedication to her career and her long nights alone. Could they ever get back that innocence? Or should she pack away that hope and enjoy having sex with an old friend who knew how to play her body like a violin? Drifting off to sleep, Kat woke sometime later to Slater's fingers stroking through her hair.

"I didn't hurt you, did I? Earlier? How's your wrist?"

"Perfectly fine. I'll grab an icepack. What time do you have to go to work?"

"Around eight." Derek pulled her closer.

"I need to get back to my place and give it a good clean."

Muscles tensed beneath her. Kat watched his defined abs sharpen, and she couldn't resist stroking a hand over his carved stomach.

"Don't go home. Stay here."

Kat froze. Was he serious? They weren't even dating. Probably wouldn't ever get back together. Was Derek asking her to move in with him?

"I think someone murdered him."

Kat wasn't following and looked up at Derek's grim face. "Who was murdered?"

"Brock."

"Brock Newman, our friendly neighborhood serial killer? The man who nearly killed me?"

"I need to sit down with Donnie and go over the details. I'm hoping Fletcher will come to the same conclusion."

"I don't understand."

"Suicide doesn't fit with his profile or that of the suspected serial killer."

"That's all you have to go on?"

"No. I'm still figuring it out. I'll sit down and explain it to you this evening. I messaged Elliot last night, and he'll be with you for the day."

Kat didn't like Derek's theory. The brief relief she'd felt evaporated and her mood darkened, but she trusted him and would wait till he'd checked things out. Kat shouldn't let her guard down so easily. Not with a lurking serial killer, and not with a sexy ex-boyfriend. Still, she couldn't stop her fingers from trailing beneath the covers. She'd always loved holding him in her hands. Derek's hips bucked as Kat worked his shaft. Feeling him grow made her feel powerful. She may be scarred and weary, but when Derek looked at her with such hunger, she felt beautiful. After he donned protection with eager hands, Kat climbed onto his powerful body and rode him hard. Living in the moment felt right. She'd save the fear and night terrors for another day.

◊ ◊ ◊

"I never pictured Charlie living in the city. You, on the other hand…"

Slater took in the modern loft conversion as Donnie shut the front door behind him. The industrial space featured high ceilings, large steel framed windows, and light wooden floors. A skylight lit up artfully placed stonework and a minimalist lounge and kitchen, and a wide metal staircase led up to a private level.

"She's always wanted to live in urban sprawl." Donnie chuckled. "We do spend time at Johnny's cabin when it all gets too much for her."

"Seriously, brother. This is some fancy shit!" This was the first time that Slater had seen their newly built home.

"I know. Charlie discovered this gutted space and threw her money at it. Elana's father—who's some fancy architect—helped with the design. I'm not complaining as it's my dream home."

"Remind me again, Elana is Charlie's best friend? The exotic-looking blonde that looks like a model…"

"Yeah. Elana was with us in Morocco when that bad shit went down."

"Oh, hell! That's the girl that Atlas is hung up over."

"The very same, but he's squatting in the friend zone." Donnie grinned and glanced over at the kitchen.

"I'm not hung up over Elana. She's just a cool chick to hang with." A voice called from the kitchen.

Slater turned in surprise. The laidback operator placing a glass in the sink was almost as quiet as Donnie and Slater hadn't even realized he was there. Dylan *Atlas* Jenkins met Slater's direct stare and turned on the tap to wash his hands. The guy looked like he could star in *Point Break* with his surfer sandals, overly long blond hair and bronzed skin. Unlike Slater, that tan came from spending way too much time in the sun.

Without glancing away, Slater yelled, "Hey, Donnie, what's Matthew fucking McConaughey doing in your kitchen?"

"Screw you." Atlas gave him the finger and Slater grinned.

"Despite your girly-ass sandals, I understand that you're a Pitbull in the field."

"Thank you, sir." Atlas dried his hands on a dish towel. "That means a lot coming from you."

"It's not coming from me—it's coming from MIT. You and I still need to visit the range sometime. And—Jesus—don't call me 'sir.'"

"Game-on. Sir—I mean Mr. Banez—Slater—"

"Stick with the last one." Slater stretched out to shake his hand, noting that they were the same rangy height.

"I gotta bail." Atlas leaned around to address Donnie who began unrolling a computer cable with precision. "Max mentioned a barbecue?"

"Yeah, late September—if we're still in-country. Can you pick up Elana on the way? I know you live in the same area."

"Sure can… so she's coming?" Atlas tried to sound casual and Slater suppressed a grin.

"She's Charlie's best friend, what do you think?"

After Atlas left, Donnie closed the door behind him. "Poor lovestruck fool."

Slater grinned and followed Donnie to a fancy glass dining table. Donnie's brick-like laptop was already flipped open and sat on a thick rubber mat.

"Where's Charlie?"

"At the pediatrician with Willow."

Slater glanced up in concern as he pulled his laptop from his backpack. "Everything okay?"

"All good. It's Willow's bi-monthly check-up."

Donnie placed what looked like another giant-looking placemat on the table before taking Slater's laptop from his surprised hands and carefully setting it on top. Slater raised his brows at his friend.

"What? It's a brand new table."

"Shift your anal-ass over and let's get started. I need to be back onsite by two."

"You're a bossy dick."

"Yeah, well this case is giving me a 'first 48' vibe. When's your next deployment?" Slater asked.

"Not for another two months. We're training up some new MIT guys soon. We'll fly out to Fort Bragg when we get the green light, and then we'll be heading back to Kenya."

"How was your last deployment?"

"Great—we took down a Salafist smuggling ring. The team misses you, bud, although Atlas is doing a stellar job."

"He's a great lad," Slater confirmed.

"And you don't miss the mud, the blood, and the beer?"

Slater grinned. "I'm still neck deep in mud. Can't get away from the blood, and let's not talk about the beer. I stay away from that shit—I'm an idiot on the beer."

Donnie's easy laugh had Slater raising his brows.

"You're always an idiot, but we still love you. Now tell me what's up. I'm guessing this is about Brock's death. The press has named him the 'Belsnickel Killer,' based on that sinister Santa Claus character from Germanic folklore."

"Yeah. The press found out about the gold tinsel and ran with it."

Slater laid out the shooting and motel scene, walking through every detail. Donnie listened intently, waiting for Slater to voice his concerns.

"This wasn't a suicide."

"I might agree, but tell me why you'd think that."

Slater kept his features composed as he explained the first part of his theory as logically as possible. "He used a Taurus PT-145 Millennium Pro Pistol. Fletcher called me earlier; they found a second gun in the room—a Sig Sauer P320 under the pillow on the other bed. A veteran wouldn't choose a damn PT-145 over a P320. The Taurus model is a discontinued weapon which is known to fire when bumped or dropped, even when the safety is on."

Donnie sat back. "So you think Brock's go-to handgun was the Sig."

"Wouldn't that be your choice for conceal carry? Would you ever buy that PT-145?"

"Not if you paid me," Donnie said, folding his arms. "There are some excellent Taurus models on the market, but the PT-145 was discontinued for a reason."

"They found a roll of gold tinsel, steel pipes, and a bag of teeth in Brock's truck. There is still no sign of his clothing—the gimp suit or the balaclava."

"Maybe he got rid of the evidence—burned or tossed it."

Slater cracked his knuckles then ran a hand through his hair. "Why bother? If Brock was planning to kill himself in a blaze of glory, he wouldn't care, especially since he left the rest of his sick arsenal lying around."

"True. What else do you have? Something I can work on?"

Slater turned his laptop screen towards Donnie. "These are the photos I snapped on-scene of the birthday card and his probable family. I need to know who they are and what kind of relationship he had with them."

"How does this relate? Many serial killers live normal everyday lives with strong familial relationships. They spend quality time with their families, and in many instances, the individuals they've established a life with, during killing sprees are not usually victims of their violence. The times when they do kill family, it's usually a member from their childhood who contributed towards their abuse."

"I agree, but the photographs don't align with this specific killer's profile." Slater tried to voice his argument. "There's no doubt that Brock Newman was a damaged and troubled man. He had major issues—especially with women. But he had a strong affection for that woman and child. The photographs are well worn and Brock's handled them a whole load. Please see if you can explore that link."

Donnie nodded. "Send them to me."

Slater rubbed a hand over his eyes and let out a long breath. "They also found drug paraphernalia in his truck. We're still waiting on the autopsy report."

"So if he didn't kill himself, then who pulled the trigger?" Donnie asked.

"Someone who knows zilch about guns. A perp who prefers handling other weapons."

"Someone who was working with Brock? A serial killing duo?"

"Shit, Donnie, I don't know, but I'm going to find out."

Chapter Fifteen

"I can't believe I agreed to this." Kat placed her bag on the back of the chair. She'd just introduced Casey to the rest of the women around the table.

"You need to chill the hell out," Charlie said, slumping back in her seat. "If anyone is drinking a shitload of shots tonight, it's you. I'm out of the mix as I have to bug out early to check on Willow."

"Donnie will be just fine." Abby laid a reassuring hand on Charlie's arm. "Tonight is the first time you've had a girl's night since the birth. Enjoy the evening."

"It just feels weird. I miss my little pumpkin."

"I know," Abby agreed. "That doesn't change. You need to get used to having 'me-time' once in a while."

Kat couldn't contribute or relate to the maternal conversation; instead, she grabbed the menu and turned to the cocktail page. Her wrist still felt a little sore, but it had come a long way over the past week since the parking lot shooting. And what a week it had been. Every night, Slater would return from the facility, and they'd spend hours in each other's arms. His delicious hands and mouth wouldn't rest until she came apart... multiple times.

"It's technically not a girl's night." Lizzy's voice carried across the table. "We have two goons watching our every move."

All eyes turned to the brawny men sitting a couple of tables down from them. Johnny and Atlas scanned the bar like it was about to be stormed.

Kat laughed. "One of those goons is your husband."

"I know, and he's been particularly goonish tonight. He gave our poor babysitter the third degree—never mind that she's sat for us before. You should check out his version of a covert nanny cam."

"Ninja boy madness," Abby said, shrugging. "Max is the same. He's perfectly happy staying home with the kids rather than finding a sitter."

"Where's Slater tonight?" Charlie asked.

"Red—the guy who runs the veteran support group, asked if Derek could open and close for him. Red has been staying in Nevada for a few days. Derek has so much on his plate, and he's been grumbling all afternoon."

Lizzy leaned on her folded arms. "I'm guessing that Slater would rather be spending that time with you..."

Kat ignored the gooey feeling she got every time she thought of her temporary sidekick. Their bedroom action couldn't last forever. "It's complicated."

"Tell me about it." Casey arm-hugged her friend. "This last month has been a field of landmines."

They ordered snacks and drinks, and Kat listened quietly as the other women talked about their respective men. She'd had that once—unwavering faith in a relationship. Now, all she had was a lonely apartment and a book deal—her life story wrapped in a glossy cover. Kat suddenly didn't want to tell her story. What were all those brave words about helping other victims, when she floundered in the surf?

Kat's pain felt too personal. She'd dedicated the past year to scribbling her suffering onto a page, hoping it would help her to heal, but she still felt brittle and frail. Kat hadn't dealt with any of her hardships.

The dawning realization had her shredding a napkin in her lap. Derek had chosen the right path—he'd seen a professional and worked with a support group. He'd risen back up, while she still sat in the dirt.

Feeling incapable of having a conversation, she excused herself and found the nearest exit. She walked out onto a small patio and took a seat. Kat's fingers worried over her scar, as she tried to envision her uncertain future.

"You can't stay out here; it's not safe." Lizzy's voice made her jump. "Johnny is watching us from behind the glass." Lizzy pointed inside. "Does Slater really believe you're still in danger?"

Kat nodded, wanting to be alone. Her foot tapped as she stared at a nearby street lamp.

"I recognize that look in your eyes." Lizzy sat down beside Kat. "I lived in that same prison for so long."

"Your finger? Because of what happened to it? I'm sorry, I shouldn't ask—"

"Yes. Not many know this, but if Slater trusts you, it's good enough for me… I was kidnapped and tortured by extremists."

"Oh, God. I'm so sorry." Kat turned to the tiny woman. Lizzy looked so put together in her black torn jeans, white tunic, and pale pink jacket. Kat couldn't imagine the terrors that Lizzy had faced.

"Slater's arm was injured during my rescue."

"I had no idea. He hasn't said anything and I'm assuming it fell under the classified umbrella. All I heard was that he was on a mission."

"Yeah—to save my dying ass. If they'd arrived even just fifteen minutes later, I wouldn't have survived. My kidnapping will always haunt me, but every day I grow stronger."

Both women had had the same recovery time—sixteen months. So why couldn't Kat heal like Lizzy had? She voiced the fear that she'd held in for so long. "My attacker stole my identity. I'm so lost. I have zero direction, or career path, and let's not talk about maintaining a personal life. I want to crawl under the covers and sleep. God, I could sleep for days."

"You're allowed to crawl under the covers, but you can't hide forever. You have to take back your existence."

"How?" Kat asked.

"One tiny step at a time. If you're not seeing a therapist, then find one. And start with what makes you smile."

Kat swallowed burning tears. "What if being around Derek makes me smile? I can't risk that, he'll destroy me."

Lizzy moved to crouch before Kat. "You do what's best for you. I can't tell you to end or start a relationship. All I can say is that you matter—your happiness matters. You can fight the fear and the darkness, because you're stronger than any evil dick-cheese. You, my sweet girl, deserve the world."

Tears sprung at Lizzy's words. Kat had known this woman all of two weeks, and Lizzy already felt like her soul sister. Leaning forward, Kat wrapped her arms around Lizzy and clung. Everything felt uncertain, but Lizzy was right. It was time to let go of anxiety and hurt. Kat needed to forgive herself and heal her soul.

After she'd wiped away the tears, they made their way back inside. Johnny stood by the door. He'd been watching their back the whole time. Lizzy wrapped her arm around the broad warrior's waist, and he bent to kiss her. Kat needed a tequila shot. She didn't usually drink, but this night would be an exception.

◊ ◊ ◊

Slater unclenched his hands and tried to relax. The small group sat in their usual circle at the weekly vet's meeting. He wouldn't have attended the session, but Red was away and had asked Slater to run the meeting and lock up after. The six other men in attendance chatted about an upcoming charity bike ride to Wyoming. Slater only half listened. The constant alertness he'd lived under for the last week had worn him down. Watching for killers lurking in the shadows, and lying awake at night listening for any sounds. And the desire. It ate at his soul. Slater couldn't get enough of his angel. He'd taken her at every angle and on every surface in his home. He wanted to be permanently buried in her sweet body, listening to those throaty moans and have her wrapped in his arms.

When he wasn't by Kat's side, his worry distracted him from the heavy work schedule. He wasn't wrong—Brock Newman was not the killer. Slater knew it in his gut. So why was Brock set up? As a distraction?

His phone buzzed, and Slater glanced at the screen and excused himself when he saw Donnie's name. After stepping into the front courtyard, Slater answered.

"What's up, super nerd?"

"Be grateful for that nerdy part of my beautiful brain—I have news on Newman's family."

Turning serious, Slater said, "Speak to me."

"The woman in those photographs is a high school sweetheart from Burley, Idaho. Her name is Sandy Johnson. They had a long-term on again-off again relationship, and that's his little girl. According to medical records and a couple of newspaper articles I've discovered, after exiting the military, Brock returned to his home town but left shortly after a bad accident."

"What kind of accident?"

"One that he blamed on PTSD. Brock drove into the back of a truck one night. Broke his arm, but his family weren't as lucky."

Slater swore and sat on a nearby bench. "How bad?"

"The girlfriend—Sandy—lost her right leg below the knee. Their little girl broke her neck. Her spinal cord was still intact, but the kid laid in traction for weeks."

"Was Brock arrested?"

"He claimed that the truck ran a red light and swerved in front of them. Brock left the state shortly after, but I'm guessing that he blamed himself. There are records of wire transfers from his bank account to Sandy—substantial amounts. Brock emptied his savings account and then some—every scrap of earnings went to that family. I guess that if he hadn't died, he'd still be supporting them. He took out a generous life insurance policy, but his 'suicide' will cause complications."

Slater stood and paced. "If Brock cared that much about their welfare, then he wouldn't have killed himself. I'm wondering if the guy was a dick because of the accident combined with his PTSD issues. I'm guessing guilt consumed him, and that's why he left Idaho."

"Yeah—I'll keep digging. By the way, I just emailed you the copies of the background checks you requested. So far, I don't see any red flags."

Slater thanked Donnie and hung up. He hadn't had the time to dig into the history of all Kat's acquaintances and friends. Slater even requested background checks on her publisher. Slater opened his email app, and debated returning to the meeting. Ignoring the urge, he clicked on Donnie's link, opened a couple of random files and scrolled through the records. Ten minutes later, his fingers paused, and Slater re-checked what he'd just read.

"Son of a bitch!" Slater took off up the stairs, not pausing until he stood before Elliot, who looked up in surprise. Adrenaline coursed through Slater's system. He forced a smile and gestured with his hand. "Elliot. A quick word?"

"Uh. Sure man." The easy-going operator stood and stepped away from the seated circle. Slater deliberately trailed behind the other man while directing him out of the public arena.

"There's a room off to the side."

They stepped into what looked like a Sunday school classroom. Kids drawings decorated the wall, and small desks filled the space. Both men wore concealed guns, but Slater still glanced around for an additional weapon if their conversation turned ugly. A pair of scissors lay on a nearby table, and Slater walked over and sat his ass on the edge of the wooden surface.

Elliot must've picked up on Slater's tension because his arms dropped to his side. "What are you doing, man?"

Slater took in Elliot's stance and physical position. "Contemplating life, and wondering in particular why it's so hard to trust these days. I mean you think you know someone. Even if you both briefly served together on a mission."

"I don't know what you mean." Elliot shifted his feet, then stilled.

"Yeah. Who gives a damn about details? Married or… not married. What's the big deal?"

"You checked my records."

"I did. The same records that indicated that you've been

divorced for three months. Separated for six. You left Kat in the mall because your 'wife' was at the dentist. Tell me, which part of that whole charade rang true?"

Judging from Elliot's flaring nostrils, Slater had just poked the bear.

"All of it," Elliot said through gritted teeth.

"Bullshit." Slater spat the word and stood. "You deceitful bastard—I left you alone with Kat—I trusted you. What else are you lying about?"

"We're divorced, but we haven't shared our status with the world. We still live together, although not for long." Elliot's eyes turned hard, and just like that, he morphed into a different man.

"My wife—ex-wife—cheated on me with her high school boyfriend while I fought on the front lines, and engaged with the enemy across the globe. Our decade-long marriage meant nothing to her, and I'm kicking her out of the house as soon as I tell our kids that their mother is a whore."

Elliot's bitter rage caught Slater off guard. He'd left Kat under the protection of this individual.

"I think you have anger issues."

"No—I have trust issues, and my personal life is none of your damn business. I lied about my situation. Big freaking deal."

"And you broke my trust while I searched for a killer. You need to leave. I'll forward you the balance of what I owe you. I appreciate your help—"

"I don't need your judgment! You don't get to terminate the contract, because I'm quitting." Elliot stepped into Slater's space.

Slater spoke, his voice low and dangerous. "Either way—if you come near Kat or me again, I'll remove the threat."

Elliot chuckled nastily. "I've got better things to do with my time."

He backed off and gave Slater the finger. *Mature.* Once Elliot had left the room, Slater followed the soldier to his car and watched him drive off. Only then did Slater reach for his phone and dial Fletcher's number.

◊ ◊ ◊

The killer had planted Nano-sized GPS tracking devices on three vehicles, including Kat's Mini Cooper—which was a waste. He didn't risk tampering with Derek's truck, but it helped to know who her friends were. He'd tracked Jayden's SUV remotely, after the officer had stopped off at Derek's place. The signal had next led to this address. After crossing the busy street, the killer parked nearby and scanned the busy bar, finding his target. He then walked over to a café across the street where he could watch Kathleen from a safe distance. Coffee wasn't good for his frayed nerves, but he ordered it anyway. He wouldn't get near, not with those two capable-looking men milling around the periphery. They'd protect that bunch of spoilt bitches with their lives. White-picket-fence assholes. After he'd finished his second cup, the killer returned to his car and started the engine. His favorite song played as he removed his upper and lower dentures and studied the artificial teeth. Thanks to the press, he now had a surprisingly accurate name. The Belsnickel Killer. Pity they'd pinned it on that idiot, Brock Newman, but at least it had taken the heat off. The FBI had backed away, and now he could hunt in peace. It had been so easy to set up the hot headed fool.

The two bodyguards hovering around Kathleen meant that Derek still harbored suspicion. Clever shithead, but Derek's quick thinking would get him killed.

Getting comfortable in the dim space, the killer clicked the false teeth together over and over, thinking back to his childhood…

The cardboard box smelled musty. His momma liked to collect Santa Claus dolls, and many times she forgot to throw out the packaging. This box used to house the biggest life-size stuffed toy and made a great hiding place amongst the rest of the junk in her room. He hated their filthy home—it made his skin crawl. Momma always had the money to buy her stupid dolls and Christmas stuff from her catalogs, even when it wasn't damn Christmas; filling out her order forms and mailing them off from the post office. She was obsessed with the tinsel and lights. Why couldn't she buy Rudy a pair of new pants that fit?

His leg began to cramp. He'd been hiding for hours.

Momma, please don't find me. Don't find me.

Rudy chanted the familiar mantra, but she always found him. He could never escape his punishment. Burning sweat trickled from his brow into his eye, and he swiped away the moisture. It was almighty hot, and he wished they had air conditioning like some of the other farms. Rudy wasn't allowed to play with the other children, except for Dash—his older brother. They weren't even allowed to go to school.

Once in a while, when Momma went to town for supplies or to the post office, Rudy would ride his bike over to one of the neighboring farms and watch the other children play. Sometimes, their parents would invite him in for lemonade or cookies. Those were the best days. Rudy always took two cookies. He never ate the second one, instead he'd stuff it in a pocket and save it for later.

When Dash had found out, and threatened to tell Momma, Rudy had offered some of his cookie stash—being the nice homemade kind, Dash took him up on his generous offer.

Payment for Rudy's deceit. Rudy was a naughty boy, and Momma punished him regularly.

"Rudy! Where the hell are ya?"

Wrapping his arms tighter around his legs, he pulled his knees to his chest as she walked in the room.

"I'm gitting tired of yer games, boy. You can't hide forever. You're not a kid no more. Take yer punishment like a man."

Perspiration dampened his back, and his clothes itched. Rudy resisted scratching his calf as she shuffled further into the room. Her skirt brushed against the box.

Please don't find me.

Rudy almost jerked at the second voice in the room. "Don't be a pussy. Momma ain't gonna give up looking. We need to help her from now on, and not act like lil bitches."

Rudy didn't want to move but didn't want to disobey his big brother either. Dash was right; he was acting like a baby. She was a single mom and needed their help. They didn't have much money, and him sassing her deserved punishing. Why was he such a bad boy? It had all started when he'd dropped a drinking glass—the one with reindeers on the side—and it had shattered across the floor. When Momma screamed and hit Rudy upside the head, he'd raised his fist. That was a mistake—one he'd have to atone for.

The itch on his leg grew worse, and he resisted the temptation to scratch. Why didn't they move to the next room? He heard them thumping around the bed. Rudy so badly wanted to scratch at his itch, but instead, squeezed his eyes shut, praying they'd leave. Finally, footsteps sounded on the wooden floor of the passage, and Rudy pulled up his worn pant leg, and scratched at the damp skin.

"There you are, you little coward."

Something slammed into the side of the box, and Rudy toppled. Momma grabbed his ankle in a manacled grip and dragged him across the floor. The carpet burned his bare skin as Rudy screamed, trying to escape. Momma was too strong, and Dash just stood back and watched. He could've stopped her. He was much bigger than other boys his age. Instead Dash glowered at Rudy, looking like he'd punch Rudy in the nose.

It was time for Rudy to grow up, yet he couldn't stop the tears from rolling down his cheeks, or the girly screams escaping from his lips. Momma dumped him onto a kitchen chair, and it rocked under his weight. Why did nothing ever work as it should in their butt-ugly home? Why couldn't they move to the city? Momma could get a job, and they could get better stuff—like new shoes without holes in 'em.

"Wipe that snot off your face and stop sniveling."

He did as he was told before clutching the kitchen table in trembling fists. Momma left, then came back holding the pliers, looking wild-eyed and wild-haired. Rudy hated that frizzy nest sitting atop her stupid head. He refused to look her way; instead, he focused on the faded Christmas decorations, and gold tinsel placed in the dusty basket in the middle of the table. Momma leaned in, screaming her practiced tirade. She wasn't wearing her false teeth, and Rudy flinched as spittle hit his cheek.

"Do I tolerate disrespect, boy?"

"No, ma'am."

"You think you can talk back to me with that pretty mouth. It ain't gonna be pretty for that much longer."

"I'm sorry, Momma." Piss soaked through his underwear, spreading down his leg. If she found out what he'd done, she'd make him pay. Rudy shifted his foot to hide the growing puddle. Dash saw the mess, shook his head, and walked out the door.

His brother didn't like to see Rudy get hurt. Dash was the only person to have Rudy's back. They'd die for each other... kill anyone that got in their way. It was them against the world.

Momma asked him a question. He heard the word "daddy."

Why did your daddy leave us? She asked that same question every time.

"He ran off with a whore," Rudy replied automatically.

"Why else?"

"Because I was a squalling baby."

"I gave birth to yer large head and sinful body. You didn't stop bawling for the first month of yer stupid life. You drove him away, and you still can't follow simple orders." She picked up the pliers.

"No, Momma. I'll do anything. Please don't. Take me off the list." He started to cry again.

"Since a pup, you've been as dumb as an adder. You're always on my naughty list. Open yer mouth."

Over the summer, she'd already pulled three of his big teeth. Rudy clenched his jaw shut, his tongue ran along the gaping holes: two back, and a front one. The back ones hurt the worst and bled the most. Rudy couldn't eat for days after a pulling. Sometimes he ran a fever. After the last tooth, he thought he was gonna die. Even his eyes and ear had hurt. Mind numbing pain that throbbed for days.

Dash told Rudy that they wouldn't grow back—it was not like losing his baby teeth. Dash had also lost a couple, but Momma hadn't punished him in a long time. Maybe she was scared of him—he had grown some.

When Rudy didn't comply, she grabbed his hair and wrenched his head back. Tears and snot ran down his throat, Rudy choked and coughed. The pliers slammed into his cheek.

"Open yer mouth, yer afflicted with evil, and this is the cure. Open! It will be over soon."

Momma threw a leg over his lap and pulled his head back even further. Finding a gap, she shoved the pliers into his mouth. Grabbing a tooth, Momma twisted and pulled with all her might. Pain exploded in his jaw, and Rudy's vision blurred as he fought for freedom. The chair tipped, and the last thing he saw was the floor rising to meet his face.

When he opened his eyes, Dash was there, holding a dirty rag to Rudy's leaking mouth. "That's a bad one—that sucker had deep roots."

Rudy moaned as Dash helped him to stand. "Lie down on the couch. I'll git some water. Stop making Momma mad, otherwise, you won't have any teeth left."

Blood poured down Rudy's throat as he sat on the torn cushions. The metallic taste made him gag, he'd soon be retching and only hoped he'd make it outside in time. Any movement escalated the pounding in his head, and Rudy kept as still as possible.

"Happy birthday, brother." Dash handed him a glass of water.

Turned out to be some eleventh birthday. Rudy would kill their bitch mother one day, and he hoped that Dash wouldn't be too mad. Rudy would do it for the both of them.

◊ ◊ ◊

Slater slapped Johnny on the shoulder and glanced around the dimly lit space, only relaxing when he saw Kat on the dance floor with Elana. Not technically dancing—more like swaying while hanging off the tall blonde. A decade ago, this would've been Slater's favorite type of hangout. Now he just wanted to be hanging out at home, maybe watching Netflix or barbecuing in the back yard.

His gaze switched back to the women. "Kat's drunk? This is your version of watching over her?"

Johnny shrugged his folded arms. "She needed to let-go—have some fun. We kept her safe."

"Speaking of keeping her safe, Elliot is no longer working for me. If he turns up, it'll be Mach 5—FUBAR shit."

"Are you serious?" Johnny turned to Slater. "What did he do?"

"Lied about his background, but the man has a whole load of fuel backing a dangerous temper."

"It's always the quiet ones… I gotta go. I'm the designated taxi."

Slater nodded a goodbye, while watching Kat stagger and giggle at something Elana said. He'd never seen her drunk before, not once in the years they'd dated. The recent stress must be wearing her down. Slater walked onto the dance floor. Time to shepherd her home. Kat turned suddenly and Slater caught her in his arms.

"Who put that wall there?" Kat pointed at his chest.

Slater snorted as he held her upright. "You okay, angel?"

Kat reached over and grabbed Elana's sleeve. "Derry! Meet my newest and bestest friend! Do you have a hair tie?"

He felt himself frown. "Do I look like I have a hair tie?"

Kat squinted at his cropped head.

"Why does she need a hair tie?"

"In case she hurls." Elana grinned.

Just at that moment, a hipster with a man bun wandered past, and Kat launched herself in his direction before Slater could stop her. She grabbed the startled man's arm. "Do you have a hair tie?"

"Um, no?"

"Wait—in that wee bun?" She reached for the stranger's head.

"Sorry." Slater grabbed her wrist and pulled her to his side.

The guy grinned and went on his way.

"Derry? Lurk at you! What is this magical madness?" Kat waved her hands up and down his torso. Slater raised his brows.

Elana—who seemed to be the sober dance partner—took a swig of beer and turned to Slater. "Honey, don't take it personally, her last Mojito received the same 'magical madness' treatment."

"She's been drinking Mojitos?"

"Two Mojitos, a couple of shots and a Gin Fizz. Guess she's a lightweight," Atlas said from behind.

"Mr. Rodzilla… you're so brave and sexy." Kat ran a hand over Slater's chest, and he grinned, enjoying the show.

"Forget the name 'Slater.' I think we have a new call sign." Atlas chuckled.

"Derry, let's go home. I want to play with your magic Excalibur."

Elana choked mid-sip and Slater couldn't help laughing out loud. Kat frowned as she swayed in place.

"Guinevere, I reckon it's time to leave."

"My name is Kat. Wait… where's the rest of the gurls?"

"They left with Johnny." Elana stifled a yawn. "They all gave you a hug, remember?"

"Casey?"

"Her boyfriend picked her up."

Slater turned to Elana and asked, "Do you need a ride?"

"I've got her." Atlas stepped forward and handed Elana a strappy handbag.

Elana shot him a cautionary glare. "I seriously need to buy a car. You're now my regular taxi driver."

"You've just moved to the city. Relax, I've got you."

Elana visibly bristled at Atlas's last statement, but followed him to the exit. The woman looked to be a formidable fortress. Slater silently wished Atlas luck with his chosen femme fatale.

It took a while for Slater to corral Kat to his truck. Her drunk babbling was darn cute, and he couldn't help smiling at her chatter. A prickling awareness had Slater turning to scan the parking garage. It wasn't all that late, and vehicles still packed the lot. After helping Kat into the passenger seat, Slater climbed in, and cut through the busy neighborhood. Finally, he glanced over at Kat, who stared at him with a wide grin.

"What?"

"What?" She parroted with a gruff tone, and licked her lips. "Your voice is so sexy. Now can I fondle Excalibur?"

"Damn woman." Slater almost jerked the wheel, steadying himself for a second time as a delicate hand slid over his thigh. Her seatbelt clicked.

"Angel-pie, no…"

Her hand crept further up. "It's so pretty."

"Shit, I mean it, Kat. You're drunk, and my junk isn't pretty. It's rugged… and manly."

Ignoring his warning, she leaned over and began loosening his jeans. This time, Slater pulled onto the shoulder as her head landed in his lap. They came to a final stop. Raising his hands from the wheel, Slater bit his lip and smiled. Ladylike snores drifted up from below. Kat lay slumped, using his crotch as a pillow.

His phone lit up with an incoming call, and Slater looked at the caller ID and groaned. Red, the stats-gagger probably wanted a play-by-play of the earlier meeting. Slater forced himself to answer, as he eyed Red's keys in the console—he still needed to get those back. After that, Slater wouldn't attend another of Red's meetings. He wanted to try out Fletcher's support group instead.

"Hey, Red, how was your trip?" Slater stroked a thumb across Kat's temple and stretched out his legs.

"Good. I'm driving back now. How was the meeting? I heard that you pulled Elliot aside, and he stormed out?"

"Uh. Yeah. We had a personal issue to discuss."

"Elliot just called me, and he's a complete wreck. He's squatting in some parking lot—talking about how everyone has betrayed him. He's in a dark place."

Interesting.

Glancing around the quiet street, Slater put the truck back in drive and pulled onto the road.

"Elliot mentioned what we spoke about?"

"No. But I'm sick of you upsetting my members. First, you drive Brock to suicide by assaulting him in a safe space, and now Elliot?"

Slater wasn't wasting time talking to this windbag. "I gotta go, buddy. I can drop your keys off in the morning."

"The rules dictate—"

"Text me your address." Slater hung up and took a calming breath. The only thing that mattered was Kat's safety. His tired brain tried to sort through his boiling emotions. Were they meant to be together? Was Slater capable of giving Kat everything she craved and then some? For the moment, they both needed sleep. Everything would be clearer in the new light of day.

Chapter Sixteen

Nausea woke her, and Kat sat up before clutching her head. "Bloody hell."

She glanced around the vaguely familiar room before groaning and flopping back on her pillow. Fuzzy memories seeped to the surface. Slow dancing with Elana... groping at Slater's junk... mauling him in the car.

Kat glanced down, happy to see that she still wore her jeans and blouse. So she hadn't stripped naked at any point—Yay for her. The smell of stale smoke and fading perfume had her nose wrinkling, and she'd overused her still tender but almost healed wrist—but how? Kat hoped it wasn't while assaulting her sober and hot-looking driver.

Rolling off the bed, she staggered to the shower and spent a good thirty minutes leaning under the spray in a dazed stupor. Swiping at the fogged up mirror, Kat grimaced at her pale complexion and added a little foundation and blush to the mix. She still looked sickly and her hair was a tangled mess. Giving up, Kat threw the brush aside and grabbed her leave-in conditioner instead.

With what felt like hours later, she finally emerged and made her way carefully to Slater's kitchen. Any sudden movements had her gritting her teeth against a throbbing headache.

"Hello, sunshine!"

Slater's voice was way too loud and chipper. Kat winced before shooting him a nasty glare.

"Oops. Did someone get up on the wrong side of club duvet?"

"Aye, and if you don't lower your voice, I'll club your arse." Kat opened the fridge and grabbed a bottle of Coke.

"Angel-pie. Don't. Here's Tylenol and a glass of water."

Kat glanced at the breakfast counter. Sure enough, a couple of pills and water sat waiting next to a tub of yogurt and a banana.

"I need caffeine." Kat carried the bottle over to the counter and took a long swig. The banana received the evil eye; she reached for the Tylenol instead.

"Drink that water. It'll be warm outside today." Derek downed his glass. "You were cute last night."

Kat turned her attention to the smug agent in the room. "What? Did we end up doing any crazy-ass shit?"

"Not me. You, however, ended up in my lap."

Wincing, Kat offered a mumbled apology before downing the rest of the Coke.

"Relax, you pawed at my crotch before falling asleep."

"Oh, God. I forced myself on you. I'm so sorry."

"If you weren't drunk, I would've cooperated in the front seat of my cab. Mr. Rodzilla felt the loss." Slater tried not to grin and failed.

"Shut yer bake. Did I call it Rodzilla?"

"In front of our friends. You also called my junk 'pretty.'"

"I'm such a nitwit. Sorry."

Slater walked past and squeezed the back of her neck. "You

had your fun, and I drove your drunk-ass home and carried it to bed. It's all good. I do like the term 'magical Excalibur.' Let's stick with that."

Kat laughed and winced as she picked up her water. "Ouch, I've tweaked my wrist."

"Probably while staggering around the dance floor."

"God, I'm a mess. I need to go home and fetch some of my things. I have all my notes in my office, and I'm set up for my webinars on that end. Can't I just stay at my apartment?"

"Not until I know you're safe."

"You know it's not up to you. If I want to go home, you can't stop me. This theory about another killer is—"

All humor gone; Slater shot her a glare. "It's not a theory."

"Really? Do you have any concrete evidence?"

"What are you saying? That you don't trust my judgment?"

"Not your judgment."

Slater narrowed his eyes. "Say it."

"I don't want to fight. I want my life back."

"What do you think is happening here?" Slater leaned his hands on the counter.

"We've had a… special time together, and I don't know where we'll end up, but that's no reason for me to stay in your home."

"Are you serious? You think I'm making shit up to keep you close?"

"I never said that."

"Yeah, you kinda did. You think I'd use your safety—and allow you to feel continual fear—as an excuse to what? Keep you locked away in my house? What the hell, Kat?"

Kat couldn't think past the headache and stood.

"We're fighting a losing battle."

Slater's words made her angry, and she waited for him to finish.

"I know why you think so poorly of me and my motivations. I was a deserter."

"You're the bravest man I've ever met, and I don't question your motives."

"I retreated from our relationship and caused irreparable damage. I never blamed you for walking out the door, because I did nothing to keep you by my side. I was so absorbed in my pain and my misery. I want to go back and give myself an ass kicking."

"Derry, what do you want? We've been dancing around our issues for weeks."

"I want what I can't have—a do-over. You—by my side."

"So should I ignore the past? Do I pretend that you didn't think about being with someone else for a brief minute? Do I forget about the anger and the hurt and all the mistakes we've made?"

"The only woman I want to be with is you. For Goddamn ever!"

"I can't think past today or my pounding head. I want my life back, my tiny apartment, and currently non-existent career."

"You want to hide."

"Aye, is that so wrong? A serial killer carved evil words onto my door, and I narrowly missed getting shot, and I'm living with an ex-boyfriend who's messing with my head."

She'd phrased it the wrong way and Derek visibly shut down. He left the room; the back door slammed closed. Derek had messed with her head, but not through any fault of his own. Desire clouded her resolve, but self-preservation called the shots.

Kat spotted Derek leaning on the deck railing as she walked

past the window. She went to her room, made the bed, and laid down. Her head pounded in time with her pulse. The space felt a little stuffy, which meant it would probably be another baking summer's day.

"When you're ready, I'll take you over to your place. Pack your bags." Kat jumped at Derek's deep voice. He leaned against the doorjamb with hands stuffed in jeans pockets, looking tired, angry, and hurt.

"Will I be safe?"

"I'll stay in your guest room. If that's not okay, then I'll be in my truck."

"Don't be silly. You can use the guest room."

"Fine. When you're ready, let me know." Derek turned and left.

His cold demeanor made her chest ache. Kat packed her things and changed into a simple pink cotton sundress with nude ballet pumps, before twisting her black tresses into a messy bun, and applying bright pink lipstick. She may feel like death, but she'd still make an effort to feel human.

Like always, Derek's gaze ran up her length, making her blush. This time his shuttered look gave nothing away. An awkward silence descended as they drove towards the freeway. Kat re-adjusted her sunglasses against the harsh glare and stared at the bright blue sky. The truck's temperature gauge clicked over to a hundred degrees, and Derek leaned over to turn up the air.

He unscrewed a bottle of water and chugged half of it. "Drink water," he said, pointing at the second bottle. "Do you mind if I make a quick stop on the way?"

Kat shrugged. "Sure, whatever."

"Red—the guy from my support group—needs his keys back."

Derek pulled over to program the address into his phone's GPS. Soon they wound their way through the suburbs before entering a quaint neighborhood. They pulled into the drive of a neat-looking one-story home.

"I'll just stay in the car."

Derek paused while opening his door. "I'm not leaving you out here, unprotected."

"I doubt the killer followed you all the way here. I'm fine."

"Kat, get out of the truck." A muscle ticked in his jaw and Kat refrained from rolling her eyes.

"Can you leave it running in the meantime? It's so hot."

Slater nodded.

Leaving her purse on the seat, she pushed open her door and slipped onto the cobbled drive. Derek met her on her side and guided her towards the house. Kat pulled away and stormed ahead. Catching up in two strides, Derek stepped around her and pressed the doorbell.

They waited in the baking sun.

"I need to piss," he said, rubbing his shoulder.

"Well, you drank a reservoir. Shite, it's warm," Kat said, wiping her dampening neck.

The sound of a deadbolt being pulled back sounded, another lock clicked, and the door opened.

Kat stepped back in surprise. "Rolf?"

"Kathleen?"

Slater stepped closer to Kat. "What the hell is going on? You two know each other?"

"We dated." Rolf supplied with casual aplomb.

Kat cut in. "One blind date."

"Why did you call him 'Rolf'?"

"That's my name. Rolf. My army mates call me Red. I'm

sorry, Derek, I didn't realize that she was your 'Kat,' not until now."

Derek looked like he'd implode, and Kat hurried to smooth over their twist of fate. "It was the blind date that I'd mentioned."

"Relax, buddy; Kathleen and I parted as friends. I'm just happy to have finally met your 'Kat,' even though it's under strange circumstances. Come in and grab some raspberry lemonade. I made it myself."

"We have to get going. I just came to hand over your keys."

"We need to talk. I need a moment of your time—I have concerns."

"It can wait." Derek turned and grabbed Kat's hand.

"Elliot called—again—and was acting pretty strange on the phone. He made threats against you and says he's being watched. I'm wondering if he's coming off prescribed meds. The guy sounds paranoid."

Kat shifted uncomfortably. That didn't sound like the Elliot she knew.

"What threats? When did he call?" Derek asked.

"This morning, around eight. We spoke for over an hour. Come in."

Derek looked grim as he stared out onto the street.

Kat wanted to get to the bottom of this. "Did you know Elliot back in Colorado?" she asked Derek.

Derek nodded. "We also served on a mission together back in the day."

"Well, I can't think while standing in this blazing heat, and my head is about to explode. I'll take a lemonade." Kat tugged at Derek's hand, and he reluctantly followed. Rolf stepped back and let them into the cool foyer. They followed him past a front living room to an open dining area. He gestured towards a couple of chairs. Kat glanced around the sparsely decorated space as she sat, feeling relief at her lucky escape. Rolf's beige personality shone in a muted space that didn't include wall hangings or photographs. The guy was as colorful as mud. Rolf disappeared into the kitchen. Derek paced the space with restless energy. When Rolf came back with two glasses of lemonade, Derek excused himself to use the bathroom, and Rolf showed him the way. The tall, iced glass called Kat's name, and she took a long sip, tasting rich berries and something sweet that she couldn't name. It tasted delicious.

Sitting back and placing the heavy glass back on the table, she uncrossed her legs and looked over at Rolf, standing in the kitchen doorway. He smiled at her oddly, and Kat smiled back. The way he hovered without making conversation creeped her out and Kat took another sip.

"Thanks for the lemonade. It's wonderful."

"A recipe from an old neighbor. It goes great with cookies— the home-baked kind."

Still… that unblinking stare… Kat looked away. Her chest felt tight, and she straightened in the chair. The cool room suddenly felt too warm, as she took in a deep breath and rolled her now numb lips. Kat's chest wheezed, and she swallowed hard. The next breath seemed worse, and this time, she couldn't swallow past her swelling throat and tongue. Panicking, Kat pushed up, her glass tipped and rolled to the floor with a dull crash.

"Help…"

Red walked over to a cabinet drawer and pulled out a webbed-looking vest. "Lemonade a little too sweet for you? It must be the honey."

"No… why?"

"Because you're on the naughty list. Kathleen, did you think you'd ever escape?"

◊ ◊ ◊

Slater used the head and glanced over at the rattling exhaust fan. He couldn't think past the noise and couldn't find a way to switch the damn thing off. He gave up and washed his hands before pausing. Elliot had fought like a tiger alongside Slater when Slater was a Green Beret. Regardless of what had happened in his personal life, the soldier had saved numerous lives. Entering Red's home, Slater decided that Elliot wasn't capable of hurting innocents. No matter how fucked up his friend was, Elliot was a stand-up guy when it came to his job. As soon as they were back in the truck, Slater would call Elliot and help him sort through his personal mess.

As Slater slipped back into the passage and glanced at the closed doors to his right, another alarm bell rang. Out of the hundreds of thousands of men in Salt Lake, Red happened to be Kat's one and only blind date? A man that Slater knew from Colorado. Slater didn't believe in coincidences and slid up to the first closed door. He didn't have much time to perform a quick search.

A sparse bedroom. The next room looked like a small library. Bookshelves lined a wall. Memorabilia and photographs took up the adjacent wall. Framed photos of a soldier that looked similar to Red or Rolf, and this man seemed larger with a hooked nose— Red's deployed brother. Another shelf held additional framed images, except these were photographs from newspapers or magazines. Slater froze when he recognized himself, and those of fellow veterans. The closet in the corner called his attention, and

Slater reached over to turn the knob, then swore.

Five sets of false teeth. Two Santa Claus dolls sitting in a nest of tinsel. Rolls of gold tinsel. A large black bag sat on the floor, and Slater pulled it out of the dark space and unzipped it. The slick rubber material caught in the dim light. Slater rose, drew his weapon, and rushed into the passage, pausing when he spotted Red standing near the entrance to the living room, peering around the wall.

"You found my private treasures."

Slater pointed his Glock at Red's forehead and placed his finger on the trigger.

"Shoot me, and you'll kill your girlfriend. You move fast, but not fast enough." Red raised his hand and waved an electronic detonator with a press trigger in the air. The psychopath's thumb hovered then rested on the button.

Slater's pulse skyrocketed. "What have you done?"

"Strapped a lovely suicide vest to Kathleen's chest. Drop your weapon, or she'll go 'boom.' And I'd hurry, she doesn't look so good."

"Son of a bitch." Clamping down on panic, Slater considered his options. He had none. Kat needed him. He hadn't heard any scuffling or commotion earlier, but the noisy bathroom fan hadn't helped. How had the sick fucker managed to strap a vest onto Kat without her screaming? For the first time in his career, Slater's gun hand trembled as he eyed the still raised button beneath the asshole's thumb. Red stood concealed behind the wall, and Slater couldn't risk shooting without triggering the bomb. If Slater held a sniper's rifle, he'd have a sporting chance to blow out the man's brain stem. Too great a risk with a handgun. If Red pressed down on the button, two pins would spring together, complete the circuit and trigger an explosion.

Red kept a safe distance. "Well, I guess you've made your decision." He wiggled the detonator, and Slater raised his hands.

"I'm dropping my weapon. Be careful with that; I doubt that you have experience with those kinds of vests. Where did you get it from?"

"I made it myself. Amazing what you find on the dark web. You thought I was in Nevada, but I've been holed up at home, building this brutal baby."

Jesus. A homemade bomb could blow any second.

Slater placed his gun on the floor and slowly rose. Too much distance sat between Slater and the target, and even if he lunged for Red, he'd be too late.

"Kick it into the corner."

Slater did as he asked. Red backed up and pointed towards the living room.

Walking past, and turning the corner had Slater wanting to collapse to his knees as he took in Kat's predicament. She sat slumped on the floor amongst broken glass next to the dining table.

Red's detonation cord ran along the floor and connected to the battery pack at the front of a suicide vest, strapped tightly to her upper body. Slater's experienced eyes took in the grim details; a crude jacket constructed with seatbelt webbing, canvas material, and leather belting. Red had attached a conservative amount of plastic explosives—a couple of pounds—enough to cause mortal injury to the person wearing the vest and anyone in the direct vicinity.

"Sweetheart, look at me."

"Can't... breathe."

Blood drained from Slater's head, as tingling pressure spread along his extremities. "Kat, please look at me. It's going to be okay."

She did as he asked, and Slater surged forward.

"One more step and I'll blow her to kingdom come." Red now stood at the opposite end of the room.

Slater froze, hands still in the air. "Her lips are blue."

"That's what happens when you're allergic to honey."

"You shitting, fucking, dickwad asshole. I'm going to destroy you."

"Now that's no way to speak to the 'Belsnickel Killer.' I prefer the name, 'Rudolph the Red.' It has a better ring. Do you know how many lives I've taken?"

"And do you know how many I've taken?" Slater countered in a deadly tone. Red shuffled back a step.

"Get to the other side of the table, before your woman becomes minced meat."

Slater reluctantly complied, each second seemed like an eternity as fear suffocated his thoughts.

"Just… let her go. Her EpiPen is in her purse—in the truck. This is between us."

"Wrong. Kathleen is the one I want—the naughty whore. You're just the dumb schmuck who couldn't get over the stupid bitch. I did it all for you, and every other brave man and woman who were betrayed by their loved ones back home."

What the hell?

"You didn't serve, did you?" Slater recalled how Red had never quite seemed like one of the guys. He'd played the part of a veteran with enough success, that no-one had ever bothered to look into his service records. And they'd all spilled their secrets in their weekly meeting while a wolf sat amongst them. Many of the veterans couldn't talk about their missions, so what did they end up sharing? All their personal challenges. Their significant others… divorces… pregnancies … marriages… betrayals. And all the while, this monster recorded their deepest secrets.

How much had Slater shared with this man? He'd started therapy three weeks before their breakup and had attended a couple of sessions at Red's local veterans support group back in Colorado. Had Slater spoken about his floundering relationship with Kat—in those first sessions? He must have. Slater sure as shit didn't share his military experiences.

"The fucking army wouldn't accept me because of my mouth. Due to my 'orthodontic appliances.'" Red pulled out a set of false teeth and waved them around before opening his mouth. The guy had no teeth. Red shoved his dentures back in, and Slater wondered if Red had periodontal disease.

"Dash got through; he's a damn hero. He only lost a few teeth, unlike me. I'm such a naughty boy." Red paced as his mentally deranged soapbox grew. "You all risk your lives every day on the front-line. All you ask for is a little loyalty in return. I saw her break your heart in the snow. You sat on your front steps and bawled like a kid. You spoke about how she'd destroyed you—after the breakup. Do you remember?"

Slater vaguely remembered drinking himself into a stupor, before attending a session. That was his breaking point, and the week he'd decided on seeing his first therapist. God, he'd placed her in the path of a psychotic maniac. Was that where Red's obsession first began?

Slater's focus was split between Kat and the detonation switch. If he could keep Red talking, he might find an opening. She didn't have much time—Kat could barely sit upright. Her raspy gasps tore at his soul.

"You were there that night?" Slater asked, inching closer.

"Yes. I came to see you at your home—about possibly volunteering in a couple of our charity events—instead, I watched the drama play out on your front steps."

Red made his way over to her side, and Slater turned to stone. "Touch her—"

"And you'll what? Make a move, and you'll kill her and possibly yourself." Red crouched and stroked the back of her neck.

"Your boyfriend is always so smooth and controlled. Bet he's not feeling all that slick at this moment—bested by a civilian. He'd do anything for you. Wouldn't you, Derek?"

"Goddamn right, son of a bitch."

"Too late." Red removed a pair of pliers from his back pocket and waved them in front of Kat. "Maybe I should take a souvenir. Such a sweet mouth." He nudged her cheek with the pliers, and Slater shook with horror. He focused on distracting the demented bastard.

"You planned our visit."

Red shrugged. "It's a Sunday—your day off. I knew you wouldn't leave her alone. She'd be by your side. I just needed to get you into my house. It went a lot more smoothly than I expected. Your toilet break was a gift. I thought I'd need to drug your ass or knock you out. I laced your glass of lemonade, but it turned out, I didn't need it."

Slater slid an inch closer. "You set up Brock to take the fall."

"I needed more time. It was easy; Brock wasn't that bright, plus, self-hatred and anger ran his life. We hung out together, and I got him hooked on cocaine. Fed him stories about your infamy in the military. How arrogant you were, and that your woman needed a good hammering from a real man. Drove over to his place when it was time, turned up the volume on the action movie we were watching, before blowing his brains out. The bastard didn't even have time to react. I took his truck for a joyride and had a little fun. I wanted to scare you, but I almost shot Kathleen in the head. I'm not good with guns—not like my brother. After I kill the both of you, I'll disappear and find a new place to hunt." Red stroked her shoulder. "Which tooth should I extract?"

Slater slid closer. "One of mine. Toss the pliers my way, and I'll do it myself."

"Awww. How sweet." Red placed his pliers back in his pocket. "I'll pick her body clean after the explosion. I'm sure I'll find teeth in the oddest of places."

Kat's whistling breaths grew more labored, and Slater's adrenaline surge almost made him hurl. "Hold on, angel. It'll be okay."

"Don't lie to her. These are her last moments. You can stand at a distance and watch her die, or you can cradle her in your arms. You want to play the 'star-crossed lover' scenario, now is your chance. If you choose this path, I'll wait until she's unconscious before pressing the trigger, and she won't feel a thing."

"She'll suffocate to death. Fuck you. Let me go to her." If Slater could get close enough to the vest, maybe he could disarm it.

Slater stepped around the table just as Red rose from his crouched position. Kat moved quickly, grabbing the broken base of the glass and thrusting the jagged edge deep into Red's thigh. Slater exploded in violent motion, racing for Red as he screamed and bent forward. The detonator almost fell from his hand. Kat grabbed Red's thumb and bent it backward.

By some miracle, Slater got to them, just as the detonator rolled to the floor. Red raised his fist to her as Slater threw himself into Red's chest, shoving him back. Red tried to scramble away and reach for the detonator. Covering the target's body with his, Slater locked Red's groping arm to his side. Slater then swung a thigh over Red's chest, trapping the man's other arm between the bastard's face and Slater's crotch. Red screamed in frustration and tried to buck. It was too late, Slater rolled sideways, locking his legs together in a death grip. Slater might be a sniper, but thanks to MIT training, he was just as deadly in hand to hand combat. Slater executed the Figure Four Jujitsu choke hold with controllable grace. After securing Red's neck between his thighs, Slater performed the death blow with a twist of his hips. He felt more than heard Red's neck snap. When the body relaxed, Slater unhooked his legs and scrambled to Kat's side.

"Kat? Sweetheart, hold on. I'm working as fast as I can."

"Bomb... first?" she whispered as she lay curled on the floor.

"Yes, angel. Bomb first." Slater ran for the kitchen and grabbed a smooth-edged knife from a knife rack. Kat couldn't hold on for much longer.

Stumbling back to the dining room, he collapsed by her unconscious side.

"No! Kat, fuck, baby. Hold on. I've got you." With shaking hands, Slater sawed through the belted straps of the vest.

"Kat, open your eyes!" She'd stopped wheezing and lay too still. The blue tinge around her mouth intensified. With a final snap, he freed her from the vest and dropped the knife. Scooping her into a fireman's carry, Slater raced for the door. It took too long to break out of their tomb and into the bright sunlight. Slater laid her on the grass next to his truck before wrenching the passenger door open.

An older woman walking a labrador, paused before taking a cautionary step back. "Oh, Lordy! Everything okay?"

"Call 911. Anaphylaxis—and please back up. There's a bomb in that home."

Slater emptied the contents of Kat's bag and scooped up the EpiPen, wasting valuable time removing it from its container. Positioning it on her outer thigh, Slater compressed the button. Placing an ear to her mouth, and a finger on her carotid pulse, he checked her vitals. Kat wasn't breathing. Slater tipped her head back and began CPR as the labrador lady spoke with a 911 operator.

"C'mon baby."

Slater's eyes burned as he performed mouth to mouth. Air wasn't getting in and her chest wasn't rising.

"Breathe, Kat! Goddamnit, breathe!"

He'd perform a fucking tracheotomy if needed. He wasn't a medic, but he knew the basics. "Please don't leave me."

Slater pushed in more air and felt the tiniest give. Taking another breath, he pushed harder. Her chest rose ever so slightly, and Slater focused on those small movements, hearing sirens in the distance. When a tiny gasp escaped her sweet mouth, Slater wanted to shout his joy.

"You've got this, baby. Pull that air in."

Kat's chest rose, and she groaned. After the fifth steady breath, Slater pulled off his shirt and wrapped it around her sliced up palm. Positioning her on his lap, Slater held her hand, rocking her as they waited for the paramedics.

Chapter Seventeen

Four years ago.
Centerville, Utah.

His brother wouldn't like what he had to say. Dash had little choice. He parked in the street and stared at Rudolph's tidy suburban home. Thanks to the money they received for their mother's property, they could both afford a small place in the city. That's all Rudy had ever wanted—order and peace. Rudy now had order, but they'd both never have peace.

Rudy wouldn't be happy with Dash's news. It would be an uncomfortable conversation, and Rudy would be mad. Tough shit. One of them had to earn a decent living, and it was Dash's duty to keep that roof over his brother's head. Rudy was different, and people sensed that. He couldn't keep a damn job.

As if sensing that his sibling had just pulled up, Rudy walked out onto his front yard and scanned the street. Dash raised a hand, and Rudy waved back, grinning like a kid. Dash climbed out of his Challenger and walked over to flop down in a chair opposite his now seated brother. They sat under the only tree.

Rudy tapped his fingers. "You look like shit. Where's your pretty girlfriend?"

Dash had been dating the same woman for over a year. A sweet little thing that he'd intended to marry. It turned out she was like the rest of the whores. One stupid fight about his impending deployment and he'd popped her in the mouth. That's what she got for talking back.

"She left me," he said glumly.

"No way, man. Are you okay?"

"Do I look okay? I bought her a fucking ring and everything."

"You loved her?" Rudy looked confused.

Dash wasn't so sure if he 'loved' her. He didn't understand the sentimental concept but nodded anyway.

"Like you love me?"

"Don't be a dick, you're my brother. That's different."

Rudy smiled then grew serious. "Did you tell her about Momma? What we did to the bitch?"

Dash glanced around the quiet neighborhood before answering. "Hell, no."

"What about the others? Did you tell her about the whores?"

"Keep your damn voice down." Dash slapped his brother across the head, and Rudy shoved back at Dash's shoulder.

"Listen. I'm going to be away for a while. I joined the army."

Rudy bolted to his feet. "Why the hell would you do that?"

"Because I need to earn enough money so that you can eat, dumbass. Besides, I can do some good killing over there." Dash felt his pants tighten at the thought.

"I'm studying to be an electrician."

"Good for you, bro. Don't stress the fuck out, because I've got your back." He'd always have Rudy's back. Standing, Dash clasped a hand to Rudy's shoulder. "I'll call you. Let you know when I bug out."

His brother grabbed Dash's wrist. "Don't... don't forget about me."

"Are you kidding! It's you and me—"

"Against the demons," Rudy finished. "Rudolph the Red and Dasher the Depraved."

Dash was definitely depraved. "Behave while I'm gone. Don't attract unnecessary attention."

"I want to kill the bitch that broke your heart."

Dash felt his eyes burn. "I dealt with her."

He made his way back to the car and turned to give one last wave. Rudy stood alone in the shade, looking like a lost boy. God help anyone who'd ever hurt Dash's brother.

◊ ◊ ◊

"Never mind calling this a circus, this is a goddamn Disney parade." Fletcher pulled up a hospital chair and stretched out his back after another two detectives walked out the door.

Kat eyed that escape route. How long did it take to discharge her? She hated hospitals; they reminded her of her previous attack and all the months spent in intensive care hooked up to monitors. Shifting restlessly on the starched sheets, Kat tried to calculate how long she'd been lying in a hospital bed.

"What time is it?" she asked.

"Around midnight," Fletcher replied.

"Bloody hell, can't I at least get dressed?" she grumbled, glancing at the man glued to her side. Her voice still sounded croaky thanks to the initial intubation in the ambulance and the ER. "You mentioned some extra clothes?"

Derek looked up wearily and glanced over at his backpack he'd retrieved earlier from his truck. "Sweatpants and a shirt. I doubt they'll fit—you'll drown."

Better than her stained and bloody dress; her hand had bled like a sieve. She wanted to adjust the tight dressing, but Derek refused to let go of her other hand, so she stared at the wall instead.

"You'll have to wait until they remove your IV," Derek said, squeezing her hand.

The next round of agents and detectives entered the room, along with two well dressed and distinguished gentlemen. Derek and Fletcher immediately stood, almost standing at attention. Numerous officials had already taken their statement. From what she'd gathered, after the paramedics rushed her to the hospital, local law enforcement had sent in a bomb squad to dismantle the suicide vest. They'd also recovered evidence of Rolf—Rudolph's killing sprees. Teeth from additional victims, two gimp suits, and more weapons. Kat felt only relief, knowing that the notorious serial killer who'd turned her life upside down, was finally dead.

There would be no more victims, and she'd helped in stopping him. The stitched up slice on her hand was so worth it. Sinking that large shard of glass into his muscled thigh had felt strangely satisfying.

Kat barely took note of the greetings and introductions in the room. She looked up when she heard the term "Director of the FBI."

A silver-haired gentleman with shrewd eyes stepped forward and offered her his hand. Derek—who still held it—reluctantly released his death grip.

"Hugo Sullivan."

Kat smiled at the boss-man as Derek stood aside and clasped his hands in front of him.

"Kathleen Flynn." Her raspy words had her clearing her sore throat.

"Do you need water?" The director waved a hand, and one of

his agent minions scurried out the room. She'd been chewing on chipped ice for the last two hours but didn't refuse the offer as the director sat at the end of the bed. He seemed like a genuine and direct leader.

"Young lady, thanks to your bravery, we have one less serial killer roaming our streets."

"Derry—I mean Agent Banez—did all the work, sir."

Nostril's flaring, Derek looked away as the director shook his head. "That's not what I've heard. I think you made an excellent team. If you need anything whatsoever, we're invested in your ongoing recovery."

Kat nodded as the director turned his attention to the stiff warrior to her right. "The training facility is looking impressive. The first of its kind under our belt. The terrain and newly built village looks so much like Afghanistan."

"Thank you, sir. That's the objective."

Kat remembered Derek mentioning that the director—along with some Washington heavy hitters—took a tour of the site over a week ago.

Folding his arms, the director squinted at Derek. "Are you sure you don't want to be in the field?"

"Sir, I've trained countless Special Forces, and black ops teams overseas. If you're sending agents to foreign war zones, I'll have them trained and ready for engagement. I'm better as a trainer."

"That's debatable. You're one lethal son of a bitch. I've read your file." The older man turned to the other agents in the room. "What were the rest of you schmucks doing while he took down the 'Belsnickel Killer'?" Ignoring the awkward clearing of throats, Director Sullivan stood and turned to Fletcher. "I want a full report, and this case wrapped up in a thorough investigation."

"Yes, sir."

"Oh, and avoid the front entrance when you leave. The press hounds have settled in for the evening."

After the federal pack had filed out the door, Derek sat back down and slid his hand over hers. Chuckling, Fletcher stood. "Banez and Sullivan are sitting in a tree, K-I-S-S-I-N-G."

"Screw off, Fletch face."

"I think Sullivan has a big crush on a certain sniper. I'm getting coffee. You guys want anything?"

"To escape?" Kat said before yawning. Her yawn turned into a smile as her white-haired doctor walked into the room.

"How soon can I leave?"

The grouchy doctor just raised his brows. "Patience, Miss Flynn. That was one close call. We had to intubate."

"I feel fine."

"You're fortunate. Delayed epinephrine injections can be associated with fatalities."

"What do you mean?" Slater looked paler than before, and Kat squeezed his hand.

"She should have received the epinephrine at the first onset of her symptoms. And delays after that could render an ineffective treatment. There's a small window of higher effectiveness."

"We didn't have a choice." Kat squeezed Derek's hand again, worrying about his darkening countenance.

"I'll run through your chart. You received a second intravenous dose of epinephrine at the ER. After stabilization, we hooked you up to supplemental oxygen, and a large volume fluid of isotonic saline. You responded well to the treatment. Not all anaphylactic patients are as fortunate."

"So you're saying she's lucky to be alive, even after I shot her in the leg with the EpiPen?" A muscle ticked in Derek's jaw.

"That is correct. Take it easy, Miss Flynn. Look after those stitches in that hand and if you have an onset of recurring symptoms—if your chest feels tight—come back in for treatment. It's rare, but it happens."

After the nurse removed her IV, Kat swung her legs over the side of the bed. "Hand me those clothes and pull the curtain."

Derek didn't move, and Kat shot him an exasperated grimace. "Earth to Derry."

"I fucked everything up. Like, literally, everything."

"I'm fine, you're fine and we get to live another day. Help me with this knot." Kat fiddled with the gown strings. "Derek?"

She looked his way and froze. He looked like he was about to toss his cookies.

"Shit and hell, what now?"

"I'm not good for you." He pushed himself up before leaning his hands heavily on the mattress.

"And you came to that half-assed conclusion, how?"

"You want me to list the reasons?"

"Enlighten me."

"Jesus, Kat. I brought a serial killer into our lives. Thanks to my selfish actions, he witnessed our breakup and marked you as his target. Then I left you vulnerable—"

"I left you, remember? I did the dumping."

"Regardless, my role was to protect the woman I loved... and yet you had to fend off a killer."

"The attack was all on that Belsnickel asshole—"

"Then I was so caught up in jealousy after discovering that Red was the man you'd dated. I was so fucking distracted that I walked you into his home? I didn't even think of what a giant-ass coincidence it all was. I offered you up as a sacrifice and left you with a psycho while I took a piss!"

"We didn't know." Kat reached out, and Derek jerked away.

"I should've known. After years of black ops training, what the hell happened to my instincts?"

"Don't do this."

He backed up against the wall. "I stood by helplessly in his home, and watched him play his depraved game. If you hadn't stabbed him in the leg, we might not be here."

"It was a distraction. I knew you'd use the opportunity to kill him."

"Then... then! I discover that I almost killed you by delaying the epinephrine."

"You saved my life! You had no choice."

"I should've run out to the truck and grabbed the EpiPen immediately after killing Red."

"And left me strapped to a bomb? Derry... be serious. You made the right call."

"I've caused you so much pain. Physical and mental." He rested his head against the wall and stared at the ceiling. "It's amazing how one incident can be the catalyst for a trail of destruction. Do you remember when we both last felt true peace—together—as a couple? It was at that cabin just before the Black Friday bombing."

Kat ignored her growing heartache, remembering moments she'd treasure forever.

Derek's mouth turned up. "I lived in a shiny and bright world with my girl, and was invincible—having no idea of what lay ahead. A month later, I held dying children in my arms, and from then on, it was a slippery slide down a gravelly hill. And instead of gaining traction, I hurtled into hell. I drank, and couldn't sleep. I lost the woman I loved. Then a grenade almost tore my arm off, and I chose to say goodbye to my MIT brothers."

Kat stared at her feet, not wanting to hear the rest.

"I wasn't the only one to tumble down that hellish hill, because I had a firm grip on your hand and dragged you down with me. It came full circle. I'm the destructive catalyst in your life."

"That's not true."

Derek straightened. "I'll take you home—to your apartment. Can you call Casey to stay with you?"

Kat tried to speak past the lump in her throat, as tears spilled.

"See?" Derek said as if her tears were proof of his ridiculous argument. "Only pain."

They swam in a whirlpool of history and heartbreak.

"You're right." Kat forced out the words and saw him jerk in response. "Not about your guilt. That's a bunch of baloney, but about us. The timing will never be right. One of us will never be ready. We're see-sawing back and forth." Kat wiped her cheek and stared at her glistening fingertips. "God, I want to take away all your pain. That's all I've ever wanted. I laid in bed at night watching as you tossed and turned. All those tortured memories that I couldn't fathom. If I could, I'd reach into your mind and draw out those nightmares, and make the Black Friday hauntings my own. When you love someone so deeply, all you want is to see them smile again. I prayed for that every day, and then I fell into the same hole."

He worked his jaw as he watched her talk, eyes shining and reflecting his pain. Kat shot him a shaky smile. "It ends now. Casey can take me home. I release you of everything. You're an incredible man, and I'm sorry I couldn't give you what you needed."

Derek shook his head, then let out a growl, before turning and walking out.

A clean break… again. This decision was for the best. Wasn't it? Kat swallowed her heartbreak and climbed calmly from the bed. Her knees shook, as she braced herself against the rail. Her life was a mess, and perhaps this was Derek's lucky escape.

Chapter Eighteen

Two days later.
Bagram Airfield, Afghanistan.

Private First Class, Dasher Hill, stood to attention as the Platoon Sergeant walked through the door. What had he done now? Aside from twiddling his thumbs for the last thirty minutes waiting for "plat-daddy" to enter the room.

"At ease. Take a seat."

Dash did as the man asked, surveying the neat office before settling his gaze back on the senior NCO. They'd never actually spoken, but the guy was known to be a hard charger that clawed his way up the ranks. Dash preferred to keep to himself, and wasn't interested in big brass posturing from above. He squatted in this dust bowl for two reasons; he loved the killing, and he needed to support his younger brother. Dash could never get enough of the killing—the more gruesome, the better. That thrill that came along with making the enemy suffer. Why couldn't his superiors leave him alone to do his job? He didn't care about fellow asshole soldiers, and their noble standards. He especially didn't care for the posturing of senior officers.

Dash raised his brows as respectfully as possible as the

blowhard across the table flipped through a file.

"You have a brother? Correct?"

Stiffening, Dash nodded his head. "Uh. Yes, sir."

"Your brother lives in Centerville—in Utah."

"Sir, what is this about?" His palms began to sweat, and Dash wiped a hand over his thigh.

His Platoon Sergeant looked up, meeting Dash's worried stare with a calm countenance. "I'm sorry to inform you, your brother—Rudolph Hill—has passed away."

"Bullshit!"

Rudy was one of the toughest fuckers on the planet.

"Sit back down. At ease, soldier.'"

A wave of dizziness had Dash complying. He shook his head before resting it in his hands. When he finally glanced up, his gaze met cool scrutiny.

"How did he die?" Dash asked.

"I'm not at liberty—"

"How did he fucking die?"

"You're coming very close to—"

"Fuck you and this damn hellhole."

"Easy. I know you're upset. We'll grant personal leave."

"And I'll take it. Now tell me how Rudy died."

"He was killed… during a federal investigation."

Dash needed all the facts. What had his damn kid brother done?

Once the Platoon Sergeant dismissed him, Dash walked out into the warm sun and paused to lean on a prefab wall of a nondescript building. His baby brother was gone. They'd killed him, and Dash wanted to scream out the pain. Instead he sunk to the dirt. Dasher was supposed to protect his little reindeer brother. He hadn't protected him from Momma, and he'd failed again. He could avenge his brother's death. That wouldn't make it right, but Dash would find the dickhead responsible for his brother's death.

Looking around the muted military base, and then down at his dust-covered boots, Dash knew he was finished with this place. Not done with the killing, just done with the Ghan.

Five days later.
Layton, Utah.

Kat counted just three reporters. A significant improvement from the first couple of frenzied days back at her apartment. She flicked the blinds shut and walked over to her freezer to pull out a tub of chocolate ice cream and sliced frozen banana. Milkshake time. Next came the milk and chocolate syrup.

The story was headline news. Thanks to sneaky informants in law enforcement, local and national news stations now possessed detailed accounts of the serial killing drama. Kat had turned her phone off, only checking her email once before giving up. Local talk shows and international news stations had all invited her to sit on their fancy sofas and talk about the "Belsnickel Killer." They could all screw off.

Casey and Abby had been incredible—delivering bags of groceries, so Kat didn't have to face the journalist mongers. Except, she hated hiding from the world, and she wasn't the only one. According to Abby, the press had also camped out on Derek's doorstep. He was now known as the handsome sniper who took down a brutal serial killer. Kat suspected that Hollywood wanted a piece of him. Surfing her television channels hadn't lasted long. She'd scowled at the simpering women lounging on talk shows, and waxing on about Derek—how the gorgeous agent could rescue them any day of the week. Those beautiful, stupid-ass talk show hosts could all have him.

Kat blinked back the tears. She'd cried way too much over the last week. Cursing, Kat swapped the ice cream scoop over to her good hand. Her stitches pulled tight and had now begun to itch. Ignoring her lousy mood, she spooned healthy amounts of ice cream into the blender.

A knock on the door had her pausing. If this was another damn reporter… Kat stomped over to the door and checked the peephole, before swinging it open with a grin.

Casey pulled her into a long hug as Elana stepped past.

"Wait, I didn't know you knew each other?" Kat looked at the two women in surprise.

"We connected at the bar the other night while you were soaking up the alcohol. Close the door—a reporter asshole is galloping up the stairs."

Kat did as Elana asked, slamming the door shut, as the skinny man shouted her name.

Elana openly examined Kat's kitchen and living room, and Kat paused to gape at the willowy girl for the hundredth time. Only one word described Elana… stunning. Kat couldn't remember ever meeting anyone with such "out of this world" beauty. She could waltz onto a production set, and they'd beg to have her in their movie. There was more to Elana than just her incredible bone structure and thick blonde hair. The woman exuded intelligence and brash confidence. If Elana walked into a room, she owned it.

Her Muslim father was an internationally renowned architect and a supporter of women's rights. And her Wyoming mother was just as incredibly beautiful. An elegant farmer's daughter from Jackson Hole.

Kat liked Elana and wanted to get to know the direct woman with the jaded yet sparkling eyes.

"Your place has a rental feel." Elana fingered a vase. "But there are some pretty touches."

And there was that honesty that Kat loved.

"Sorry. I'm being rude."

"No, you're right. This apartment isn't exactly home. It's a transitional spot until I get my life back on track."

Elana nodded. "What are you making in the kitchen?"

"Arse and shit! The ice cream is melting. You guys want a wee milkshake?"

"I won't say no. How are you feeling, friend?" Casey climbed on the nearest barstool, and Elana walked up to the counter and leaned on her elbows.

Kat busied herself with the shakes. "Honestly? I feel like shite. Don't get me wrong; I'm glad my attacker is no longer a threat to me or anyone else. I just... hell. I miss Derek. I feel like I've traveled back in time to our first breakup."

The other women said nothing as she blended the chocolate concoction. Kat pulled two more glass mugs from the freezer and carefully poured the girls and herself a generous helping. Once they'd settled in with wide straws, Casey shot Kat a sympathetic look.

"Would it help to know that Derek is a complete wreck?"

"You've seen him?"

"He came over yesterday and sat on my couch like a grumpy gargoyle. I had work to do and tapped away on my laptop while he stared at the wall for two hours."

Kat snorted. "He blames himself for any bad luck that may have come my way. Hell, if I stub my toe, I'm sure he'll find a way to make it his fault."

"Maybe you should try harder," Elana said, licking ice cream off her thumb.

Casey and Kat gaped at Elana's bluntness as she licked another finger.

"What? You make good milkshakes."

"I need to 'try' harder?" Kat placed her glass on the counter.

"Do you want to be with Derek?"

"I don't know."

"Well, do you love him?"

"Of course, I love him."

"Then what's the problem? It won't be easy. Do you think you're the only couple to face difficulties? Relationships are hard work, especially if you're starting over together."

Kat gnawed on her bottom lip, considering Elana's words. "What if he doesn't love me anymore? I get that he 'loves' me as a person. That doesn't mean he's in love with me—all the butterflies and 'stars in your eyes' kind of stuff."

"There's only one way to find out, ask him."

Elana may be too direct for even Kat, who internally rejected that suggestion. Kat shook her head, and Elana sighed.

"No offense, honey, but hiding in this small apartment isn't going to get you answers. I know all about building barriers. You and I both have walls—we've just erected them under different circumstances."

"Derek has walls too," Kat stated defensively.

"Of course, he does. You can't expect a man who's gone through as much as he has not to have fortification." Elana scraped at the bottom of her glass with her straw. "Stop hiding behind a screen. I do the opposite—I run, and refuse to settle for anyone or anything. Is that a healthy flaw? No, but I own it."

"Is that why you and Atlas… you know."

"Me and Atlas what? We're just close friends."

"You don't find him attractive?"

"He's darn cute, but way too laid back for me. I want someone who has their shit together."

"You mean like a hefty 401K."

"No. Just… he's so happy-go-lucky and sweet. He's too sweet."

"Aye, he's really sweet. So sweet that I heard he saved your life in Morocco."

"He did. Numerous times. He's just too young." Elana looked perturbed.

"Is Atlas younger than you?" Casey asked in confusion.

"No—he's two years older than me."

Casey rolled her eyes. "You're a crazy girl."

"I'm just saying," Kat persisted. "I think there's a lot more to Atlas than he reveals to the world. I heard from Lizzy that he tried out for the Olympics as a snowboarder before he joined the military. He's also extremely loyal and protective of his teammates."

"How about another round of milkshakes?" Elana said, changing the subject. "This time you'll show me how to make them."

Chapter Nineteen

Three weeks later.

His shoulder screamed in pain, and Slater stretched his neck before adjusting his stance. He surveyed the deck of the newly built facility, feeling proud of what he'd accomplished so far. Agents, top dogs, and dignitaries were gathered in small groups in the clubhouse and on its extensive lawn. The catering company did a great job serving up platters of roasted meats and salads to the masses. Opening day had finally arrived, and now a different form of hard work lay before him.

He'd already selected a team for his training division. Black ops men he'd worked with in the past and a couple of agents with former military training. They wouldn't take on the first round of students until his newly elected team was up to standard.

Another senator walked up to Slater and shook his hand. That's all he'd done all day, schmooze with the swaggering politicians. Aside from Elliot who'd popped in to see the facility. The two men had mended their fences, and Elliot seemed to be in a better place emotionally. Slater almost swayed from exhaustion. He'd practically lived onsite for the past month, and his body felt the harsh effects from lack of sleep and endless manual labor. Slater's bed called his name—someone else also called his name, haunting his dreams and occasional nightmares.

Silky black hair, and serious indigo eyes. Pretty lips pressed to his chest... Slater could no longer stay away from Kat. He wasn't heading to his bed tonight; he was heading to hers. He couldn't get through four weeks without her. Slater huffed out a breath and turned to check the ice buckets at the bar.

"Congratulations." The husky voice from behind had him slowly turning.

Blinking against the mirage, Slater took a step back. "Angel?"

A navy fitted dress with ivory lace trim on the cap sleeves and the neckline drew his attention. Three pretty, pearl-colored buttons decorated the sleeves and the conservative, yet shapely pin-up look had his mouth watering.

"How did you find this place, or get clearance? If I knew you wanted to come, I would've made a plan."

Kat smiled. "I have friends in high places."

"Ah. Director Sullivan."

"He left his business card in my hospital room. Sullivan owed me."

Slater laughed and shook his head.

Kat slowly scanned the grounds. "The facility looks great. I guess all the ninja stuff is tucked away in these hills?"

"It sure is. We have seven sites spread across the mountain, built to look like war zones or potential ambush points." Slater pointed to the right and Kat leaned towards him. Her familiar scent made his chest tighten. "There's also a command and control center a mile up the road. Multi-story training structures further up the mountain. Two additional training villages. There is an explosives range a few miles away, and we have two small arm ranges at the back of the clubhouse."

As if on cue, two gunshots broke the silence and Kat jerked in surprise. "That's loud!"

"Sniper rifle. If you stand out back, you'll need hearing protection. Wait till you hear the helicopter 134 mini-gun. We set it up out back. 2400 bullets per minute."

"And you need that, why?"

"I don't, but some senior cowboys in the bureau thought it would be a nifty attraction for opening day. It's on their dime." Slater leaned closer. "They're charging those politician pricks 50k to fire the damn thing for five seconds."

Kat snorted. "Boys and their wee toys."

Slater traced a finger over her wrist, and she turned to face him. She stood so close, and he couldn't move away.

"I was coming to you—tonight."

The small frown creasing her brow, indicated that she didn't believe him. A young female walked up, and Slater inwardly groaned. The woman was beautiful—nothing compared to Kat. The up and coming actress was the wife of an elderly local mayor, and she had a wandering eye.

"Mr. Banez, I've heard so much about you. We haven't had a chance to talk." She laid her manicured nails on his forearm, and Slater resisted the urge to shake her off.

"Kathleen Flynn. Nice to meet you." Kat thrust her hand in between them, and the actress stepped back.

"Sabrina Winchester."

The way she eyed Kat's light scar had Slater gritting his teeth. Another man walked up to their small circle with a predatory stare. Slater recognized the man as a well-known international journalist and talk show guru who would run a story on the facility. The light in his eyes unsettled Slater who wanted to shield Kat from the vulture.

"This is a surprise. Kathleen Flynn and Derek Banez—together in the same room. Your story has the makings of a Hollywood blockbuster."

"We're not interested." Slater wanted to punch the well-respected host in the nose.

"Fair enough. Perhaps you'd reconsider after the release of Miss Flynn's book. It would help her ratings."

"My book release has been canceled."

Slater jerked around. "What? Why?"

"I'll publish it one day. But I'm not ready. It's still too raw." She reached over to squeeze his hand.

"That's a pity, Miss Flynn. Your story is a gripping one. Imagine the two of you in front of the cameras. A powerful war hero sitting beside his broken and scarred princess. The woman he saved from the clutches of an infamous serial killer. The Ted Bundy hoopla has nothing on this. Use the scar to secure your future."

Temper flaring, Slater stepped forward. "I'm about to rip your head off."

"Is that what you said to Rudolph Hill? Mr. Banez, I like your passion."

"Let's get something straight… Kathleen is anything but broken. She's the powerful hero who stopped a killer, not me. And if you mention her scar again, I'll pound you into the ground."

Kat's hand pulled on Derek's wrist. "It's okay. I take no offense." She turned to the journalist. "Mr…?"

"Fred Dane," he replied, obviously offended that she didn't know his name.

"Mr. Dane. This scar defines me, but not in the way you'd like to think. I hated staring at my reflection. In fact, after my first surgery, I draped a cloth over my bathroom mirror where it remained for months."

Slater frowned at her words, as the other two members of their sour group shifted uncomfortably.

Kat continued. "As the months passed, my scar faded, but I still dreamed of being whole again, with an unblemished face. And you're right, I was broken. And then suddenly... I wasn't. This scar and that attack left me in pieces. I exploded from the inside out—mentally, and spiritually. I've put myself back together again, and the last month helped greatly in my healing process." Kat turned to Slater and held his attention.

"I'm grateful for this scar, because it made me into a better person. I'm stronger, and more resilient, and I like the new me. I'm a little darker and I love that depth and unique perspective that comes from living through hell. And Derry, I love the way you look at me. You see my courage, and who I am on the inside. I now see what you see, and I thank you for that."

Ignoring the two now gaping interlopers, and not bothering with polite conversation, Slater gripped Kat's arm, and led her away.

"I didn't mean to climb on my soapbox."

"No, Kat. That was amazing and—"

"You have work to do, and I'm keeping you from mingling with your guests."

"The only guest I care about is you."

Kat pulled in a breath and grabbed his hand. "I've used the last few weeks to figure out my direction, and how we fit into each other's lives. I'm even seeing a therapist."

Derek pulled away. "I'm so proud of you, angel. You deserve to be happy and whole, and we've already had this conversation. I'm not good for you."

"Yet you still planned on seeing me later tonight?"

She had him there. "I needed to hold you. To touch this incredible skin."

"So... like a one-night stand?" Kat stepped back into his space.

"You and I have never been a one-night anything."

"Because we have this unbreakable link." Kat tangled her fingers in his. "How about we do things your way? Let's have that one-night stand."

"Are you crazy?"

She ran a finger down his chest. "We both need to release steam. One night of raw and animalistic sex and we'll fuck each other till we collapse. Work our way out of each other's system," Kat finished breathlessly.

Her vulgar words made him instantly hard, and Slater pulled her down the passage to an unused back office where they had privacy. This new Kat held a sexy confidence that confused his already love-befuddled brain.

"Is that what you want?" Slater shut the door. "And after that? What happens tomorrow?"

"No tomorrow. Just stroking and sucking and licking. Feeling you thrust—"

"Shit, Kat." He pushed her against the wall.

"We love on each other, until we can't stand."

Slater groaned. "I need to play host to the peacocks in the next room."

"I can wait all day."

That made one of them. Slater stroked her jaw and tasted her red lips that parted under his eager exploration. Savoring the growing heat, Slater tangled his tongue with hers, and pulled her hips to his. Finally, he pulled away.

"God, I want you so badly. Help yourself to a drink and find a cool place to sit."

Kat hummed her agreement as she wiped red lipstick from his lips with her thumb.

Slater turned to leave, and her whispered words stopped him. "I just shoved my panties in your right pocket." He nearly went cross-eyed, and almost ran back to the clubhouse before he stripped her naked and imprisoned her against the wall.

◊ ◊ ◊

That was the boldest move she'd ever made. Kat couldn't believe she'd mustered up the courage to seduce Derek in broad daylight. It had to be Elana's influence. She'd planned the "panty" move for weeks and now felt like a wicked seductress. Kat had always been a passive partner to Derek's outgoing and sometimes intense personality. Retreat and surrender weren't a winning combination. Their relationship was worth fighting for, and by God, she'd fight him every inch of the way, both in and out of the bedroom. So what if seducing Derek was playing dirty.

Kat started out as Slater's saintly and hardworking little girlfriend, but she was no longer that kid. She was now a grown-ass woman with wants and needs. And, Kat sure didn't need some vanilla-ass boyfriend.

She wanted Derek, a dangerous soldier with a dark past, another scarred human who knew pain, a tortured soul who reached out to her whenever she was near and who soothed her hurts before his own. Their dark pasts held each other up. Kat needed Derek by her side and wouldn't accept anything less.

By the time he locked up, it was late. Kat didn't care as she stared at Slater with hunger. They left her car and took his truck. Ten minutes later, they turned away from the property and drove along a dimly lit sand road.

"We're in the middle of nowhere." Derek's voice came out as almost a growl. He reached over and ran fingers over her exposed knee. "I've been touching your lacy bits in my pocket all night. Are you really not wearing any panties?"

Kat widened her legs, and her dress climbed up her pale thighs. "See for yourself."

"Oh, my hell." Derek stretched out his hand and slid it up her thigh. Fingertips touched damp folds, and Kat bucked in her seat.

"I can't wait. Hang-on." Derek spotted a small side road, pulled the truck onto the rough path and slammed to a stop. With swift moves, he unclipped his belt, then hers. Next, his hand slipped back beneath her dress. This time his thumb stroked and circled her clit, and Kat watched him, moaning at the erotic sight. Muscles in his forearm twitched as he rolled his hand, seeking better access.

"Raise your feet, put a foot on the dash."

Kat slipped off her shoes and did as he ordered, lifting herself into a better position, and eliciting a growl from Derek. He twisted a leg towards him. Kat slid into an awkward slouch against the passenger door, but she didn't care. Legs splayed, she gasped as he leaned in. Feeling his tongue licking her folds felt like heaven. A thumb slipped inside, and Derek began to suck. Her head slammed back into something sharp, and her hands grasped for traction. Kat ignored the discomfort, as he pulled her closer and shoved his tongue in deep.

"Don't... don't stop. Oh... my. Oh, shit."

Masterful swirls had her wanting to scream his name. Fingers replaced his thumb, and with one firm stroke, Kat came apart in the passenger seat of his truck.

Derek pulled her back up and watched her with glistening eyes. "I've never been this hard before. I'll be inside you all night."

"I want that."

"Let's get home."

They drove in silence. Derek pulled into his driveway and came around to her door. Lifting her down carefully, he led them inside. The passage was as far as they got.

"Dress—off—now."

She complied, watching him strip. A naked Derek was a sight to behold, and Kat barely had time to admire his hard physique before he raised her in his arms and positioned himself at her entrance. "What were the words you used? Animalistic? Raw? You want this?"

"All of it."

With one powerful thrust, he was fully impaled. Kat hooked her legs around his waist and held on. The next surge slammed her against the wall. Kat clenched around his cock, as her nails dug into his shoulder. He pulled out and rammed back in, and she bit his neck, revelling in the salty taste of his skin. He smelled like gunpowder and raw male.

Derek held her in place, and headed for his small dining table. Placing her on the edge, he pulled in and out with powerful strokes. Kat gripped the edge of the table as it shook under their wanton need.

"No tomorrow." Buried deep, he stroked her cheek.

"No tomorrow." Kat echoed his whispered words before wrapping her arms around his neck. He began to move again, and she closed her eyes, feeling every sensation. His strong hands gripping her hips, and his breath in her ear. The stubble against her cheek. Every part of him touched her, and she'd missed this so desperately. She felt him lose control, and they fell into an intimate and violent rhythm. Too soon, she spun into ecstacy, crying her release. Derek followed, calling her name.

◊ ◊ ◊

Slater's phone buzzed on the bedside table, and he rolled away, ignoring the call. A minute later, and it rang again. Slater hadn't slept this heavily in years and battled to surface. He reached for Kat, but all he found were empty sheets. Slater cracked open an eye. A piece of paper sat on her pillow, and Slater reached over to grab it.

Called an Uber. Tomorrow came.
Kat.

What the hell?

Slater sat up and rubbed his face. What time was it, and what time had she left? Was she still here? Perhaps he could catch her.

Slater stumbled from bed and groaned. Thanks to old war injuries, bones protested and clicked into place. His shoulder felt stiff—he'd held a smoking hot woman in his arms for most of the night.

He checked the front rooms and almost opened his front door before he caught himself. Traumatizing the neighbors with his buck-naked bits wasn't the best idea. Checking through a window, he figured she'd left.

Slater walked to his living room, noting the blanket laying on the floor. He couldn't help grinning. After the table, they'd moved to the floor where he'd just held her while they'd dozed. Later they'd mauled each other in the shower. Finally falling into bed, they'd slept for a few hours before she'd roused him with her mouth around his cock. They'd taken their time, playing and exploring each other's bodies. Then he'd made slow love to her.

After they'd collapsed into an exhausted tangle, he'd told her how much he loved her. She hadn't said anything in return, just snuggled in close and pressed a kiss to his chest.

And now she was gone? What did that mean?

Making his way back to the bedroom, Slater picked up his phone and called Kat's number. No answer—she was probably sleeping. Sighing, he sat at the end of the bed and called Donnie—who'd been lighting up his phone.

"Are you only just waking up now? It's 0900."

"Screw off; I had that facility opening shebang yesterday."

"Oh, yeah. How did it go?" Donnie asked.

"Long and drawn out. I need to start training agents and earning my keep."

"Nice, don't forget the barbecue tomorrow—at Max and Abby's. The entire tribe will be there, and then some."

Slater almost forgot. "I'll check what I'll need to bring. What's up? Why the urgent phone calls?"

"You know me; I can't resist digging. I found out a little more about Rudolph Hill's background. He was one fucked up kid."

Slater rolled his shoulder. "Fletcher mentioned that he might have killed his mother in Kansas. They're re-examining her death and have exhumed the body. She died in a house fire, but there are signs of antemortem torture. It's a really small town miles away from anywhere. I think the closest town is Haysville, so they didn't have the resources to thoroughly investigate her death."

"Yeah. According to the Swanford community, Gretchen Hill was one kooky bird who was obsessed with Christmas paraphernalia. She'd hang Santas and reindeer all around her property—no matter what time of year. She even had a weird Santa scarecrow that terrified the local kids in the neighborhood."

"That explains her kids' names. Rudolph and Dasher."

"Exactly. Mrs. Hill kept to herself and carried a shotgun wherever she went. She once threatened to shoot another farmer's horse because it defecated on her driveway. The local Swanford police arrested her twice. Once for shoving another woman in the post office and once for spitting in the local sheriff's face."

"Sounds delightful." Slater yawned and stood.

"Bro, I just read a whole load of statements from their town."

"Are you hacking databases you shouldn't be?" Slater opened a drawer and pulled out a pair of boxer shorts.

Donnie ignored the joking accusation. "Rudolph was considered the gentler of the two brothers. Dasher, on the other hand…"

"Was the town bully?"

"More like the town psycho. Both boys moved away after their mother died, and disappeared into thin air. According to local police, Dasher is the prime suspect in the rape and murder of three fellow schoolgirls. Crimes committed eight years ago— even before their mother's death. And they're not the only ones looking for him. Layton Police in Utah are seeking Dasher for questioning over the disappearance of a former girlfriend. They're waiting on solid evidence. They recently recovered the remains—she's been missing for four years."

"Wait, let me confirm. You're talking about Dasher—not Rudolph?" Slater asked.

"Yeah. Dasher Hill. Turns out both brothers have been killing for years. Victims turning up everywhere. They're linking numerous missing women to Dasher as well as Rudolph."

"Where is he now? Wasn't he on deployment?"

"Personal leave. Dasher left Bagram six days ago and flew into

Atlanta. Wasn't listed on any connecting flights from Atlanta."
Donnie sounded concerned.

"Why Atlanta, and not Utah?"

"Not sure. He's going to be a problem. Your agency is now getting involved. Watch your six, brother."

Not liking the news, Slater tried to call Kat's phone again, and it went to voicemail. He was heading her way. Slater tossed the phone on the bed, and an incoming message from Kat had him picking it back up.

I'm boarding a flight to San Francisco. Last minute possible consulting job. Be back tomorrow morning. If you want to talk, let me know.

Slater didn't like her out of his sight, but her being on an unplanned trip would keep her out of harm's way.

Do you know the client? Call me when you get there. I need to know you're safe.

Her reply made him smile.

Yes. She's a regular customer. You're a wee worry-wort. Thanks for letting me mount Excalibur last night. It was a magical joy ride.

Love for his woman slammed through Slater. His woman. That's who she'd always been. They were welded together for all eternity. The universe knew that unbreakable truth, so why were they both fighting their fate? Slater jumped in the shower. The edgy feeling grew as the day wore on, and he called Fletcher who confirmed that they were forming a task force. Dasher's local army buddy had a home in Atlanta, and they thought he might be staying in the city for a few days. The sooner he was caught, the better.

Chapter Twenty

Slater walked into the multi-floored mountain home and made his way to the kitchen.

Abby greeted him with a hug and helped him to unload the bags of salad supplies and chips he'd brought. He looked around the busy living area, spotting Charlie on the sofa with Willow. Lizzy sat on a bar stool loading up a tortilla chip with a hummus-looking dip.

"Where are Gabe and Valentino?"

"At a school friend's birthday party in Salt Lake. I'm picking them up later," Lizzy said between bites. "You wanna help set-up?"

"Because you're doing an excellent job helping—eating all the guests' food."

She stuck out her tongue and shoveled in another chip. "I am a guest, and I haven't had breakfast. It's already eleven."

Slater arm-hugged the teeny blonde and made his way out back to greet the rest of his teammates. The view from the raised and newly built deck was impressive. The large home sat nestled in the foothills of a small mountain. Hiking paths led away from the back yard into the woods.

Johnny and Max stood below, cleaning the grill, and Slater

walked over. Max balanced Lucy in his arms as he unpacked meat from a cooler. She looked so much like Max, with his same hair color and ghostly eyes, that it blew Slater's mind. The resemblance grew every time he saw her.

"Swater!" She held out her arms, and Max transferred the little tyke in a blue unicorn dress to Slater.

He blew raspberries in her neck, and she broke out into giggles. As Lucy fingered his collar, Slater surveyed the yard.

"Shoot, buddy. You've done a lot of work."

Slater supposed Max had the means. His family and extended family owned a spread of land in Colorado. Max had sold his generous acreage and instead bought the place in Utah.

"It's getting there." Max surveyed the landscaped layout, and Slater did the same.

Max had built the raised deck above stacked boulders. Instead of getting rid of the indigenous layout, they'd used natural elements. Different levels and steps divided up the space. A grassy area encircled a pool and a massive, circular, stone bench. Lavender bushes and heat-loving plants dotted the vast yard and rockery, and shrubbery covered the remaining area.

"Abby knows her flora. She's the one with the green thumb, I just carved out the bare bones and brought in a landscaping team."

"Could you have craned in any more Thor-type rocks, you Finnish miscreant?"

"Debatable." Max's light eyes sparkled. "They were just lying around this neck of the woods."

"Uh-huh. Where's your sauna—your slice of Finland?" Slater asked.

"Don't start. We are planning on building a hot tub near the games room." Max pointed to the sliding doors situated on the ground level leading into the house.

"Of course you are. Love this view." Slater glanced out at the impressive hillside and adjacent canyon. "Can I just bunk at your place permanently?"

"Why don't you buy a home this end?"

"'Cause I'm not loaded with the moola. Who are those dudes?" Slater nodded at the two couples walking down the steps.

"Gary Cox and Tyler Wood and their wives. Part of a Delta team that we worked with on the last deployment. A good bunch of lads."

Slater's phone buzzed in his pocket. Kat's text message had him relaxing. She was safe, and her plane had just landed in Salt Lake.

Lucy grabbed for the phone and Slater handed it over. "Kat says she's heading over."

Johnny raised his brows. "So you guys are back together?"

"I don't know, man. There's so much history—we're wading through mud."

"If you love her, then it's all worth it. Look at Lizzy and me. I screwed things up with her when we first 'dated.' We got through it, and she's the best thing that's ever happened to me. She's my goddamn life."

"Language." Max nodded at Lucy.

Johnny grimaced. "Sorry, man."

Lucy pointed at the sparkling pool, and Slater carried her over. She wriggled to get down, and he ignored her struggles. "I'm guessing you ain't going in without your armbands or life jacket. Sorry, little bug."

"Fishy. Mommy."

"Yes, mommy is a fish." Slater had seen Abby swimming her

laps, and she swam like an Olympic athlete.

Atlas loped down the stairs and walked over to greet the guys, and Elana followed him out to the yard.

Their matching blond heads shone in the bright sunlight, and Slater noted what a beautiful couple they made—even if they were just "friends." Both tall, tanned and good-looking. When Donnie walked onto the deck, Slater handed Lucy over to Elana. "Can you watch her for a second? I need to talk to Donnie."

"And what makes you think I know anything about babies! Kids aren't my thing."

"She's almost a toddler. You'll be fine."

Ignoring Elana's horrified expression, Slater raced up the stairs. "Any new developments?"

Donnie leaned his forearms on the wooden railing. "You know about the impending raid on the Atlanta home?"

"Yeah. Fletcher called me earlier. They've traced Dasher Hill's cell phone to that area."

"Well, then we're on the same page. There's talk of his involvement in more deaths in his home town. This is big."

Slater nodded. "The brothers killed together as kids, starting with their mother."

"I think Dasher began way before that."

There were some evil shitheads in the world. Slater should know... he'd eliminated a good number in his time. Stretching his shoulder, he pulled out his phone and called Kat. She was ten minutes out. The lawn below filled up with milling guests. Feeling restless, he went inside to see how he could help.

◊ ◊ ◊

Kat ignored her nerves as she made her way to the kitchen. She'd be laying it all out on the table today. Almost begging Derek to take a chance on their relationship, and she'd be doing it at his former team leader's home. She wasn't leaving without a final answer. After greeting some of her friends, Kat grabbed a glass of wine and walked out into the back yard. Thankful that she'd worn casual jeans and a tank top for the flight, Kat glanced around at the summery atmosphere, taking in the smell of grilled steak and green pine forest. Abby crouched next to the pool, securing a life vest to Lucy. Charlie sat under the trees with her pram. Nearby, Johnny stood behind his wife, his arm wrapped around Lizzy's shoulders, as their sweet dog lay at her feet. The rest of the men stood in a huddle around the grill.

There were a few strangers that Kat hadn't met. Some big burly men and elegant-looking women. Not seeing Derek, she smiled politely as she made her way over to Charlie and the snack table.

"How's little Willow?"

"Ornery." Charlie dangled a pacifier in the kid's face. "I'll head inside and put her down. She cried all night. Poor Donnie insisted on staying up with her. He must've walked a hole in the carpet trying to get her to settle."

"I'll head in with you. I think I need to piddle." Looking thoughtful, Lizzy jiggled her hips. "Yip, I need to pee. And I'll be picking up the kids soon."

Kat couldn't help laughing. "What the hell was that?"

"What?"

"That hip shaking move?"

"That's her bladder capacity measurement tool." Johnny's eyes sparkled with humor. "Lizbug does it in bed at night. Jiggles her ass and decides whether it's worthy of a trip to the bathroom."

"What? It works. If you feel the tickle, you need to piddle."

Lizzy was definitely a new bestie. Kat loved the quirky firecracker who bent down and swept up her little spaniel. Then she planted a kiss on Johnny's lips.

"Be careful driving, baby. Do you want me to come along?"

Lizzy rolled her eyes. "What am I? Like five? I'll be back in thirty."

After the women had left, Johnny turned to Kat. "I think Slater has spotted you." He pointed to the deck.

Sure enough, Derek headed towards them with laser focus.

"I'll leave you two alone. Whatever happens, sort out your mess—the one preventing you from staying together or living apart. You both deserve happiness."

Kat smiled at the muscular giant. "I want what you have with Lizzy."

"Then take it." He raised his beer and walked to the grill.

"Are you having fun? Sorry, I helped Max carry fold-out tables from the basement." Derek looked robust and very male in his jeans, light gray t-shirt, and a layered, dark gray, button-up shirt.

"I am having fun, surrounded by friends."

Derek slid up and ran a hand over her waist. "Am I your friend?"

Kat stared into his warm eyes, and her mouth turned up. "You're my everything."

Ignoring the surprised look, she stood on her toes and pressed a soft kiss to his firm lips. Strong fingers cupped her jaw as he angled the kiss, his tongue slipped into her welcoming mouth, and Kat gripped the front of his shirt. He smelled like laundry detergent and cedar, his scent reminding her of the night before... rolling in his sheets and feeling those firm hands running over her naked skin.

Derek's lips migrated to her cheek and kissed her scar.

"You're my everything too. I love you so damn much."

"Then let's do this, and I'll promise to look after that brawny heart." Kat placed a hand on his chest. "This time it's for today, tomorrow and forever. We've both lived through hell, and deserve our slice of heaven."

"Angel-pie." Derek gazed at her with such warmth. "I'll spend my life making you happy—if you can deal with my revised over-communication strategy and my ass sticking to you like glue. You'll be sick of my face."

"Never." Kat smiled and traced his jaw. "It's the sexiest and kindest face on the planet."

"Erm. Sorry to interrupt. Brother, we need more ice and soft drinks. The MIT4 boys are swinging by later. Can you run over to Walmart with me? I'll need extra hands."

Derek growled at the sound of Donnie's voice, but he didn't let go of Kat's face. Thumbs stroked the corner of her lips. "God, I love you."

"I love you too."

Donnie groaned, and Derek laughed. "We're going, dickhead." He kissed Kat's forehead. "I'll see you in five."

Once he'd gone five steps, he turned and yelled at the crowd. "Kathleen Flynn is the love of my freaking life and is now officially my girlfriend!"

Their friends whooped, and she shook her head, her wide grin reflecting her joy. "You're a wee idiot."

"But I'm your wee idiot." Derek held his hand to his heart as he retreated up the path.

◊ ◊ ◊

The Walmart lines took too long. It was a Saturday, and everybody, including their aunties and grandmothers, littered the aisles. Once they'd loaded the six bags of ice and five packs of soft drinks, and were back in the truck, Slater answered the call from Fletcher.

"Have you found Dasher Hill?"

"No. The only thing we recovered at the scene was his U.S. phone."

"So he could be anywhere. And I killed his brother."

Fletcher agreed and Slater's neck prickled with dread. Fletcher mentioned their next steps, and after Slater hung up, he exchanged a worried glance with Donnie.

"You and Kat need an assigned protection detail, at least until they've caught this unstable asshole."

"Already handled. Fletcher is arranging the logistics. Thank God she's with the rest of the team."

They drove in silence. Once they'd arrived back at Max's place, Slater would whisk her off to a controllable location.

They pulled into the drive, and both men carried in the first load. The house sat quiet, and Charlie waved a hand in greeting as she ascended the stairs to the bedrooms. Slater ran back out and pulled a bag of ice from the vehicle to hand over to Donnie, who could schlep in the rest of the soft drinks. Slater was heading out to the back yard to join Kat. Although she was safe and surrounded by capable men, he needed her with him. His phone buzzed with an incoming call. *Unknown number.*

Slater didn't usually answer random calls but knew it could be one of the new agents on his

team. Still, he debated sending it to voicemail. He pressed the answer button.

"Derek Banez." The calm voice sounded unfamiliar.

"Who is this?"

"You killed my brother."

Dasher Hill.

The bag of ice whacked against Slater's leg as he pivoted on the paved driveway.

"Now, your woman will die."

Dropping the ice and his phone, Slater ignored Donnie's curse from behind, and chose the shortest route to the back yard, heading for the side lane he'd used earlier. The connecting door sat open, and he barged through, and down the cobbled steps.

Slater barreled around the corner of the home and scanned the yard. Kat stood on the opposite end, chatting to Johnny. Slater's world slowed as he opened his mouth to yell her name.

He was too late. Kat's head jerked. A millisecond later, the report from the gunshot ricocheted through the hills. Kat fell, her body slamming into the concrete bench. Slater's brain stuttered, then went berserk as he roared out his pain. His legs wouldn't move, but he forced himself forward as Johnny threw himself onto Kat. The world didn't just slow; it flashed by in snapshots of chaos. More gunshots echoed and screams filled the air.

Max raced by, as a flowerpot exploded to Slater's right. A bullet whizzed past, almost grazing Slater's cheek. Someone ripped him backward and slammed him to the floor. Air whooshed from his lungs as he struggled to stay focused on Kat's still form.

"That's what he wants!" Donnie's face loomed in Slater's blurring vision. "Dasher Hill wants you! Stay down."

Hill could have him. Slater's life was over when he'd seen Kat fall under the sniper's bullet. Tears ran as he mouthed her name, trying to elbow Donnie in the face. Glass panes shattered as bullets peppered the back of the cabin.

"I won't let you kill yourself. Help me save my wife and baby! They're alone in the house."

Slater shook his head to clear it. Was this another nightmare? Please, God, let him wake in his bed and find his Kat curled into his side.

Chapter Twenty-One

Max covered the salads with foil and threw away a couple of used plastic cups. He glanced up when he heard his daughter's happy shout from the pool. Lucy was cradled in her mom's arms in the shallow end as Abby bobbed in the water. God, he had a sexy wife. Her hair was piled on top of her head in a loose up-do. Wet tendrils clung to her face, and that look in her eyes as she gazed at their daughter... pure love. Abby looked at Max the same way—like he could wield a hammer and move mountains. Slater was right—technically, Max had moved whole boulders into their yard, and so what if he'd used a crane. Max grinned at the thought. He'd do it a thousand times over for her. His wife loved pottering in the garden, just as much as she enjoyed teaching art students in their art studio.

He'd married a serene and gentle celestial Goddess, and they had two beautiful children. Life was pretty fucking perfect, and Max hated leaving them when he faced deployments. Every moment together was a gift to be cherished.

Max bent over to pick up a plastic wrapper when he heard the first rifle shot. Disbelief anchored him to the spot for a split second. He took off running, registering Slater's guttural cries, as more shots echoed through the valley.

Abby stood centered in the rectangular pool. Eyes wide, with frozen horror, she clung to their daughter. They made an easy and attractive target through a sniper's scope and Max pushed harder into his already all-out sprint.

Max shouted at his wife. "Get to the far right!"

Low rockery with a small waterfall lay in that corner. Max thanked his lucky stars, that he'd gone with real rocks and not faux shotcrete when he designed the landscaped area surrounding the pool. Abby pushed sideways just as a bullet sliced the water, an inch away from her shoulder. Paved cement exploded on the far side of the pool and Max executed a shallow dive, as Abby swam to the deep end, all while sheltering Lucy. He caught up to them in two powerful strokes and covered them with his body as he corralled them to shelter.

The cover wasn't ideal—too low—but if Max could press them to the corner, under the pool rim and obscuring rockery, the Sniper wouldn't have a clear enough shot.

Lucy began to cry. "Oweee!"

Her little head sat just above water level, and her parents' bodies sandwiched her, as they crouched.

"Oweee, dadda!"

Yeah, he was smashing her against Abby, but he had no choice. "Hold on, little Lulu." Max looked into Abby's terrified green eyes.

"Tell me you weren't shot." He didn't see any evidence, but he wasn't taking chances.

"I… I don't think so," Abby replied.

A bullet slammed into the rocks just above their heads, chipping away a whole chunk. Max swore, then yelled at his team.

"Alpha Two! Juliet Two! Delta Two! Sierra Two! Location and fucking status?"

Nothing.

"Someone fucking answer me!"

Donnie replied from near the deck. "Juliet and Alpha are down. Delta and Sierra are clear to engage." Donnie's reply had Max torn between relief and alarm. Johnny and Atlas had been shot? How badly were they injured? And Slater had just watched Kat fall. Would he be stable enough to assist Donnie in neutralizing this sniper bastard? The rest of the team were either injured or pinned down, and they all needed Slater's skillset. The sniper sat way too far up the hill to hear their shouted conversation or Max's orders.

"Delta, engage and don't stop until he's taken his last fucking breath! Use the Scorpion. The keys are hanging by the front door. You know where my weapons are."

"Copy that!" Donnie yelled.

Max owned a Scorpion MK1—an off-road beast. And as per a MIT2 pact, all the men on the team had access to their respective members' gun vaults. The safe combination was a mutually agreed upon code. Now it was a waiting game while his men hunted.

A volley of bullets slammed into the rockery. Abby screamed and Max sheltered them with as much of his body mass as he could, but he couldn't save his own hide, and a bullet ate through the rock edge and sliced through a muscled shoulder. White hot pain shot down Max's arm, and he roared, struggling to hold on.

Abby's sobs sounded like they came from a distance. "No... baby. Oh, please no."

Pulling in steady breaths, Max tried to reassure her. "Just... a flesh... wound."

The surrounding water turned crimson as his blood ran down his chest in a steady stream.

"Max. Please don't do this. Stay and protect our baby. Let me make a run for it, without my body taking up all this space, you'll both be safe—"

"Don't even think it," he said through gritted teeth. "Promise me, if I pass out or get shot again, you'll leave me to sink. Don't expose yourself and our baby. You stay where you are and protect Lulu. Promise me."

"Max... no."

"Promise me, that you'll live. Our child will live."

Abby nodded through the tears.

Ignoring his throbbing arm, Max drew her to him and tried to nestle her in the corner as best he could.

◊ ◊ ◊

Slater—a super soldier—was no match for Donnie's martial art skills. The analyst made brief work of wrestling Slater into the sliding door that led to the games room. Then, he pinned Slater to the wall. "Get your head on straight."

"Kat..." Grief expanded with every breath.

"I know, buddy. I'm so fucking sorry. Jesus."

"I couldn't... save her."

"None of us could. Listen to me. Johnny is with her and he'll look after her... either way."

Slater couldn't draw a breath, and dropped to his haunches as gaping sobs took over.

"Listen to me. You go out there, and he'll execute you. We eliminate him—not the other way around. I need to find my wife and baby." Donnie's voice broke on the last word. "Help me. We find them and then we go hunting. Help me, dammit."

"Retribution," Slater said in a wooden voice, tasting salty tears on his lips.

"Yeah. Retri-fucking-bution."

Slater had no other choice. Dasher Hill wouldn't leave his sniper's nest until he'd eliminated everyone Slater cared about. Another shot rang out, jerking Slater from the shocked haze, and he followed Donnie up the stairs to the first floor as his buddy called Charlie's name.

"Donnie? Oh, thank God." Charlie stood up from behind the solid granite counter and Donnie rushed towards her.

"Get back down!"

Clutching Willow, she did as he ordered. Her phone lay beside her. "I called 911. They're aware there's an active shooter. I told them which direction they should approach from—just from what I've guessed."

Charlie sounded surprisingly steady. Probably from their time in Morocco. Donnie mentioned numerous gunfights and car chases.

"The basement is the safest place in this house. No windows, solid brick walls built below ground level."

"You've been in Max's basement?" Charlie asked.

"It's a nice basement. Prepper-type shelves loaded with supplies. The shooter can't see you up here, but we'd worry about stray bullets. And there's still a chance you might get shot if you leave from the front."

"I was almost hit when he first started shooting. I came downstairs to fetch Willow's bottle. I left her... alone for a second. She could've been shot." Now Charlie's expression reflected the abject horror that they all felt.

Donnie's hand shook as he grasped her arm. "C'mon, Firebird. Let's get you both to safety."

"I'll get the weaponry," Slater stated.

They lunged in opposite directions, both men re-emerging into the kitchen at the same time. Slater held a SSG 3000 sniper rifle and it's ammunition—an older but durable weapon with excellent accuracy. He handed Donnie an AR15 rifle. Both men already carried concealed handguns as backup weapons. Donnie grabbed the keys to the Scorpion, and they moved out. They'd have to circle around, and that would take time. But tracking targets was second nature to the two experienced operatives.

◊ ◊ ◊

His thigh burned like a bitch and the pain woke Johnny. Someone lay beneath him, and he immediately tried to alleviate some of his weight.

Black hair and something warm and wet obscured his vision. Raising his head, Johnny looked down.

"Johnny, move your legs!" Atlas yelled from somewhere behind him. "You're still exposed."

The last few moments slammed back into focus. Kat getting shot. Johnny trying to cover her body. Him, dragging her behind a concrete bench. Then the pain. Looking down, Johnny realized that Atlas was right. Half of Johnny's body still lay exposed.

"If you move, he'll know you're alive. He's picking off survivors. You'll have to move quick."

"Where is he?"

"About 400 yards away to the East."

"Atlas, are you hurt?"

"Atlas was shot in the calf trying to protect me," Elana yelled out.

"I did protect you, and I wasn't shot, it looks like a bad shrapnel injury. Now, stay still."

Bracing himself for the pain, Johnny launched himself forward on his good leg, using his momentum to drag Kat along. She hadn't stirred beneath him, but he'd felt her blood soaking his shirt.

Concrete chips flew as the sniper fired off more rounds.

Sucking in short breaths, Johnny counted to ten. He wanted to vomit and glanced down at his leaking leg. His outer thigh wasn't as bad as he'd first thought. A missing chunk from a grazing bullet. Now that he was behind a solid barrier, Johnny pulled off his shirt and tore it up, before scanning the area. Spotting a sturdy stick lying in a nearby flowerbed a few feet away, Johnny rolled sideways and reached for the piece of wood. Screaming out the pain, he rolled back, avoiding the volley of bullets aimed his way. The wooden stick gave him a mechanical advantage as he placed the constricting band around his thigh in a makeshift tourniquet. Eliminating the arterial flow to his thigh had Johnny shouting through gritted teeth as pain spiked from his hip to his toes. When he was sure he wouldn't pass out, Johnny swiped at his sweating brow and prepared himself for treating Kat. If she still breathed. He'd seen the blood spray in his periphery as she'd fallen. A definite head shot.

He rolled to the side, expecting to see brain matter. All he saw was blood, and an intact head. He gently turned her towards him. Her face looked whole and serene. A car door slammed in the distance, a dog yapped, and Johnny froze. He recognized Valentino's raised voice immediately. Lizzy had arrived with the kids, and was walking into an ambush.

Johnny began yelling her name and Max and Abby joined in; fear apparent in their voices. The two little boys sounded louder as they laughed and shouted amongst themselves, closer to Lizzy's proximity. Johnny doubted she'd heard his warning shouts above the children's noisy racket. It sounded like they were walking down the side lane, heading directly towards the back yard.

Neither Johnny nor Max would get to them in time. Johnny would watch his wife and son die. Both men moved out of cover to save their loved ones. Valentino rounded the corner and stopped in his tracks, realizing something was wrong. Little Gabe joined him, as Lizzy and their dog came up from the rear. Blood poured down Max's arm as he hoisted himself onto the side of the pool, roaring for them to retreat. Johnny dragged himself towards his family, screaming their names.

Elana threw herself in their direction, zeroing in with such ferocity that all three of the startled newcomers stepped back. Atlas shouted her name. Shots split the air just as she ducked and grabbed each boy by the chest, driving them back behind the wall. Lizzy stumbled back up the lane to keep from getting trampled, and Ray yelped in surprise.

"Elana!" Atlas called.

The sniper turned his attention to Johnny, who'd dragged himself into the open. A bullet zipped past. Shaking and sweating, Johnny hauled himself back to cover, praying that Max had done the same. Burning pain licked up his leg, throbbing in time with his pulse.

"Lizzy, tell me you're all okay? Someone answer me." Johnny needed to hear his wife's voice.

"We're fine." Elana and Lizzy shouted in unison.

"I love you, John. Hold on, baby!"

Lizzy's voice calmed his panic, and he closed his eyes and pictured her safe and unhurt. They would survive this horror.

Atlas heaved out a groan before yelling to Elana, "You're crazy, and brave and damn stupid."

"I know! And I now have access to the house. We're getting these kids to safety and then I'm finding medical supplies."

"Don't you come back out here," Atlas warned, but Elana didn't reply.

◊ ◊ ◊

Donnie eased up on the gas, slowing just enough for Slater to leap from the vehicle. Splitting up made more sense as they would close in from both sides. Unless Donnie had a clear shot, he'd mostly provide a distraction while Slater narrowed in on the target. Rolling to his feet, Slater raced up the hillside, not caring as branches and bushes tore at his skin.

Hatred like he'd never felt before burned through his soul. He could almost taste the bloodlust rising above the black nothingness. Peace could never be his friend and death would never stray too far from Slater's world. He'd always be a killer that destroyed his prey. The last months of healing fell away as his legs ate up the distance.

Finally, he dove to the ground and used his scope to zero in on any anomalies. He waited and listened until he heard Dasher fire another round. Using the "crack and thump" method to locate his enemy's position, Slater turned in the general direction. The quick lapse between the crack of a bullet, and the lower sounding thump—the discharge of the rifle—helped Slater to narrow in on Dasher's hide lying just 300 feet away. Slater now slowed the hunt, creeping towards the concealed bastard. The sound of an engine meant that Donnie had circled to the opposite side of the target and was heading back down the mountain.

Finally, close enough to hear Dasher's curse, Slater slowly raised his rifle back into position. A large tree trunk obstructed Slater's view, but he couldn't miss seeing the shots aimed at Donnie and the Scorpion.

"Is that you, Banez? You fucking prick! Drive your lazy ass over here. I'm not done until I have your head on a damn pike."

Shifting, Slater moved in a low crawl over rock and gravel, keeping his body flat and taking his time to settle in as silently as possible.

"Nobody fucks with my brother. You see what happens when you touch the Hill brothers? I take away your world. Your precious bitch is dead."

Slater squeezed his eyes shut against the rage. Taking a moment to exist in the nightmarish forest, Slater breathed in the scent of pine and earth. The smell conjured up the night he'd given Kat the Jade pendant—an image of making love to her against a tree in a snowy woodland. Her trusting gaze and that slight smile as he'd told her he loved her for the first time.

Slater wanted to howl out his pain, instead he set his jaw and decided on his own potential sniper's nest. A good angle and a clear shot. Dasher was an infantry soldier in the army, and his basic training might hold up against civilians. Slater was no civilian and the asshole was now in his line of sight.

Slater avoided a fallen log. Any large objects would naturally draw a target's eye. A nest of damp leaves in a trough of earth was the better choice and Slater rolled into his chosen spot. Hugging the earth, in a familiar prone position edged him into full-on sniper mode as he aimed down the scope. Mother nature provided excellent camouflage and he automatically calculated distance and wind velocity. It was a calm day amongst the still trees—2mph at the most and Slater made his windage adjustment on the rifle. It was immediately obvious that Dasher wasn't a trained sniper. His camouflage and movement discipline was poor, and he rested his weapon on a boulder, exposing most of his body mass to the enemy.

Aiming slightly off target and rejecting a head shot—an 'instant' stop—Slater squeezed the trigger.

He reloaded and took his time loping up the hill. The sight of the man spurting blood into the dirt warmed Slater's ashen heart. The bastard's rifle now lay a few feet away and Slater kicked it aside.

"Who did you think you were fucking with?" Slater ran his eyes over the gaping shoulder wound. Rifle bullets could cause more carnage than a hand-gun because of the higher velocity. The fallen man would bleed out in minutes. "I purposely aimed for your trigger arm. That gives us time to talk."

The distant hum of an engine closed in.

Dasher groaned and tried to roll over. Slater placed his foot over the grisly injury, grinding the soldier into the dirt. "Your journey is over."

"Slater?" Donnie approached on foot from the left. "You don't want to execute an unarmed man in cold blood."

"He killed my Kat, and he's not walking away. Both our lives are now over."

"No, they're not. You're surrounded by people who love you."

"And how many of them died today?"

"We can't say until we get back to the cabin. Bro, please. Kat wouldn't want this. He's dead already."

Would Slater allow his inner demons to have the last word? If he doled out justice in this secluded space, Slater knew Donnie would lie to protect him. The temptation was worth the corruption of his soul. Slater didn't just want to execute the man at his feet, he wanted to bury the psychotic bastard alive. Take him apart slowly, limb by limb. Then Dasher's thin lips turned up in a smile.

"Buddy?" Donnie placed a hand on Slater's arm.

Slater nodded his surrender while staring into Dasher's hate-filled eyes. Donnie called Charlie and confirmed their status, giving the all clear. Then Donnie dialed 911 and did the same.

Lowering the rifle, Slater stepped back. "He gets medical attention after everyone else, but he won't survive that injury."

Memories from the last five years flickered before reality slammed in. Slater didn't want to be standing on this mountain side with an empty-headed psychopath. Slater wanted to hold Kat, and cradle her in his arms one last time.

"Banez..." Dasher shifted. "I'll see you in hell."

"Probably. I'm already there."

Donnie pulled the plastic restraints from his pocket. He hadn't taken two steps when Slater aimed and fired. Dasher's head exploded like a melon.

"What the hell!" Donnie swung around.

"He had a second weapon."

Slater pointed at a secondary weapon—a pistol—that Dasher had tried to pull from a back holster.

Slater had counted on Dasher's feeble attempt to turn the tables. Any trained soldier wouldn't rely on just one weapon. When Dasher's uninjured arm had edged towards the concealed gun, it had given Slater the excuse he'd needed.

Slater walked towards their off-road vehicle. "Keep him company or not. I don't give a damn, I'm heading back."

Catching up, Donnie ran around to the passenger side and they exchanged haunted glances as they climbed in, praying they hadn't been too late to save their friends.

Chapter Twenty-Two

The cabin looked like a war-zone. Slater ignored the approaching sirens, and raced across the torn up lawn, looking for signs of Kat and Johnny.

Towels covered two deceased bodies on the grass, and Slater staggered, heaving out a breath.

"Kat's inside," Max said from behind. Slater turned to face the grim operator who resembled a pale vampire. His wet t-shirt was soaked in blood, and he'd draped a blue towel over his shoulders.

"You shouldn't be standing." Abby grabbed her husband's waist and tried to steer him back towards the games room.

Slater got there first, maneuvering around the couple and taking in the carnage. The snooker and ping-pong table were tossed on their sides against the wall. The wooden floor was slick with water and blood. Hearing Johnny's shout for more towels, Slater turned to see his injured medic friend working frantically to staunch a patient's blood flow. Lizzy worked by his side. The Delta operator—Tyler Woods—lay at their feet, gut shot and clutching to Lizzy's arm while Tyler's wife sobbed nearby.

Elana sat in another corner and held a towel to Atlas's lower leg. "Kat is in the living room."

Slater's world shifted. Literally tilted, and he braced himself against the wall, fighting the wave of dizziness. Kat was upstairs, in the next room.

Rolling away, he stepped around the zombie-like victims and the injured, and climbed the stairs. Charlie sat in the passage, clinging to her little girl and to a terrified Lucy, and Donnie rushed up and wrapped them in a solid embrace.

The rest of the house sounded strangely quiet—aside from Abby rushing past with two rolls of McNett self-adhering wrap.

Scanning the room, Slater's eyes fell on the sofa, spotting Kat's raven hair draped over the side. He made his way over on numb legs and sank down beside her. The thick, blood-soaked tape wrapped around her head had him frowning. When her chest rose and fell, he let out a choked sob. Dazed eyes returned his stare. Kat was alive?

"The bullet grazed her skull. She's missing a chunk of hair and skin—she'll need stitches—plus she's barely conscious," Abby said from the kitchen. He looked up at the calm woman, now wearing blood-stained shorts over her damp bathing suit.

"She's... alive?"

"Irish luck, I'd say. Kat hit her head when she fell, and Johnny is worried. She's drifting in and out, and is not fully awake."

A mix of panic and relief had Slater's hand hovering above Kat's cheek. She lay so still, and it reminded him of the vision in Lagos. That time, he'd tried to touch her, and she'd evaporated like smoke. Maybe he did have a TBI. A traumatic brain injury would mean that none of this was real, instead the day was a night terror gone horribly wrong.

When his fingers traced her silken skin, Slater slid to his knees beside the couch, and lay his head on her chest. Kat moaned his name as his hands clutched her shoulders, stroked her arms and touched the pulse in her neck. Warm skin meant she was alive, and he focused on her steady breaths. Slater whispered her name over and over in the muffled silence.

Death hadn't strayed far. It had danced with every one of them today. Wives, girlfriends and children were not exempt from the wicked markings of a maniacal lunatic.

◊ ◊ ◊

Elana held the new wrappings in place as Abby folded the tape tightly around Atlas's lower leg. No-one said a word. She looked just as shell-shocked as Elana felt, and Atlas now lay too still. When Abby was done, she raced back to Max to check on his shoulder.

Rolling off her knees, Elana shoved the old soaked bandages aside and shifted up against the wall. With a grunt, she lifted Atlas's head onto her lap. He barely registered the move, as his eyes drifted closed. Worry over his leg had her stroking his forehead. For the first time, Elana could stare at the handsome soldier without fearing that she'd lead him on in any way. His combination of laidback lethality, chivalry and kindness fascinated her. A death-dealing puppy dog that followed her everywhere. Not everywhere—there was a whole side to Elana that Atlas never saw. A private and dangerous world.

She shouldn't care this much about a man. How had they grown so close, even though she tried to push him away with her prickly persona? Atlas didn't care. His persistent attitude had embedded him in her world, and she now looked forward to his nightly phone calls. Aside from his deployments, he hadn't missed a call since their return from their Moroccan adventure.

Elana had made it clear in North Africa that they could only ever be friends. He'd seemed to accept that, and that's why his nightly calls had at first seemed strange. But she'd soon looked forward to hearing his voice. He would ask her how her day went, and then they'd chat about anything and everything. Atlas would do most of the talking, and she'd listen as she'd get ready for bed. Elana was the first to admit that he was her security blanket. It wasn't healthy, but she'd relied on him in a foreign place, while injured and terrified of the armed mercenaries chasing them down.

But Elana's world held no safety. There were no barriers against evil, and the less that Atlas knew of her secret life, the better.

How would he react? He'd freak the hell out. No-one could know, not her family, or Charlie or Atlas. They'd put a stop to her operation, and the cause was too important. There were lives on the line. Some things in life took precedence over relationships and having a personal life.

Elana's head felt heavy, and her limbs began to tremble in earnest as she glanced over at Johnny and Lizzy. They were covered in blood, working side by side to save the life of a friend—Johnny's Delta buddy. The room looked like a scene from a horror film, and Elana suppressed a sob. She couldn't look out the window and see the couple who didn't make it. The other Delta Force soldier, Gary Cox had died trying to protect his wife. They'd both fallen under a hail of bullets. Elana didn't know the guy but her heart hurt for the deceased couple. It could've easily been any one of Atlas's team members or their respective wives.

"Hey."

A hand grasped her wrist, and Elana jumped. She looked down at pale green eyes.

"You okay?" Atlas asked in a slurred voice.

He lay on a bloody floor, bleeding heavily from a leg wound, and he was asking Elana if she was okay?

"I'm fine, Captain America. You're the one who's injured. Where are the damn paramedics!"

His mouth turned up. "Captain America?"

"You flew through the air and flattened me to the ground. Those man muscles saved my life."

Eyes twinkled. "I should get injured more often... you're comparing me to a super... hero. And you noticed my muscles?"

"Hard not to. How many hours did you say that your team works out in a day?"

"Too... many." Atlas grimaced.

Elana frowned and stroked his hair. "Hold on. Help will be here soon. I'll go and check with Abby."

"Don't leave." He squeezed her hand. "That feels good—you—touching my hair."

"Well, since you're injured and all." Elana swallowed, remembering a different time where his fingers had run through her hair as she'd lain in a fevered haze.

Voices lit up the passage and black boots thundered down the stairs. Elana breathed a sigh of relief as officers barged into the room. She ignored their drawn guns and yelled for paramedics.

It took far too much time for the first responders to clear the way. When they finally loaded Atlas onto a gurney, Elana stepped back and let go of his hand. She'd call and stop by to visit a couple of times, but any more time spent with the handsome warrior would be unwise. It was time for her to detach herself from his world.

The metallic smell of blood, and suddenly cloying air, had Elana pushing through the chaos and heading for the front door. Staggering onto the lawn, she collapsed to her knees. Charlie called her name and Elana looked to her left. The large shaded tree sheltered her best friend and the four kids somewhat from the insanity. Elana lurched over on shaking legs and sank to the bench. She gathered the three older kids and hugged them to her chest. Charlie joined in and Elana reveled in the familiar touch of her friend.

A paramedic checked them over and handed out blankets, and Elana couldn't tear her eyes away from Kat being loaded in an ambulance. Slater ran alongside and the look in his eyes for Kat rattled Elana. Worry, fear and absolute love. Charlie, and all of her friends had found good men who'd all demonstrated bravery and loyalty. Elana should believe in love—her parents' marriage was a perfect example of the glorified emotion. So why did Elana believe that it was all a myth—at least for her? And why did she run in the opposite direction, whenever her heart considered taking a chance? Why did seeing a couple in the throes of love send Elana into a panic?

Elana knew why. Her heart and faith in herself had died a long time ago at midnight, on a deserted street in Jackson Hole.

Epilogue

Two months later.
The Piece Club.

"I am sorting the blue ones!"

Gladys glared at Atlas. "No, you're all googly-eyed and staring at the pretty girl at the next table. Now concentrate!"

Elana looked up from the adjacent table causing Atlas's cheeks to redden.

Kat suppressed a giggle, nudging Slater in the ribs. He squeezed her waist back, feeling just as amused.

"Don't grin like a dick, you're supposed to be sifting through the blue bits." Atlas glared at Slater who'd wrapped Kat in his arms, as she perched on his lap and worked on the top corner.

"My hands are otherwise occupied." Slater held her close, and took in her delicate perfume. The noisy chaos in the packed room had him relaxing into his chair. The center had hosted a charity event for a PTSD awareness day. The hall was filled with mostly elderly Vietnam veterans, but there was also a healthy scattering of younger vets from local support groups. Due to their delayed deployment, the MIT2 team had also turned up. Johnny and Atlas were still recovering physically from the shooting. In a month's time, they'd all be back in the field.

The tragic day in the mountains had taken a heavy toll on the team and their loved ones. This was the first time they'd hooked up socially since the attack. Max stood apart from the rest of the crowd. He'd positioned himself in the opposite corner, almost standing guard. Slater knew that stance and the PTSD dynamic that kept Max on his toes. His arm may finally be free of a sling, but that wasn't the only damage the man carried with him from that day. With a quick kiss to Kat's cheek, Slater shifted her off his lap and stood.

He hated letting her go, even for a second. Since her stay in the hospital, he'd clung to his Kat. After being shot, she'd hit her head on the concrete bench on the way down, and then on the paving. The angle of the fall meant that she'd experienced minor swelling on the brain. The doctors had induced a four-day coma, and administered anti-seizure medication. Slater had spent two weeks by her side as she'd slowly recovered.

The last couple of months had been the worst of his life, but they were finally out of the woods. Kat still experienced severe headaches and spoke with slurred speech after a long or tiring day. They were told this would be temporary. Slater watched her like a hawk. Any sign of exhaustion, and he'd whisk her home.

They'd shaved the side of her head around the injury site, so Kat insisted on wearing beanies or flat caps whenever possible until her hair grew out. Slater hated how self-conscious she felt. He told her everyday how beautiful she was, and today, she decided to wear her hair down and ignore any odd looks. Of course, she'd been welcomed warmly into her "Piece Club" fold, and was now the recipient of fussing friends.

With a quick hand squeeze, he left Kat at their table and headed towards the man who was his forever brother, old leader and loyal friend.

Max pushed off the wall. "Hey, bro, everything okay?" His ghostly eyes checked over Kat, then darted around the room.

"I was about to ask you the same thing. Why are you hovering in the corner like a buzzing drone? Choose a table."

Max glanced at his wife sitting with Lizzy and Charlie, and Gabe waved at them from the kiddie's corner where he built a children's puzzle with Valentino. The two boys were inseparable.

"I don't feel like sitting," Max said, folding his arms.

"Or talking apparently."

"Are you trying to be a dick?"

"Not trying. I've always been one. One who's suffered from PTSD and recognizes that look in your eyes."

"Jeez, Slater." A muscle ticked in Max's jaw.

"I heard you're selling your house."

"And I heard you're looking to buy. You want it?"

"Why?" Slater asked. "You've done so much work on that place?"

Max dropped his arms and turned; all humor gone. "Because the kids are terrified of the yard. And Abby tries to hide a flash of fear, every time she glances at the surrounding hills."

"I'm sorry, man."

"And I fucking can't look at that swimming pool without seeing visions of my wife and daughter being mowed down in the water. What if I hadn't gotten to them in time?"

"But, you did."

"Others weren't so lucky. Gary and his wife—"

"That's not your fault." They'd all attended the couple's funeral and Slater thought about their deaths every day. "It's my fault. Place it on my shoulders. I can take it."

Max pushed Slater against the wall and leaned in. "If you ever spew that kind of horse shit again, I'll kick your ass."

"Fair enough. As long as you promise to get some help, and attend a few meetings with me."

Max nodded and stepped back.

"Besides," Slater said. "I think we're out of the woods. It's smooth sailing from here on out."

"You can't know that." Max snorted.

"I can. I feel it in my bones. I think we're all going to live long and happy lives. Eighty-year-old grumpy fuckers, squatting in your wooden Finnish sauna."

"I'm thinking that you're the one that really wants that sauna. You can't let it go." Max's mouth turned up.

"Hell, no. So I can gaze at your naked, scantily clad balls? That's Abby's job."

Chuckling, Max asked, "When's the wedding?"

Slater frowned at Max's words. "What?"

"How long has that engagement ring been rolling around in your pocket?"

Slater glanced down, shifting his hip to the wall. "Observant bastard. You saw that?"

"You're planning the proposal for today?"

"Tonight... I think."

"Why not now?" Max asked.

"Are you damn crazy?"

"Kat's surrounded by everyone she loves, including her parents."

That was true. Her parents sat at Kat's table. They'd spent the last month in Utah, after the shooting. Slater adored the gentle couple, and he'd asked her father's permission two days ago.

"Go, she's waiting. We only have a limited time on the planet with our loved ones."

And Slater and Kat had already spent too much time apart. Max was right. This was the perfect moment. Ignoring his sudden nerves, Slater headed her way.

Kat was examining a puzzle piece, and looked up as he approached. He crouched beside her chair and she frowned as he covered her hand with his.

"I never saw the bigger picture when we first met—I didn't know my own direction in life or that I'd shatter into a thousand puzzle pieces, or that you'd put me back together again. First by walking away and then by returning to my world and reassembling me—and us. It's like the universe always knew we were the perfect fit."

Kat cupped his cheek, her eyes glistening.

He swallowed past the lump in his throat. "I want the complicated 2000-piece puzzle that is loving you, and chocolate milkshakes, and long swims together, and squabbling over breakfast, and lazy chats on the deck."

Slater produced the ring box from his pocket. He knew she'd love the square, center cut diamond mounted above the band, surrounded by rows of diamonds and a single center row of small, round, red Jadeite stones.

"I had to include the Jade. It saved your life and gave you back to me."

"It's so grand," Kat whispered. "Like my dear Derry." She looked up. "Aye—yes—I want complicated, and to be with my true soul mate." She laid a hand over his chest. "This heart is mine, just as mine is yours."

Cheering filled the room. Overcome with emotion, Slater pressed a long kiss to her lips, before whispering, "I'm glad you love me for more than just my pretty Rodzilla."

Kat giggled, and Slater pressed her close, reveling in the sweet sound.

The End.

Watch out for "Kite on the Rocks." (MIT Book #5)
This is Atlas and Elana's story. Filled with international
intrigue and subterfuge.

Kite on the Rocks
Prologue

Layton, Utah.
The Creekside Community Center.

Dylan *Atlas* Jenkins knew all of her quirks, thanks to the months spent getting to know her. And thanks to their past adventures in Morocco. But, something seemed different, Elana held a nervous energy he'd never seen before.

She sat at an adjacent table at the Veterans charity day—an event held at a local recreation center. Tables filled the room, and everyone built military-themed puzzles. Boxes of 1000-piece puzzles were on sale in the corner of the room, and all profits went to the *Special Operations Warrior Foundation*.

Derek *Slater* Banez had just proposed to his girlfriend, Kat. The room cheered at her acceptance. After congratulating the happy couple, Atlas zoned back in on his jumpy friend. Elana Celik was more than just a friend—at least in his head and his imaginings.

Hell, she was like a tall goddess. He knew he'd fallen for her from the first moment he'd seen her photograph on her Facebook page. And then, when he'd rescued her from an assassin in Morocco, he'd never wanted to let her go. The memory rose of cradling an unconscious Elana in his arms as they ran through the streets of Ait Benhaddou, her blood soaking his shirt, and his surge of possessiveness. Atlas never believed in insta-love or the concept of love, but he couldn't explain the connection he felt for the elusive blonde bombshell.

Elana checked her phone for the hundredth time. Glancing at the screen, she rose and exited the busy room. Atlas stood, ignoring his cramping leg. He still recovered from the shrapnel injury that had sliced apart his calf muscle two months ago.

His only focus was on Elana who'd withdrawn from their friendship around the same time as his injury. She'd visited him in the hospital a couple of times, but wasn't taking his phone calls, and Atlas missed her company. Perhaps she'd met someone. That would suck, but he'd have to deal with remaining in the friend zone. They needed to talk and now was as good a time as any.

Catching a glimpse of the slender woman pushing through the front doors into the darkening lot, he trailed behind. Elana turned away from the parking lot and pulled out a second phone. Powering it up, she slipped around the opposite corner.

His neck prickled and following his instincts, Atlas slowed and eased along the wall. Her voice sounded clear on the autumn breeze.

"I said I'd be there... I'm on my way... I set the location—not you."

Atlas frowned at her words. Elana shuffled farther away, and he stepped closer.

"Do you want the package or not?"

What in the hell?

"At the entrance to the canyon... I'll be there in thirty... It's none of your business where I am… yes… I'm coming alone."

Retreating towards the lit entrance, Atlas almost growled out his concern. What the hell was Elana doing? And who was on the other end of that call? Adrenaline surged as he considered all the possibilities. As far as he knew, Elana was completing her Masters in a Bachelor of Arts in Human Rights Studies, and was a college student who worked for her father in a part-time capacity. Who was she now mixed up with?

He thought back to everything he knew about her, which was a surprisingly small amount, considering how much time they'd spent in each other's company. Elana's mother was from Wyoming and had met Elana's Muslim father in Turkey back in the day. They'd married and moved to Jackson Hole. Her father was a human rights activist and lecturer who'd written numerous books on women's rights. He was also a well-renowned architect who raised incredible homes for the rich and famous in Hollywood. Elana adored her parents, although from what Atlas had gathered, they weren't around that much during her youth.

Elana's alluring beauty stemmed from her father's Islamic heritage and her mother's Germanic beauty. Their daughter was well-traveled and regularly stayed with family members across Europe, also speaking multiple languages. Elana seemed stable, but sometimes, appearances could be deceiving, and she now hung out with his team and their respective loved ones. If Elana was mixing with a dangerous crowd and endangering his friends in any way, Atlas needed to know.

He chose a concealed doorway and watched her walk back into the building. Atlas climbed into his Jeep. Five minutes later, she re-emerged and headed for her brand new BMW. As an elite covert operative, Atlas had been trained to follow jumpy extremists from an undetected distance, and so trailing her through the city was a piece of cake.

When Atlas spotted her pulling into a rundown diner, at the mouth of a canyon, he kept on driving. Parking in the empty lot would be obvious, and he drove to a lookout point a mile down the road. Digging through his hiking pack in the trunk, Atlas retrieved a digital camera and attached a telephoto lens. Tucking his handgun into his holster, he broke out into a limping run along the deserted highway. His still healing calf muscle hindered his progress, and Atlas hoped he hadn't wasted too much time.

Her fingers tapped on the tabletop, and Elana immediately caught herself and withdrew her hand from the sticky surface. The diner sat empty, and when the lone waitress handed her a menu, Elana put it aside. The health department should close down the filthy place—it probably broke numerous health code violations. That's why Elana had chosen the spot. No cameras, hardly any customers or prying eyes. Still, she wore a baseball cap and a hoodie and sat slumped in the corner. Elana glanced at her watch. She'd been five minutes early, and now there was a minute left. The man would be on time. She knew it in her gut. He wasn't the type to mess around—a player who knew the game.

Another deadly player came to mind. Atlas Jenkins. He must've been in the bathroom when she'd left the center. She'd wanted to see him one last time. That aura of safety boosted her confidence. The athletic warrior stood taller than her, which was saying a lot as Elana sat at almost six feet. That wide, white-toothed smile, and the way his forehead creased into a cute frown whenever his brows rose. Tousled blond locks paired with stubbled sexiness, and the small laugh lines that crinkled at the corner of his pale green eyes. Those sexy lips that always sported a cheeky grin. The guy must know how irresistible he was to the opposite sex. Pity that she had no room for him in her crazy life.

Ignoring the nervous fluttering in her stomach, Elana straightened her back and scanned the lot. Was she doing this? She'd taken her enterprise to the next level, and this might be a foolish move. She hadn't yet swum with a shark this deadly, and when his truck's lights lit up the lot, Elana held her breath and willed herself to relax.

The door pushed open, and Dimitri Kazak headed straight for her booth, sharp eyes darting around the empty space. He'd brought along a friend. Both men were large—over six feet of built muscle. Unlike Atlas, they exuded an air of weighty and solemn violence. Holy shit, she was out of her league. Elana suppressed the urge to run for the door. Both men were obviously armed, and they sat assuredly across from her, making direct eye contact. She willed herself not to look away.

"Let's not waste time, Miss Celik—hand over the package."

Elana hesitated. "Dimitri, who's your friend?" She'd purposely used his first name even though it was the first time they'd met in person.

"This is Foster. He works with me."

Elana held out her hand. The other man grumbled and exchanged a look with Dimitri. Not twitching, she raised her brows, and Foster passed along his ID. When she was satisfied, Elana handed it back, then slipped a hand into her hoodie pocket and pulled out the baggy.

After glancing around, she slid the package across the table. "If you stick to your agreement, I'll send another gift your way."

"Fair enough. But if you screw us over in any way…"

"I know what I'm doing. I'll be in touch." Elana stood on

rubbery legs and concentrated on striding for the door. She'd done it... she'd actually done it. Now, there was no stopping her.

"Elana," Dimitri called.

She paused with her hand on the door.

"You're playing a dangerous game. Be careful who you trust."

With a nod, Elana pushed out and breathed in the fresh air. Not pausing to look around, she headed for her car and for safety.

◊ ◊ ◊

Atlas watched her leave, tempted to follow and confront her. Instead, he focused on the two burly men still sitting in the diner. He hadn't been able to hear the conversation from his exterior lookout point in the concealing tree line, but he'd seen her hand off the ambiguous package, and he'd snapped several good photos of the two thugs and their vehicle. If they'd made any aggressive moves towards Elana, he would've charged the place, weapons blazing.

His damaged leg screamed in agony. Atlas limped back to his vehicle and made a call to the only man he knew that could help him to unravel the mystery meeting. Dave *Donnie* Wilson, the analyst on MIT2—his covert team, answered and Atlas began to talk. Elana didn't know it yet, but he had her back. If she were into something illegal, Atlas would cross that bridge when needed. Until then, he'd fight like hell to keep her out of harm's way.

ACKNOWLEDGMENTS

Jade in the Snow addresses several issues close to my heart. Slater's story was always going to be a complicated one. I wanted to highlight the challenges of PTSD and facing a future when everything has gone to hell. Many of my loved ones and friends suffer from combat PTSD. Too often, it's patched up with a band-aid, and these warriors never get the help that they deserve. No-one should have to struggle alone

As an allergy sufferer, I wanted to write a character who deals with the possibility of true anaphylaxis. Too often, kids and adults are targeted due to this medical condition. 25% of children are bullied, teased, or harassed because of a food allergy, and not just by fellow students. 21% of the perpetrators are teachers or adults. An allergy might be dismissed or not taken seriously, leading to contaminated surfaces or foods. Even now, as an adult, I still need to be cautious of the reactions/ dismissals of others, especially in restaurants or at a new friend's home.

Finally, I'd like to thank all those that contributed to Jade in the Snow with their research and patience. Geoff Perrin, thanks for your help on the covert/ military side of things. Kendra Hilditch, you're a sweetheart, and thanks to you, Kathleen Flynn now has some Irish flair. To my sweet family—love you all so damn much. To my editor, Joan Turner, at JRT Editing—thanks for all that you do, and making time for *Jade in the Snow* while settling into your hectic new routine. My cover artist—Syd Gill—I love the red and white cover!

Lastly to Derek Slater Banez. You're fictional and only my imaginings. Just hope I've done you justice. Because, damn, it's hard writing a funny character with loads of one-liners.

Louise Dawn writes heart pounding romantic suspense. She's also a graphic designer and fine artist in Utah. Louise loves travelling and has lived in many countries before choosing the States as her home. Her passion is reading and writing fast paced stories simmering in romance. If you enjoyed this book, consider leaving a review. It's appreciated by authors both new and established.

Chat with her on Facebook @
https://www.facebook.com/authorlouisedawn

Follow her on Twitter @ https://twitter.com/louisedawnwrite

Or check out her character's development on Pinterest @
https://www.pinterest.com/louisedawnwrite/boards/